FROCK IN HELL

YVONNE VINCENT

First published in 2021 by Yvonne Vincent.
Copyright © 2021 Yvonne Vincent. All rights reserved

By Yvonne Vincent:

The Big Blue Jobbie
The Big Blue Jobbie #2
The Wee Hairy Anthology

Frock In Hell

Losers Club (Losers Club Book 1)
The Laird's Ladle (Losers Club Book 2)
The Angels' Share (Losers Club Book 3)
Sleighed! (Losers Club Book 4)
The Juniper Key (Losers Club Book 5)
Beacon Brodie (Losers Club Book 6)

To Mum and Dad. Forever in my heart.

PROLOGUE

I held my breath for a few moments, then let it out in a long moan as the pain wrenched my gut. I looked at Tony, sitting there with the big bag full of whale song and aromatherapy oils, looking for all the world like a startled garden gnome.

'I'm fairly sure it shouldn't be this sore, this early,' I gasped.

'Should I get someone to come and do a fanny check? Half an hour ago they were telling me to go home. Half an hour ago they said you were nowhere near. I'll get the fanny nurse. Right, yes, that's what I'll do.' Tony strode purposefully out of the bathroom, still babbling about fanny nurses, and I said a silent prayer that, by the time he got to the nurses station, he'd remember they were called midwives.

Half an hour earlier, a midwife had been trying to persuade Tony to go home and had only let him stay because I asked if I could have a bath. When my waters broke at 2am, we'd hit the panic button, grabbed the bag and headed to the hospital. I'd barely had time to throw on a pair of clean knickers before Tony had me out the door and into the car, so when I heard that a bath was an option, I leapt (okay, lumbered) at the chance.

The fanny nurse arrived, with Tony bringing up the rear. By this time, the contractions were coming fast and strong. I fixed a beady eye on the fanny nurse.

'I think I need my epidural now.'

'Well, Katie, we'll just pop you on the ward and check how far apart your contractions are, then we'll have a wee look at that cervix, dear,' said the fanny nurse. I realised I couldn't keep calling her the fanny nurse because at some point I'd say it out loud. I'm the sort of person who would do that. I once refused to go to the Citreon garage for fear I'd accidentally say Shitreon. Having spent the last while joking with Tony about fanny nurses, it was only a matter of time before my gob got the better of me. I squinted at her nametag. Fork me, her name was actually Fanny.

'Look, Fanny.' I tried not to laugh as I saw Tony's head shoot up. He clearly hadn't seen the nametag and was expecting me to add the word 'nurse'. I could see him anticipating telling the hilarious tale to all our friends. Another wave of pain started. 'I'm not even sure I can make it to the ward. The pain is pretty constant'

'Nonsense, here we go, now pop your t-shirt on, we'll just wrap the towel around your bottom half. There you are. It's not far.'

I shuffled down the corridor, a hospital towel barely covering my bum, hunched over in pain. Tony was once more lugging the bag of 'all the things you could ever need for a nice, relaxing birth.'

'Bloody hell,' he whispered, 'I think there's a cow trapped in that room over there.' It was a mark of how anxious Tony was, that he was making daft jokes. Of the two of us, Tony was the sensible one. The responsible one. The one who made life decisions for sound financial reasons.

From a room behind us came a lowing sound. Some poor cow was, indeed, mooing her heart out as a contraction hit. I felt a tiny bit sorry for her, but at the same time decided that I would definitely not be making that sound, just in case there were people like me around to take the piss.

'Maybe there's a whole farmyard here,' I snickered, 'D'you hear that other one? Definitely a horse.'

Fanny guided us into the ward and I scrambled onto the bed. A couple of other midwives, fanny nurses, whatever, appeared and they wheeled a machine towards me, unravelling a big brown belt as they went. However, the moment my bum touched sheet, I'd hit a wall of unrelenting pain.

'Hush now. The other patients are sleeping,' said Fanny, as a loud moo burst forth. It occurred to me that I should tell Tony that if he got lost, he should just ask for the bovine ward, then I realised that the noise had come from me. Oh bugger. And why had they put me in here where people were sleeping? Why wasn't I on the labour ward? And what, for the love of gas and air, were they doing with that effing belt.

'I want my epidural!' I howled, writhing around the bed in agony as three women tried to wrap the big strap around me.

'If you put the belt on, we can get a readout of your contractions. Can you stay still for just a moment?'

No, I could fucking not stay fucking still, because I was being tortured by an invisible hand and all the fanny nurses were making it worse with their belty thing and they weren't listening so they may as well just eff off.

'I want my epidural now! Will you please listen?! Give me my epidural now! I am not having contractions. I am having one big, very huge, giant contraction. I want my epidural now!'

'Well, that's just not possible, Katie dear. Forty five minutes ago you were nowhere near ready. It's far too early for your epidural. You must have a very low pain threshold.'

You. Cheeky. Witch.

'Will you please listen to me!' I cried, deciding that an appeal to the collective common sense of the fanny nurses was probably a better option than punching Fanny's lights out. I writhed on the bed, the towel long since cast aside and my lady garden out for all to see. The nurses continued to try to strap me in, while Fanny stayed down the business end, presumably trying to work out how she was going to check my cervix without getting kicked in the face. She had no way of knowing that she would be accidentally kicked in the face, no matter how hard she tried to avoid it. Low pain threshold, my arse.

Then, suddenly, I paused in my thrashing. Something felt different. Like when a poo comes. Only not a poo. Oh, bloody hell, I hope not a poo. Please, God, don't let it be a poo. I don't want to shit myself in front of all these people. Hang on, did I just say that out loud?

I could see the belty people out of the corner of my eye, delighted that I was finally still. I could see Fanny, thinking that she'd triumphed over the silly, first-time mother who was Making A Fuss. I could see Tony, looking apprehensive, because he knew that either something was wrong or I was about to say something outrageous. And he wasn't sure which was the lesser of the two evils.

'I have to push now.'

Tony later told me that Fanny went pale. Fanny knew that she'd been a big twat, but fair play to her, she charged around ordering a wheelchair and phoning the labour ward. Then, with me clinging on to the arms of the wheelchair for dear life and still screaming for my epidural ('Oh, it's too late for that now, Katie dear.'), we all charged through the hospital to the labour ward. As ever, poor Tony was bringing up the rear with the bag of 'all the things we would never need for a nice, relaxing birth because now everything had gone tits up and it was definitely NOT relaxing'. I focused on keeping a hospital blanket tucked over my bare nether regions, although I feared that, while screeching round one particularly sharp corner, I may have had a legs akimbo moment and accidentally flashed an old man outside Cardiology. Oh well, at least his ECG would make interesting reading.

'Ooh, Katie dear,' said Fanny, as we finally burst through the doors, 'I've never seen such a quick labour and birth. I'm going off shift now but would you mind if I stayed?'

'No problem.' I looked at Tony, who was wheezing after his unexpected sprint and looked like he should have stopped for a quick check-up at Cardiology. 'Is that okay with you?'

Tony dumped the heavy bag on a chair, then had second thoughts, moved it, and dumped his backside on the chair instead. He just nodded at me and slumped back. A nurse passed him a tissue and some water and I could vaguely hear her talking kindly to him, coaching him to breathe in through the nose and out through the mouth, but by this time I was up on the bed and more concerned with my own breathing.

Before my mind separated itself from my pain-wracked body, I turned to Fanny and said, sweetly, 'Could you hold my hand please?' Then I took a deep breath, surrendered to the agony and squeezed that hand until I felt the bones grind.

. . .

Fifteen minutes later, I was holding our beautiful, perfect daughter. Tony sat on the bed next to me, tenderly stroking each of our heads. I turned my face towards him, radiant with happiness, and whispered, 'I'm so relieved I didn't shit myself.'

Tony whispered back, 'And I'm so relieved I didn't throw up when I cut the cord. Are you sure you want her to take my surname?'

'Definitely. April Frock makes her sound like a Spring wardrobe.'

We gazed down at our daughter. April Meadows, millennium baby, born 1st January 2000. A special day and a special child, who would go on to do special, wonderful things. We would bring this little poppet up with love and tolerance. We would teach her kindness and respect. She would be the brightest star in the universe and we would be the best parents ever. She had Tony for numbers and rules and being thoroughly decent. She had me for adventures and stories and amazing cooking. Together, the three of us were setting off on the best adventure of our lives. Being a family.

A man in rolled up shirt sleeves entered the room and began pulling on some surgical gloves.

'Now, away with you Tony,' I said a little too loudly, 'The fanny doctor's here.'

PART ONE
KATIE

CHAPTER 1

I felt the shock thud into my stomach and almost dropped the phone.

'She's been what?'

'Look, I'm really sorry Miss Frock. We were at this club last night and I saw her with this randomer. He was well shifty, like. Next thing I know, the cops have her. I didn't know if I should tell you. Sorry, Miss Frock. Sorry.'

'It's okay, Janine. You're her friend and it's hard to know what to do for the best. Leave it with me. I'll sort it out. And by the way, Janine…'

'Yes, Miss Frock?'

'I'm not your teacher any more. You can call me Katie.'

'Right-o, Miss Frock. Bye.'

I put my phone back on the nightstand and sat up in bed. The big, furry lump at my feet gave a growl of protest at being so rudely disturbed, but didn't move.

'C'mon Archie. Stir your hairy bum and go out for a pee. April's been a twat again, but we still have you, don't we, momma's good boy? And who's the bestest good boy in the world?'

I leaned over and gave our Beagle a hug. Tears sprang to my eyes and, a moment later, when Archie began to squirm, I realised I was perhaps squeezing a little too hard. Well, it's not as if I had anyone else to hug. What time was it? 5am. Where was Tony this time? Mumbai? No, that was last month. Somewhere beginning with M. Moscow? Marrakesh? Aha! Milton Keynes. At least we were in the same bloody time zone, for once.

I met Tony when he had just finished his marketing degree. He was the least creative person I knew, but, somehow, he ended up making corporate films. The project management and the market research appealed to the anal retentive in him. Lots of lovely spreadsheets and data to analyse. So, Tony did the meeting and greeting of clients, the budgets and the businessy side of things at JT Productions. His partner, Jack, was in charge of the sexy side - filming and graphics.

I called Tony. No reply. I called again. No reply. I texted 'Call me asap. April in the shit again.'

I called Jack. After a few rings, the phone was answered with a cheery, 'Who is this, who disturbs my lovemaking? Speak now and have a bloody good reason.'

'Jack, it's Katie. Listen, I can't get hold of Tony. Is he with you?'

'Not unless he's a 34DD signorina with a savant-like grasp of the Karma Sutra.'

Milan! That was it!

'Oh, lordy. Sorry, Jack. Listen, if you speak to him, can you get him to call me? It's urgent.'

I threw on my clothes and was letting Archie out the back door when I realised I'd forgotten to put on a bra. To bra or not to bra? That is the question. Whether it is nobler in boob…bollocks to it. It's not like the police would be looking at my chest. My nipples pointing due south were hardly likely to be integral to their enquiries. They weren't going to say, 'Now, Miss Frock, before we move onto the matter of your daughter having a bag of drugs, we'd just like to ask a few questions about your droopy breasts.'

Archie padded into the kitchen, leaving a trail of muddy footprints, and I shut the back door. As he settled down into his kitchen bed, one of at least five dotted around the house, I gave his ears a scratch and sighed.

'Right, old chap, I'm off to dig April out of yet another hole. Be a good boy and if you fancy mopping the floor while I'm away, you really would be the bestest boy in the world.'

. . .

By the time I arrived at the police station it was nearly 6am. 7am in Milan time. Where the hell was Tony? Why hadn't he called? I loved that man to the very depths of his data-driven soul but how could someone so bloody organised never look at his messages? He never opened letters either. It drove me nuts, having to go through his letters once a month, so I could clear the mail before it piled up so high that anyone looking through the letterbox would think we'd died and been eaten by Archie. Not that people would look through the letterbox. It had long since been taped shut after Archie nearly took the fingers off Dennis, the postman. No amount of large Christmas tips would make Dennis forgive us for Finger-gate. He was a very grumpy man at the best of times and I suspected that Finger-gate was why he kept ignoring the No Junk Mail sign on our mailbox. If I died and was eaten by Archie, how long would it take anyone to notice? Work might ring in a few days to check I was okay. Tony might be concerned that he was about to go on another trip and had no clean underpants. April would need to borrow a fiver at some point. Hmm. Probably about three weeks before anyone was sure I was gone. By which time I'd be little brown Archie parcels all over the back lawn and nobody would know what had happened to me. Maybe the police would think Tony and April had murdered me. Maybe I should leave a note for the police to say I wasn't murdered, just in case I did suddenly die.

"Dear police,
I died and Archie ate me. I definitely wasn't murdered by my family. You can DNA test Archie's poo if you like. However, the back garden is like a dog shit minefield, so enter at your own risk.
Love Katie xxx"

I went up to the front desk, which was womanned by a stern-looking tank in a starched grey shirt.
'Hello, I'm here for April Meadows.'

The tank checked her computer, then slowly turned and readied her guns.

'Are you her solicitor?'

I looked down at my tatty old top, spag bol stain down the front and nipples gaily poking through the thin material, about level with my belly button. I thought that surely solicitors made a bit more of an effort. After all, they were highly paid professionals, who probably had cleaners and assistants and people to do their ironing. I was a cook at the local pub. My shepherd's pie was legendary but it was never going to make my fortune. The cleaner, ironer and chief bottle washer in our house was always going to be me and, really, when you're skivvy to a bunch of ingrates, the dress code does tend to be less button-down collar and more button-fallen-off blouse. I decided that the tank was taking the piss.

'I'm her mother,' I said through gritted teeth. Thanks to our daughter, this wasn't my first early morning visit to a police station and I knew, from bitter experience, that arguing with the cow on the counter achieved nothing, other than less information and a longer wait.

'Right,' said the woman, looking me up and down, 'I'll let someone know you're here. But you know you can't go in, right? She's over eighteen.'

Like I wasn't perfectly aware, having had my vagina reduced to a pound of mince by the little darling over twenty-one years ago.

'It's fine. I'm only here to find out what's happening and pick her up when she's ready.'

I settled myself into one of the plastic chairs bolted to the floor, pulled a paperback out of my handbag and got ready for a long wait. The police do things on their own time. They have mysterious rituals like custody procedures to observe, and have little regard for knackered, middle-aged women, who are fervently praying that the mysterious custody procedures involve a cavity search, so as to teach their wayward little fecker of a daughter a lesson.

I decided to stop being angry with April for being a constant worry. Stop being angry with Tony for being who he is. Stop being angry with the counter cow for judging me. Stop being angry with the junkie two seats over, who kept shoving his hands down his pants to scratch his balls, before giving his fingers an experimental sniff. I would simply regard the next few hours of waiting as valuable me-time to enjoy my book.

Two hours later, I had just gotten to a good bit. Detective Chief Inspector Drake was making his way through the abandoned warehouse in pursuit of the killer. Superintendent Flowers had expressly forbidden him from taking part in the investigation because the chief suspect was Barnaby Drake, the DCI's nephew. The DNA results from the murder weapon had come back in half an hour and they were a match to Barnaby. But DCI Drake knew that someone with super-hacking skills must have tampered with the police station computer and changed the results. It had to be an inside job…

'Excuse me, Mrs Meadows?'

I looked up to see a twelve-year-old policeman gazing down at me.

'Frock. Katie Frock. Yes, hi, is April okay? What's happening?'

'I can't go into much detail, but April had a small amount of cocaine on her when she was arrested. She was with a man who we've been watching for some time and we think he perhaps slipped it into her bag when he spotted us. We have some loose ends to tie up but, if all goes well, April should be out in an hour or so.'

'Have you DNA tested the drugs bag? DNA results come back much faster than they used to, you know.'

The twelve-year-old looked at me for a moment, like he was trying to decide whether he should check *me* for drugs. Maybe hallucinogens.

'Erm…that's okay…as I say, April should be out in about an hour,' he said, slowly backing away.

'S'cuse me mate,' asked the junkie, stirring from his personal grooming. 'Have you got a light?'

'No, and if you want to smoke, you'll have to go outside.'

The police officer left and the junkie extracted his hands from his underpants. He popped a finger in his mouth and ran his nail between his teeth.

'Vitamins,' he said, winking at me as he hauled himself off his chair and wandered towards the door, taking the faint odour of old cheese with him. I watched as he pulled open the door, and made a mental note to never touch a door handle in a public place again.

. . .

DCI Drake had just cornered the suspect, when April came through the door that led to the custody suite. Standing there in last night's glad rags, all panda eyes and wild hair, she looked ready for the walk of shame. And walk of shame it would be. I let her open the police station door, then all the way to my beaten-up Honda Civic, I berated her.

'How could you be so stupid? You're twenty-one years old, for God's sake. Too old to be hanging around with a bad crowd and getting into trouble. Even at fifteen it wasn't acceptable but at least we could blame it on the terrible teens. I'd expected you to have grown out of it by now and be doing something useful with your life. But no, you have to find the lowest common denominator every bloody time.'

And lots more of the same. It was a long walk to the car park. A long walk where I knew I was wasting my breath. Nothing would change until April wanted to change. As long as we kept digging her out of holes, we were just enabling her. I'd said the same to Tony, but she was his blind spot and he was incapable of tough love when it came to April. She was a bright, clever girl-woman, who was also a complete brat and Tony couldn't see it.

April flung herself into the front seat of the car. She'd had plenty of time to compose her speech of penitence, no doubt including a large section on how it wasn't her fault, and she opened her mouth to deliver it.

'Save it,' I told her. 'Your Dad's not here to butter up and I seriously don't give a hoot. I'm tired, April. Tired of the years of worrying. Tired of the years of you not helping around the house. Tired of picking up the bloody pieces every time.'

'I'm sorry mum. He was dealing drugs in the club. I didn't know he was a bad lad. He just seemed flush with cash and was buying me drinks all night. I mean, who's going to turn down free drinks!'

'April, nothing is free. You did know he was a bad lad, you just chose to go along with it because it was easy and he gave you stuff. You don't work hard for anything and you're floating through life on a series of part-time jobs, hoping that someone will magically come along and pay for the lifestyle you aspire to. That's not going to happen. If you want things, you have to earn them. Your father is away all the time because he wants to earn good money to support his family. I hate it when he's away and I hate it that you always seem to get in trouble when there's only me here to deal with it. I love you, but you're selfish and lazy. You're also a grown up, which is why this is the last time I'm bailing you out.'

'Fine. But you're not perfect, yourself. I mean, look at the state of you. No wonder Dad works away all the time. You're just a drudge. You think you're so high and mighty but you don't work either. A part-time job cooking in a pub is hardly earning your way. You're relying on Dad to pay for everything and give you stuff, so you can't tell me that I'm selfish and lazy. You're just as bad.'

'I can't believe you said that. You know full well that I had my own career before you came along. I put that aside because we agreed it was the best thing for our family and you're choosing to see that as a selfish and lazy decision?'

'Yeah, well I'm twenty-one now and you're *still* a part-time cook in a small-town pub. So, you *are* swanning around, relying on someone else to support you.'

She had a point, I privately conceded. Why hadn't I gone back to the career I loved? I supposed I'd just become institutionalised. For years, I hadn't thought beyond the daily round of picking other people's underwear off the bathroom floor. My life had somehow turned into an endless cycle of housework, interspersed with cooking pies for drunk people. However, I wasn't going to let the little minx win the argument.

'Fair enough. Then, as a twenty-one-year-old who no longer needs to be looked after by her mother, you can do your fair share of the housework from now on. If you don't pick up after yourself, you'll find your stuff in the bin. There will be no more 'borrowing' fivers, no more make-up slipped into the shopping basket as a treat, no more stealing my wine. Mum and Dad's taxis is closed and you can start paying board.'

April looked at me defiantly and crossed her arms over her ample bosom, which was the only thing she'd inherited from me. She was all Tony, down to her weirdly long toes and ability to ignore text messages.

'Fine,' she huffed.

The rest of the journey passed in silence. April was no doubt silently scheming a way to get around these most unreasonable demands that she behave like a grown-up and contribute. I was still pondering the question of when exactly I'd forgotten about my own hopes and dreams.

As we pulled into our drive, my phone rang. It was Tony.

'Sorry, sorry. I just got your message. Is everything okay?'

'Yeah, I'm just home now. It's all sorted, nothing to worry about. Some lad put coke in April's bag and she was arrested but they're not taking any further action. When will you be home?'

'I'll be back on Friday night. Sorry you had to do this on your own.'

Yes, everybody's sorry, except possibly April.

'We need to talk,' I said, 'But it can keep until you get home on Friday. I'm really missing you.'

'Okay. Got to dash. Meeting a signor about a dog. Quite literally. Ha ha. The CEO wants his dog in the film but he's a yappy little fucker. The dog's as good as gold though. Ha ha. Speak soon.'

I locked the car and trudged into the house, to be met by a wildly ecstatic Archie. April had disappeared off to her room and would probably sleep for the rest of the day, before reappearing about 6pm to demand why we never had any decent food in this house. I sat down on the sofa and Archie crawled onto my lap.

'What happened to me, Archie? I used to be pretty and fun. Now I'm pitching up at police stations in the early hours, looking like a walking advert for giving up on life. Even the cheesy balls junkie was having a better time than me.'

Archie just let out a small fart and glared at me like it was all my fault.

CHAPTER 2

Holy guacamole, the pub was busy today. Had the whole world taken the day off to eat shepherd's pie in our beer garden? It was a sunny Friday afternoon and I heartily wished that I could down tools and drink beer. Instead, I'd nipped out the back door and was sharing an illicit cigarette with Maggie, the landlady.

'Maggie, did you always dream of owning a pub?'

'Did I shite,' said Maggie, delivering that last word with a good dose of Scottish relish. 'I used to be an actress, but it didn't last.'

'Why not?'

'Promise not to tell anyone? Right, I was doing fine. Just starting to get some good parts, when this eejit wanted a blow job before he'd give me a TV role. I said okay. I mean, what's the difference, I'd been giving them oot for free for years, so I reckoned I may as well get something for my troubles. Anyway, d'ye remember that big gas explosion in Sauchiehall Street in 1989?'

I nodded vaguely, not really remembering and unsure whether I should be appalled by the sexual assault or amazed by Maggie's pragmatic approach to it.

'Aye, well, we were just getting down to business when BANG. I damn near bit his cock off. They pulled us out of the rubble with me still attached and it made the Scottish Sun. The roles dried up a wee bit after that.'

'Oh my word, I do remember it! Maggie Banks. That was you?!'

Maggie shook her head ruefully. 'Aye. The headline was "Suckyhall Street". There's no coming back from that.'

I looked at the little Scotswoman, all prim and proper, with not a hair out of place on her helmet of a blonde bob. It was hard to imagine her biting the top off a carrot, never mind a…jeez, the two of them had been all over the papers at the time. After a moment's silence, I asked her, 'So how did you end up running a pub in Northumberland?'

'I met Bob. He interviewed me for the local paper and was a bit kinder than the rest of the press. I took him out for a drink to say thanks and we just got talking. Then we did more talking. And some other things.' She grinned lasciviously and I could see a hint of the lass from Suckyhall Street. 'His Mum and Dad had the Plough before us and when they retired, we took over.'

'Do you ever regret giving up acting?'

'Sometimes, but it's more like a fond memory. I mean, other than that last starring role, of course. I do wonder what my life would have been like now if I'd carried on, but the Sauchiehall Street thing would have followed me everywhere. Anyway, we've been here for thirty years now and it's us who are thinking of retiring.'

With that, she stubbed her cigarette out in the ancient Brown Ale ashtray and made to go back into the pub. Pausing at the door, she turned to me and said, 'No sense in looking back, Katie, when there's plenty to look forward to.'

I finished my cigarette, mulling over Maggie's words of wisdom.

The rest of the shift went by in a blur of sausage and mash, pies, steaks and thrice cooked chips. I'd tried to introduce some different items to the menu over the years, but the locals firmly rejected anything they deemed to be 'foreign muck'. It was so hot in the kitchen that, by 9pm, I was convinced my hat would make a sucking sound when I removed it. The sheer relief of being able to shake my hair out and take the apron off was indescribable.

I quickly made my way through the pub, trying to avoid eye

contact with Davey, one of the regulars who propped up the end of the bar every weekend. Fifteen years ago, Davey had been a cheeky charmer with a ready smile and a steady darts hand. His charm had long since faded into a vague seediness and the man who had once danced shirtless on the pool table, now perched unsteadily on a bar stool, rubbing his expanding beer belly and belching for England. Years of beers, I thought. They'd ruined him. The problem was, Davey still imagined himself the cheeky charmer, so any conversation with him quickly became awkward.

'Hellooo, Katie Kitty Cat.'

'Hi Davey. Can't stop. I'm just off home.'

'Aww c'mere and talk to your old mate. Hey, Katie. Want to go to a party?'

'Not now, Davey.'

'A party in my pants,' he slurred, howling with laughter and grabbing his crotch. Yep. Seediness maybe not so vague.

I don't know what made me do it. I'd always felt pity for Davey, but I tried to be decent to him. Anything else would be like kicking a dog. Unfortunately, in a flash of anger, I decided to kick that metaphorical dog.

'For fucks sake Davey. Do you even hear yourself? You're not funny. Stop sitting there like a pissed-up bookend every weekend and go do something useful.'

As soon as the words were out of my mouth, I regretted them. Never mind kicking a dog, Davey looked like I'd just punched him in the throat.

'Oh, Davey, I'm sorry. It's been a long day and I had no right to take it out on you.'

'S'okay, Katie pet,' he said, staring glumly into his pint, 'I'm a loser. I know it.'

'You're not a loser, Davey. You're just lost and I think you need help to find your way back again. I'm really sorry.' I patted his shoulder, but he said nothing and carried on looking into his pint, like a borderline alcoholic psychic with a crystal ball of real ale. I doubted there was any future for him in there.

· · ·

After being trapped in a boiling kitchen all day, the walk home should have felt like a cool release. Instead, it felt like there was a boulder in my stomach. I would carry the Davey thing for days. Stupid, gobby Katie. Why didn't I just keep my mouth shut? And now I had to go home and have 'The Big Talk' with Tony.

For the past few days, I'd been rehearsing The Big Talk. Like April, Tony wielded logic like a rapier and my impassioned arguments generally fell apart within minutes. Well, this time, Tony-me-boy, prepare to be amazed. For the missus has marshalled her mind troops. The infantry will charge with all the facts about how April is a spoiled brat and you give into her every demand. The archers will pierce you with their arrows of how you undermine any rules I make. Then the cavalry will sweep in from the sides and trample you with all the things we need to do to make her wake up and take responsibility for herself. Also, you never open your post and it's extremely irritating. Yes, that will do nicely.

I wandered down the drive to our lovely, Victorian pile. It was rather too enormous for three people, but it had been a labour of love for Tony and I. We used every penny of our savings to buy it, just after April was born. We'd moved from London, where house prices were high, to the North, where everything seemed shockingly cheap. The moment we saw the big, leaky, mouldy heap, we knew it was ours. For the first year, we'd lived in three rooms, while we saved up enough to fix the roof. Bank of Mum and Dad eventually came to the rescue, when my parents visited and refused to let any granddaughter of theirs live in a squat. Twenty years later, it was our home; the slightly imperfect, beating heart of our family. I didn't care that the radiators were temperamental or the walls were strangers to right-angles. There was a big kitchen in there, with a big table, where we had read stories, done homework, thrown parties, had sex, cried when my Mum died and pulled ticks off Archie's bum. We'd also eaten at the table, but only after giving it a good scrub. That kitchen was where I created all the marvellous recipes that I would one day unleash upon the world, hoarding them in my special recipe folder, which nobody was allowed to touch. This home we had built, this little family – they were my whole world. Come on, Katie. Get over yourself and appreciate what you have.

By the time I opened the front door, narrowly avoiding getting my nose bitten by an overenthusiastic Archie, I'd pushed the Davey boulder into my lower intestines (where it would no doubt liquify and make an appearance tomorrow – stress always gave me the trots). I was feeling quite content and ready for a calm discussion with Tony.

Tony heard me come in and emerged from the living room, taking me in his arms and squeezing me tightly.

'Ah, ah, oh,' I spluttered, squirming to loosen his grip enough to breathe a tiny bit.

'Oh, I've missed you, my gorgeous creature,' said Tony, lying his craggy face off. It was yet another thing I loved about him. He never really aged, his face just got more interesting. It was all angles and furrows, with big eyebrows and slightly gross, hairy, middle-aged man ears that he either didn't know or didn't care about.

'I stink of chips and my hair looks like I combed it with the arse end of a hedgehog,' I said matter-of-factly, 'But I missed you too, you big lummox.'

'What exactly is a lummox?' he asked, letting me go.

'I've no idea. It's just one of those words isn't it? Like hell in a hand-basket. What's a hand-basket?'

'I'm going to have to google it or it'll annoy me all night.'

Tony wandered off to get his phone and I shouted after him that I was going to have a quick shower. I pounded upstairs to our bedroom, pursued by Archie, who liked to station himself outside the en-suite door, just in case I was doing something in there that he ought to know about. Or perhaps he was a fan of off-key Abba parodies.

'Wash that bum, nice and clean, scrubbing the Dancing Queen,' I warbled, as I rinsed my hair. 'Friday night and the leg hair's gross. Take a razor to some of those.'

I was starting on 'Waterpoo, I've just washed my bum, now I need the loo' when the bathroom door opened. Tony came in, followed by Archie.

'A stupid, clumsy person,' he announced. Tony, not Archie. If Archie could talk, I'd shit myself. That dog was the keeper of all my secrets and had heard me do many private things of a night time, when Tony was away. Most of them requiring a full set of batteries and some fine motor skills.

'I take it back, then. You're not clumsy.' I popped my head around the shower door and grinned at him.

'Ooh, come here, you saucy wench,' said Tony, stripping off his clothes. It would have been spontaneous and romantic if he hadn't stopped to fold them and place them in a neat pile on the loo seat. And if he'd remembered to take off his socks. He stepped into the shower and pulled me close.

'You'll never guess what Maggie told me today,' I said. 'Do you remember that big gas explosion in Sauchiehall Street in Glasgow years ago?'

We stood under the shower together, enjoying the warmth of the water on our bodies, while I regaled Tony with Maggie's misadventures and he squidged my boobs together to make them look like bum cleavage. When I finished the tale, Tony suggested that maybe I could give him one of those. Minus the biting, of course.

I obligingly did the sexiest slither to my knees that I could muster, without knocking the shower door open with my backside and giving Archie something to talk to the other dogs about. I put my hands on Tony's thighs and I could feel the muscles, tight with anticipation. Lower and lower I went, gazing up at Tony through the steam and coquettishly biting my lip. My knee touched the floor and I leaned towards Tony's erection. My knee went back. My knee kept going back. Very fast. The words 'bloody soap!' flashed through my mind, as the rest of me shot forward and, with full force, headbutted Tony in the testicles.

I couldn't recall ever seeing someone go green before. I thought it only happened in cartoons. Tony's face was definitely a greenish-grey. He stood there silently for a moment, eyes bulging, before slowly crumpling to the floor. As he hunched over his squashed cherries, heaving and gasping for breath, the shower door swung open. I must have hit it with my bottom after all. The door hung there for a few second then, with a crack, fell off its hinges, narrowly missing Archie. Okay, maybe I'd destroyed it with my bottom.

Scrambling upright, I hit the shower off button and surveyed the damage. One broken shower cubicle, one broken husband and loads of blood. Where was all the blood coming from? Oh my days, what was going on with my face? I stepped out of the shower, almost tripping over Archie, who seemed delighted to finally have it confirmed that things definitely happened in the bathroom that he ought to know about.

The best thing about heated bathroom mirrors is that they never steam up. Which is why I could see immediately that I'd bitten clean through my bottom lip and the source of all the blood was me. Already my lip was swelling and a piece of mangled flesh was flapping from it. Definitely a stitches job, I thought. And there'll be no more of the other kind of job for quite some time, assuming Tony's testicles ever recover. I quickly grabbed a handful of toilet roll and pressed it to my lip to staunch the bleeding.

A high-pitched whine, like an animal in pain, came from behind me. Archie? Had Archie been hurt after all? I turned towards the source, to see that Tony had regained his voice, albeit in soprano. At least that meant he was breathing. I leaned over him and gently rubbed his shoulder.

'Oh da god. Are you okay? Sorry. It uz tha soak. Ery, ery sorry,' I said through my fat lip. I could see tears forming in Tony's eyes and I felt my own eyes well up in sympathy.

'Eeeeeeeeeeeeeeeeeeeeeee,' Tony whined.

'Talk to gee, Tony. Clease,' I sobbed.

'Eeeeeeeeeeeeeeeeeeeeeee.'

'Oscital. Need oscital. Acril! Acril!' I wailed.

I grabbed my pink dressing gown and threw it over Tony, then, still holding the wad of toilet roll to my bleeding face, I dangled my knickers one-handed in front of me and attempted to kick my leg through the hole. On the third time of getting them caught between my toes, I gave up on the knickers and, somehow, managed to swing myself into my work trousers instead.

Just as I covered my top half with my work t-shirt, April appeared at the bathroom door.

'Bloody hell, parents. What have you two been up to? Some weird, old people's sex thing? No, don't tell me.' She put her hands over her ears. 'La la la la la la not listening,'

'Thor thuck's sake, Acril. Helc nee ith your thather. I headgutted his galls and git dy lick. Stock laughing. It's not thunny.'

'You headbutted Dad in the balls and you want me to stop laughing?' I gave her my most murderous glare. 'Okay, okay, I'll help you. Let's get him onto the bed.'

We cautiously approached the keening, fluffy, pink lump in the shower and each took a side. Slowly, we supported Tony, still hunched over, as far as the bed, whereupon he collapsed and rolled into a foetal ball.

'Keys!' I declared. 'Garden keys!' April stared at me blankly. 'Throzen keys. In the threezer!'

I swear I saw a lightbulb go on over April's head, as she decoded my fat lip lingo. She scuttled off downstairs and returned a few minutes later with a bag of frozen peas. Gently, I lifted the dressing gown, prised Tony's hand off his balls and placed a bag of peas over his dangly bits. As the cold hit, his eyes bulged.

'Eeeeeeeeeeeeeeeeeeeeeeeee!'

Ah, maybe frozen things on the todger wasn't the way to go here. I carefully extracted the bag of peas and clutched them to my swollen lip instead. Popping the dressing gown back over his bits, to preserve what little dignity was left to him, I gave Tony's back a sympathetic rub and whispered that I was going to take him to oscital.

'Keys!' I told April. She looked at me, confused once more. She'd already provided peas. 'Car keys! Need oscital thor lick and galls. Get in car. And get Dad's slickers.'

'Hospital, lip, balls, keys, slippers.' April charged off to raid my handbag for my car keys and hunt for Tony's slippers.

I rolled Tony to the edge of the bed, swung his legs over the side and gently peeled off his wet socks. He was still looking rather green around the gills, but his breathing had steadied. I pulled him to his feet and, grasping his elbow, steered him downstairs, where April waited, keys and slippers in hand. Together, we supported him out to the car. As he was still hunched over, a gentle nudge was all it took to collapse him into the passenger seat, where he sat staring into the distance, locked in his own world of pain. Lordy, what had I done to the poor man?

April drove us to the local Accident and Emergency department. Normally, I'd be grumbling at her for driving too fast, but tonight, as I sat in the back with my bag of rapidly melting peas, I was quite relieved that our daughter regarded road signs as merely advisory. My car, the old jalopy, was slightly less pleased and, as we screeched to a halt in the hospital car park, it gave a little cough and died. Fingers crossed, it would be fine after a little rest.

April bounded across the road and disappeared through the hospital entrance. She returned a few minutes later with a wheelchair and, between us, we hauled Tony out of the car, swung his bum around and carefully lowered him onto the seat. He sat there, big, hairy, long-toed feet poking out the bottom of my pink fluffy robe, looking for all the world like a cross-dressing hobbit. I flicked the hem over his swollen precious and turned to get my bag from the car.

I was quite proud of April for taking charge and behaving like a responsible grown-up. She had really stepped up in a crisis. And, even more importantly, she hadn't asked questions. There really was no explaining this one. Her poor Dad, who held us together with his common sense, his lists and his correct way to load a dishwasher. He must be dying a little on the inside right now.

As I rummaged for my bag in the footwell, I glanced across at the driver's side to see April reaching into the back seat for her bag. 'Sensible, brilliant girl,' I thought. Then I had another thought. 'If we're here, who's looking after Tony?'

'Eeeeeeeeeeeeeeeeeeeeeee!'

I turned in time to see a pink hobbit slowly trundling into the path of an oncoming Porsche. Oh my flipping word, there was just no keeping this man safe tonight. I dashed across the car park and managed to grab the front of the wheelchair, using my feet as brakes. The Porsche whizzed past and I slackened my grip. The wheelchair once more trundled backwards, taking me with it, and I fell forwards, firmly planting a fist in Tony's groin.

'Gollocks. Tony, are you okay? Greathe, Tony, greathe.'

Tony didn't breathe. He wheezed and, once more, went a worrying shade of green.

'Acril! Get Dad in oscital.'

April passed me the car keys, grabbed the handles of the wheelchair and steered her father quickly towards A&E. I locked the car and scurried after them, terrified that I might have done some lasting damage.

I entered the packed waiting room to find April calmly explaining to the receptionist, 'As far as I can tell, my Mum headbutted him in the balls then punched him in the balls. And she bit through her lip.'

'It oz an accident!' I cried.

The receptionist looked at me, standing there with my bleeding, mangled lip, and said, sceptically, 'I see. I'll just take some details and we'll get you triaged.'

An hour later, we were still sitting in the waiting room; Tony in his wheelchair (by this time we'd discovered the thing had brakes), me squirming about on a plastic seat that seemed designed to simultaneously numb the bum and cut off circulation to one's legs, and April ignoring both of us in favour of Instagramming the night's disasters to her friends. I'd managed to stop her posting a picture of her father's bruised manly bits, which had made an accidental guest appearance when the hem of his robe slipped, but I wasn't quick enough to catch her surreptitiously photographing the two of us and captioning it #my parents literally suck. Ah, she'd guessed what we were up to, then.

Tony had fully recovered the power of speech by this time, although he still looked nauseous. He hadn't said much, though. Just sat there, with a thousand-yard stare, focusing on the pain in his stomach and boy bits. I'd apologised a thousand times already, but, again, I felt the need to explain.

'I so sorry, Tony. I slicked. Kneeled on the gloody soak.' He looked at me uncomprehendingly. 'Soak! S-O-A-Key. Then the gloody heelchair nade ne lose ny galance. I heel like a...' I couldn't think of a way to say 'complete twat' through my swollen lip, so I opted for, '...giant tit.'

Tony reached over and patted my knee. 'I know it was an accident. Love you, but finding it hard to be nice right now. Just sit quietly and rest your lip, eh?'

At some point over the next half hour, they moved us to a cubicle and helped Tony onto the bed. As time went by, I could feel my lip swelling and stiffening and I reckoned that, at this rate, I wouldn't be able to talk at all. How was I going to speak to Tony about Acril..sorry..April? I'd been wondering if, maybe, he could find a way to be at home more often and I could look for a better job. Perhaps us both working good jobs and him being around more would make April less dependent on me, set a good example and give me something of my own, get me out more. People always talked about finding themselves and, despite my earlier comforting words to Davey, I was never quite sure what they meant. I suspected it was some sort of millennial bullshit, where everyone was on a deep and meaningful journey. In my case, though, I had disappeared somewhere in the piles of dirty nappies circa 2000-2002 and never properly re-emerged. Sure, working in the pub provided some me-time and pocket money. But I never actually spent anything because I never went anywhere. With Tony always away, we'd fallen out of the habit of going out, content just to order a takeaway and cuddle on the sofa when he returned home, knackered. I couldn't remember the last time I'd put on make-up, bought a dress and…oh, shoes…I used to love shoes.

The doctor arrived. Tony had somehow blocked the pain by falling asleep, so I gave him a gentle nudge.

'Tony, the…er…uh…' I decided that my lip was now too immobile to say urologist. 'The cock doctor's here.' Honestly, I'd make an excellent ventriloquist.

I possibly said 'cock doctor' a little too loudly because the urologist glared disapprovingly at my bloody face, then summoned a nurse to take me away, while he examined Tony. Maybe I needed to work on throwing my voice so that other people didn't realise it was me who'd said the rude thing. The nurse kindly steered me to another cubicle, telling me, 'We'll take a look at that lip.'

She patched me up with some anaesthetic and a few stitches. My mouth would hurt tomorrow, but for now there was some blessed relief. My stress levels had started to come down and I was just beginning to relax, when she asked, 'Is everything okay at home?'

I looked at her in confusion, then did a mental checklist. Garage – full of highly organised old junk, thanks to Tony. Housework – vaguely done, enough not to frighten unexpected visitors away, provided they remained downstairs. Food – fridge full of nutritious items, wine and chocolate (carefully hidden in the vegetable drawer where Aprils fear to tread). I nodded enthusiastically. Yes, everything in my home seemed pretty normal.

The nurse said, 'Because, you know, there are people who can help.'

Help? Well, if somebody was willing to come and do the ironing, I would shove them in the direction of that particular mountain and wish them Godspeed. Then it dawned on me. She thought Tony had given me the fat lip.

I heard a loud groan from the other cubicle. Tony was probably having a similar conversation right now. The urologist would be gently probing his balls and suggesting a support group. Flibberty gibbet, Tony would probably rather I punched him in the balls again than go to a support group for anything. I mean, he could talk about feelings and share the odd confidence with me and even April, but the thought of 'sharing' with other human beings was anathema to him. One of the reasons Tony didn't have addictions or psychological problems was because the thought of talking to other human beings about feelings scared the shit out of him. Which was probably a psychological problem in itself, but, hey ho, nobody's perfect. I knew when he was stressed because his CD collection would suddenly be organised alphabetically and strict instructions would be issued to myself and April that we were not to mess it up again. Lots of displacement activity would go on, such as a sudden desire to apply a lawn treatment. I'd tried suggesting that he do something useful with his restlessness, like maybe pick up the dog shit before he applied the lawn treatment, but he dealt with his feelings by being useful and organised about the stuff he could control and I would have to wait patiently, until he either got over his worries or decided to talk to me. Although, if there was a support group where they all just sat around building stuff and ignoring each other, Tony would totally be up for that.

'Hone is good,' I told the nurse, 'Just trying sexy shenanigans and nutted husgand in the nuts. Hurt lick.'

'Oh, I think that lick definitely hurt. You won't be licking again for a while.'

'No, L-I-Key!'

'Yep, definitely no likey,' said the nurse, with a twinkle in her eye. She knew exactly what I meant and the minute she got out of here, she'd be telling anyone who'd listen. Thuck my thucking life.

CHAPTER 3

By the following Friday, Tony's bruised baubles had calmed down. The urologist had assured him that there was no lasting damage and he should use ice for the swelling and paracetamol for the pain. April had taken to calling him Numb Nuts and, brief moment of level-headedness gone, she was back to her usual party-going, Instagramming self. She'd borrowed my car to go to the shopping mall and returned it with a scratch on the side, which absolutely was definitely not her fault. Apparently, a highly inconsiderate pillar had been in the way. I didn't have the energy or the lip movement to argue.

The only saving grace of our injuries was that Tony was working from home. It gave us a chance to catch up with each other, spend some quality time together and take Archie for a hobble around the park. The stitches in my lip felt tight and sore, so I decided to postpone The Big Talk with Tony and, instead, just enjoy pottering about with him.

Jack, of course, had been straight on the phone the day after the accident. He followed April on Instagram, so there was no chance of Tony being able to claim illness or domestic emergency as his reason for avoiding a client meet and greet in Chicago.

'Hey, is that the Beavis and Head Butt residence?' he snickered.

Tony took the phone into the study before I could grab it off him and give his partner a barely intelligible piece of my mind. Jack appeared a few days later, bearing flowers to apologise for all the mickey-taking. Although, he still couldn't resist saying things like 'that sucks' and 'well, blow me, actually don't.' Having agreed that Tony would teleconference all the client meetings for the next few weeks, Jack left with a cheery, 'I'll head off now. Gerrit? Head?' Yeah, thucking hilarious.

Tony had called Maggie at the pub and told her I wouldn't be in for a week or two, mainly because my lip was so sore I couldn't sleep. I pleaded with him not to tell her what had happened. After the story she'd confided in me, she'd never let me live this one down and the whole pub would find out. Jeez, Davey would have a field day. If the mild sexual harassment he gave out now was anything to go by, I could expect an offer of a full-blown S & M session. He was a joiner by trade, so it was probably all in a day's work for him to build a dungeon in the bungalow he shared with his ageing mother. She'd think it was just her darling son being creative, which was also the excuse she gave for his alcohol problem and occasional lack of hygiene. Not sure how she'd explain finding me suspended from her ceiling by a pair of nipple clamps, though. Ugh. The thought of Davey's sweaty beer belly hanging over leather pants was putting me off my ice cream, which was the only comfortable, split-lip-friendly food we owned. I really hoped Davey didn't follow April on Instagram.

Maggie said she'd manage through this weekend, with a reduced menu and the stock of pies I kept in the freezer, but she was worried about next weekend. I told Tony to let her know that I'd ask my friend, Suzy, if she could help out.

Tony came off the phone and asked, 'So, are you going to explain to Suzy why you're off work?' Oh, bugger. I hadn't thought of that. No, I was definitely not going to explain this one to Suzy. She was a lovely person. Total mumzilla, though. Lord help you if you had a bad word to say about her perfect children. But, otherwise, a real sweetheart. In fact, she was so nice that I wasn't sure she'd even heard of a bj. Her children were probably some sort of immaculate conception, because I really couldn't imagine Suzy and her husband, Graham, ever unbuttoning their matching pyjamas. Suzy was PTA Mum, through and through. She did school fundraisers, church coffee mornings and meals on wheels. A thoroughly decent and kind human being, she was a Brown Owl with 'chairwoman of the WI' firmly in her sights. She was also an ace at being bossy, being super-organised and cooking for multitudes.

I needed to think of an explanation for my fat lip. One which didn't involve breaking anything, lest she offer to send Graham round to fix it. Graham was a DIY whizz and loved nothing more than getting his screwdriver collection out. Tony was a DIY trier, who didn't mind my occasional emergency calls to Graham, when it looked like Tony's efforts were going to electrocute us all/burn the house down/cause us to never be able to pee in the downstairs loo again. As long as I provided a steady supply of chocolate biscuits (banned by Suzy, who kept one eye on Graham's expanding waistline), Graham would happily fix anything. I didn't have the heart to break something on purpose and, anyway, how would we explain Tony walking around gingerly instead of being at work? Graham would surely spot the recently organised CD collection and realise something was wrong.

I considered saying I'd slipped in the shower, but with six children, not all of whom were the precious little cherubs she professed them to be, Suzy was like a human lie detector and she'd know something was up. She'd ask how exactly I'd slipped, on what exactly I'd bashed my lip etc. etc. I wasn't good at that level of detail. My lies usually only went as far as assuring Tony I'd vacuumed the living room, whereas I'd actually spent the day on the sofa, eating ice cream and binge-watching cop shows. If he expressed doubts about the state of the carpet, I would tartly remind him that the last time he vacuumed was when we got the new vacuum cleaner in 2013 and he'd pushed the thing around the living room, stopping every square foot to exclaim, 'Look how much it's picking up! I knew it was worth spending extra on a really good one.' I would also slip in the fact that the 'new' vacuum cleaner was quite old now and not nearly as effective as it used to be. This statement would send him off on a manly mission to research vacuum cleaners and compile spreadsheets on the pros and cons of their various features. Leaving me to sit back on the sofa, unmute the telly and scoff some more of the delicious ice cream. I could manipulate my husband in the name of ice cream, but I could not tell my best friend a bare-faced lie.

So, plan B then. Well, plan Z. Desperate times mean desperate measures.

'Acril! Acril!'

April came bounding into the kitchen, full of beans after a nice long lie. When you're twenty-one and indolent, mornings are to be avoided at all costs.

'Oh my God, Mum. You'll never believe what Janine's done. You know that lad who works in Blue?'

'No.'

'The one with the face tattoo who crashed his Dad's car into the bus stop in Year 10?'

'No.'

'Well, he Snapchatted her and…'

'Acril, I thorty-thithe years old. No idea who he is or hot Glue is or Snackchat. Can you cother ny shi…shi..shits at the kug clease?'

April was used to the fat lip lingo by now.

'If I cover your shifts at the pub, does that mean I get to keep your wages?'

'Yes. And I'll show you how to cook the…' I struggled to find a word that didn't contain b, f, v, w, p or m, '…things.'

I took down my sacred recipe folder from the shelf and handed it to April.

'You look athter this. It's years o' ny hard 'ork. Read it, then tonorrow you and I'll get cooking.'

It was truly exhausting, planning out everything I said so that it would make sense. However, April was past the stage of trying to get me to say 'Peter Piper picked a peck of pickled peppers' on camera so she could plaster my hilarious misery all over TikTok. She appreciated that I was passing on something precious and solemnly took the recipe folder.

'I promise I'll look after it, Mum. I know it's not just pies in here. It's all your cooking experiments, right from when you were my age. I'll guard it with my life,' she assured me.

'You getter,' I warned her, 'Or I'll nurder you.'

. . .

April proved surprisingly adept in the kitchen. Having barely lifted a finger in her life, she took to cooking with enthusiasm. Together, we spent the next few days making pub food and, as the swelling reduced, my mouth started working properly again. I filled her head with instructions on hygiene, ordering ingredients and cooking to order. By the following Friday morning, my crash course in pub cooking was done and I packed her off to the Plough with some degree of confidence.

'This has been the best week,' I told Tony. 'It's been great to spend so much time with you and April. I wanted to talk to you about her. Do you think we could sit down for a moment, because a lot of things have been playing on my mind recently?'

Tony gently lowered himself onto a kitchen chair. It would be a few weeks before he could sit normally again and, more than once, he'd commented on how much we take for granted until we can't do it anymore. He had meant sitting, but I suspected that he was also frustrated by having to work from home.

I launched into my prepared speech.

'I'm worried that April isn't a teenager, but she's still acting like one. And I don't think we're helping by continually bailing her out. Giving her extra money and rescuing her every time she gets into trouble means she never has to properly deal with the consequences of her actions. I know she was great at the hospital and she's been brilliant about covering for me at the pub, but generally she doesn't take responsibility for anything and is a bit of a freeloader. So, I was thinking that you and I need to agree on what we'll do and we both need to stick to it. I know you hate saying no to her, but we both need to do that. No extra money, no Dad's taxi at 3am, she can fund her own wardrobe. She's on a part-time wage but living the lifestyle of someone on a decent salary and as long as we continue to plug the gaps, she will never have the impetus to go to university or get a decent job.'

I looked at Tony to see how he was taking this. We'd clashed over April needing some tough love before and Tony had never been able to stick to agreed parenting strategies. The minute April whined, Tony caved.

'I disagree,' he said. 'She's a bit of a late bloomer, sure, but she's getting there. She needs to know we support her. If we push her too hard, there's a chance we'll push her away.'

'Tony, you're not the one rescuing her from parties that have got out of hand, picking her up from police stations, patching her up when she gets so drunk she falls over and breaks a rib. You're always away when these things happen and it's me who's on call. I see her going out that door on a Saturday night and only get to sleep when I hear her key in the lock at stupid o'clock on the Sunday morning.'

'It's just typical young people stuff. If she was away at university, we wouldn't know half of what she gets up to.'

'But she's not at uni. She's not anywhere and she never will be if we keep fixing everything for her. If you think that all of this is okay, stop travelling for work, stay at home and you deal with it. Because I've had enough.'

There was a moment's stunned silence, then Tony said, 'Don't be ridiculous. You know I can't be home all the time. We have a deal. It's worked for years.'

'Not any more. Not for me, anyway. I really appreciate how lucky I am that we've been able afford for me to stay at home for our daughter. But she's an adult now, in years at least, and I'm tired of dealing with her shit. I'm sick of being on my own. I want to go back to work full-time and pick up my career again. I don't feel like me. April called me a drudge and she's right. When did I become this person? If you're not prepared to make changes in how we manage April, there's no point in me doing it alone. But neither am I going to sit around, waiting for the wheels to come off. I'm going to start looking for a job. Which means that you and April need to accept that I'll be around less and, if you want someone to bail her out at 3am, you'll have to make other arrangements. Because it won't be me.'

Goodness! Where did that come from? Before this moment, I hadn't actually thought about actually applying for actual jobs. It was only a vague idea. Maybe it wasn't such a bad idea, though. Pushing the two of them to be less reliant on me. Carving out something for myself that I could be proud of. Or was I being selfish? Tony had worked so hard to build up the business for us all. We'd agreed that I'd be a stay at home mum so he could do that. The first few years had been tough and he had missed out on so many important moments with April.

First tooth. First steps. First word. First day at school. He'd really felt the sacrifice deeply. In the end, he and Jack had turned the company into a huge success, but, to this day, it came at a cost. The constant travel was wearing and, with fifty only a few years away, Tony was finding it harder and harder to adjust his body clock. Maybe a nudge in the direction of slowing down was due. He was a great father, who worshipped the ground on which April's strappy, knock-off Manolo Blahnik's tottered. However, he was a very absent father, with a rather rosy view of his offspring. Maybe a nudge in the direction of dealing with April's shit was also due. Maybe it wasn't selfish of me to want some goals for myself.

Tony pushed back his chair, winced and stood up.

'If you want to get another job, fine. I completely support you in that. But I can't stop what I'm doing. Other people rely on me and I need to rely on you. I think you're wrong about April. She'll be okay and we just need to support her.'

With that, he carefully walked off and closeted himself in his study for the rest of the day. No doubt doing very important video conferences and, I suspected, organising his CD collection by year of release.

CHAPTER 4

In the second week of hothousing with Tony, or Frockdown, as I was now calling it, I got my stitches out. Yay! The nurse pronounced me 'healing nicely' and sent me home with leaflets on wounds and infections. I already had the leaflets from the night in A&E, but she seemed so pleased with my healing powers that I didn't have the heart to turn them down.

I could have gone back to work, but I was enjoying the time off and, so far, neither Maggie nor April had complained. Tony and I had reached an impasse on the April problem. She hadn't poisoned anyone at the pub yet, so Tony kept dropping hints that she was definitely on the right track. I debated whether to tell him that Maggie had phoned to say that April got drunk after work last weekend, fell asleep on the pool table for an hour then gave Davey an impromptu lap dance. Davey FFS. The girl could sure pick 'em. I followed my new policy of letting her do her own thing and pretended I hadn't heard. 'La la la, Maggie. Not listening.'

I'd spent the week applying for jobs in kitchens. I hadn't worked as a sous-chef for twenty years, so I reckoned I'd have to start at the bottom. It would be pretty crappy, but I'd just have to work my way up again. Perhaps enrol in a college course to help me on my way. The thought of sitting in a room full of kids, learning about kitchen hygiene and boiling bloody eggs or whatever, filled me with dread. However, if that was what I needed to do, I'd do it.

On the upside, I'd kept my hand in all these years; cooking at the Plough, filling in for the domestic science teacher at the high school (she was slightly over-fond of the cooking sherry and sometimes needed a "rest") and helping out with catering for functions at a local hotel. Hardly haute cuisine but at least it gave me something to put on my CV. It was, therefore, a wonderful surprise when I opened my e-mails on my last Friday of Frockdown, to find a message from Duns, the swankiest hotel chain in the North of England.

"Dear Miss Frock,

Thank you for your recent application for the post of Commis Chef in our new hotel, The Northumberland Grand.

We would like to invite you to an interview at our headquarters in The Yorkshire Grand. Several dates are available. Please click on the link below to book a suitable time.

Congratulations on your success at the application stage and we look forward to meeting you.

Kind regards,

Gerald Smart
    Executive Chef"

Holy guacamole! An actual interview. I hadn't expected to hear anything for weeks and here I was, first interview about to happen. When would be a good time to start shitting myself? I clicked on the link. All the slots were next week. These people didn't hang about. I chose a slot and decided that now would be a good time to start shitting myself.

'Tony! Tony!'

I rushed through to the study, to find Tony sitting with his work headphones on, seemingly engrossed in a call.

'I know you're only wearing them so we won't talk to you. They're not even plugged in. Listen, I got an interview for the Northumberland Grand job. It's next week. I'm so darn excited, I can hardly breathe. Or maybe that's fear. Nope, definitely excitement.'

I was hopping up and down so much that Tony became briefly mesmerised by my boobs.

'Tony! Face, up here!'

'Sorry. Interview. Wow.'

'It's in York next Friday. I'll need new clothes. And shoes. What if they ask me to cook something? I'll need to practice! And I'll need a bag. And interview answers. What do even they ask at interviews these days? I need Google. Oh yes, a train ticket. Shall I stay overnight?'

Tony looked happy for me, but I knew that he'd mull it over and the doubts would creep in. I could expect a TONY Talk later. TONY Talks were a bit like TED Talks, except the speaker was rather grumpy and delivered what he called 'constructive criticism' with all the subtleness of one of Archie's farts. I'd previously had TONY Talks on such illuminating subjects as The Most Space Efficient Way To Load A Dishwasher, How To Put Bins Out, Negotiation Strategies When Car Shopping (As Opposed To Squealing 'I Want The Red One, GIMME') and Yes, The Highway Code Is Still An Actual Thing. The latter TONY Talk had started with a critique of my lane discipline on the dual carriageway and ended with me doing an emergency stop on a roundabout so that I could scream at him. After which, any time I drove Tony into town, he said nothing, but I could see it was killing him.

I merrily skipped off to do some googling and train ticket booking. He could burst my bubble with common sense and a dash of mansplaining later. For now, I was going to swim in my little lake of happiness and enjoy the moment. I decided not to tell April because I didn't want Maggie to find out from someone else. I intended to tell

Maggie about my job hunt, but there didn't seem any point in worrying her when it was unlikely that I'd be immediately successful. However, I couldn't keep the news to myself, so I rang Suzy.

'Hey, Suze, fancy going for a coffee and a wander round the shops tomorrow?'

'That sounds good. I haven't seen you for ages. I have to drop Poppy off at school, then take Marigold to the dentist. How about I meet you at Bernie's at half ten?'

Did I mention that Suzy's children are named after plants? In addition to Poppy and Marigold, she has Lily, Rose, Moss and Basil. I'm not entirely sure that Moss is a plant, but given that she was going to call him Cypress… And poor Basil. Ahead of him lay a lifetime of people shouting 'Boom Boom!' at him or doing silly walks. Hopefully she'd have Basil with her tomorrow and I could sniff his baby head and call him Baz. I was determined to make him cool Baz, rather than Basil The Posh Boy Who Gets Wedgies.

'Great. See you there.'

I came off the phone, looking forward to my coffee date with Suzy. Then I remembered my lip. I'd forgotten that I'd have to explain the lip. I checked it in the mirror. Bloody great scar but it wasn't too scabby any more. Nothing that couldn't be hidden behind a dab of concealer and some dark lipstick. Suzy would want to know why I was suddenly wearing make-up, but I'd just tell her I was practicing for the job interview and would she like to help me pick out some interview clothes? Suzy loved dressing other people. My wardrobe was full of tasteful items and chic accessories bought on shopping trips with Suzy. Alas, there was little need for silk scarves and cashmere in a pub kitchen, so most of the stuff rarely got an airing. Sometimes I'd put on a little black dress and wellies to walk Archie, just for the hell of it, but mostly I was a jeans and trainers gal. Which is why Tony was so surprised when he walked into the kitchen a couple of hours later and found me tottering around in a pair of heels I'd unearthed from under the bed.

'Wotcha doing?' he asked.

'Just practicing for my interview.'

'You know that most people practice sensible answers to the questions they might be asked?'

'Yes, but most people have walked in high heels at some point in the last few years. I'm somewhat out of practice,' I said, wobbling precariously as a heel struck the grout between floor tiles.

'Unless you're a man…mostly,' Tony pointed out. 'Anyway, why don't you just wear what you're comfortable in?'

'Because I haven't dressed up in ages and I'm quite looking forward to being smart. I'm going clothes shopping with Suzy tomorrow.'

'What are you going to tell her about your lip?'

'I'm not. I'll put on lipstick, tell her about the interview and take her to fancy shops. She'll be so distracted by clothes and organising me that she won't notice the lip. If she does notice, I'll just tell her I was practicing high heels and fell over. That would be a very me thing to do,' I said, promptly tripping over Archie's water bowl and grabbing the table to save myself. I swivelled my bum into a chair, deciding to take a break from my deportment class.

I spent the rest of the day going over my old notes from college and brushing up on my health and safety knowledge, courtesy of the internet. That evening, I had an urgent thought. Sauces! What if they asked me about sauces? I went off on an internet adventure, googling the menus of posh restaurants so I could see what was hot and what was not. Then I went to bed and dreamt that I was drowning in a pool of blackberry and port.

By ten the next morning, I was clean, made-up and neatly dressed. Well, I say neatly dressed; the trainers had been ditched for a pair of pumps and my clothes didn't stink of chip fat/pies/Archie. I jumped in the old jalopy and beat a path to the shops. Suzy was on time every time and, even though she had never commented on my habitual lateness, there was always an 'I'm not angry, I'm just disappointed' air about her that left me feeling vaguely ashamed of myself.

Despite the early start, I only made it to Bernie's by the skin of my teeth.

'Sorry I'm nearly late,' I told Suzy, sweeping Baz into my arms for a big sniff…erm…hug. 'I took a wrong turn and ended up going all over the place. At one point I was outside that club, Blue. D'you know, there's a lad with a face tattoo works in there? He crashed his Dad's car into a bus stop when he was in year 10.' That was the extent of my local gossip. Having missed weekends at the pub recently, I was fresh out of who was sleeping with who (or, if rumours were true about a local dairy farmer, who was sleeping with what).

'Oh, I know who you mean. Joe or Jed or something. He was a little…,' Suzy covered Basil's teeny-weeny cute baby ears, '…bugger at school. Also a bit thick. Broke into the head's office and carved his name on the desk. Investigation was very short and he was kicked out forthwith. Anyway, what's going on with you? Make up on, nice shoes. I smell a rat.'

I ordered a latte and told Suzy about the interview. And about April. And about Tony refusing to do tough love, but also refusing to be at home more often to do his share of Apriling. Obviously, I left out the tale of the testicles and me being off work.

'Oh, poor you,' she said, helping herself to a bit of Basil's half chewed biscuit. 'How does Tony feel about you going back to work full time?'

'He hasn't said much, although there has been a lot of lawn mowing going on. He said he was supportive, but I'm not sure he took me seriously when I first told him I was going to apply for jobs. I was having a bit of a rant at the time. I'm just waiting for the TONY talk.'

'It'll be a bucket of cold water for them both, the first time you're not there to bail April out or iron Tony's shirts for his work trip.'

'I'm already done with April. Even if I don't get this job, she's going to have to sort herself out. I just want to get a bit of myself back. I feel like I've been running around after them for years and…I don't know…Tony and I haven't even been out anywhere in forever. April called me a drudge and she's right. I used to wear heels and too much lipstick. I had adventures! Now, I think my social life is buzzing because I talked to an old lady at a bus stop. Am I being selfish, Suzy? Is this just some sort of mid-life crisis?

'Yes and yes, m'dear. But you've looked after them all for twenty-one years and you've earned the right to a mid-life crisis. So, in the words of Wham!, if you're going to do, do it right. Let's go and get you some clothes. And, while you're at it, just be thankful you're not a bloke. Golf club membership and a Jag. Ugh.'

'Graham having a mid-life moment too?'

'Yes. He only needs a twenty-six-year-old blonde and he'll have the bloody set. No, no, no,' she said, waving off my worried look, 'Panic ye not. Graham's far too fond of his home comforts for that sort of nonsense. And his bank account. With six children, he knows I'd cheerfully bleed him dry. Far cheaper to buy a ridiculous car and have a heart attack every time the little blighters smear chocolate on his leather seats.'

With that settled, we hit the shops.

Several hours later, I returned home, my arms full of bags and my heart full of happiness. The day had been utter bliss. Posh lunch. Posh clothes. Two ladies pretending they were posh and one baby ruining the effect by projectile vomiting milk over their shoes. Archie waylaid me at the door, signalling his utter joy at my arrival by rolling on his back and, as I bent down to pet him, sending a jet of pee over the new top that I'd 'kept on' because it was so pretty. He'd clearly been taking lessons from Baz.

Tony emerged from the utility room, clutching a packet of batteries.

'Hello, love. Good day? I've just been organising the batteries. I needed a couple for my computer mouse and we're a bit short of AAs. I bought some a few months ago, just before I went on that trip to South America. D'you remember? Any idea where they've gone?'

I did indeed remember. He was gone for a month and Archie got so used to falling asleep to the gentle buzz of Roberta Rabbit that it had taken him ages to get back to normal when Tony returned.

'Nope, not a clue.'

'Anyway, I'm glad you're back. I've been thinking about this job and I wanted to talk to you.'

Uh oh. Here we go. The TONY talk. Brace yourself, dear Katie, for we are about to go down the rabbit hole. And not even a nice Roberta Rabbit hole. No – the rabbit hole where Tony pours doubt on my reasoning and stamps all over my lovely day because he has not listened to a fucking word I've said about me being unhappy and is worried he won't have clean undercrackers to go to Moscow or wherever the fuck he's planning on swanning off to next. Well, I am not playing that game right now.

'Can it wait, love? I'm just in, I'm covered in dog pee and I want to get these bags away before April sees them and "borrows" all the things she takes a fancy to.'

'Righty-ho. I'll put the kettle on and see you in the kitchen in ten.'

There was clearly no avoiding this. I lugged my bags upstairs and emptied all the beautiful clothes, shoes and accessories onto the bed. The wardrobe was heaving with every dress I'd bought since 1998 and I put some of the old things onto already overloaded hangers to make way for the lovely new things. I made a vow to have a proper clear out soon. If I was going to be smart, sassy, worky Katie, I really needed to start being organised. However, peeling off the dog wee top and popping on a clean t-shirt would be a good start.

Of course, Archie was "helping", just in case things went on that he ought to know about. I scooped him up in my arms and buried my face in his furry neck.

'C'mon Arch. Suppose we better face the music. If you could roll over and pee on Tony when he gets annoying, I'll give you fifty dog treats.'

In the kitchen, Tony had put biscuits on a plate and was busy making mugs of tea. His mother put biscuits on a plate, even when there weren't any visitors, so Tony assumed that everyone put biscuits on a plate. When we first lived together, he was horrified that I just helped myself to a couple straight out of the packet. I'd never been able to disabuse him of the notion that nice people, proper people, served biscuits on plates. He considered April and I biscuit heathens and, even if our daughter was a brat, I was happy to have at least passed on the art of proper chocolate biscuit scoffing. I grabbed two Jaffa Cakes from the packet and stared defiantly at Tony. He just sighed.

'I've been thinking about this job business. It'll be long hours, you know. You're right about April, she can be a handful, and if you're at work and I'm away then there will be nobody here for her. And Archie will be left on his own too.'

'Suzy has already said she'll walk Archie if we need her to. April's twenty-one, Tony. She's an adult. You made the point yourself that she could be off at uni doing anything and we wouldn't know about it.'

'Yes, but you also made the point that she isn't. I'm really pleased that you got the interview. Let's not put the cart before the horse, you might not even get the job, so it's probably a moot point. But, say you do, it's going to be very disruptive if you take it.'

'Disruptive to whom? You, because you'll have to do your own washing when you get home from a trip? Disruptive to April, because there's nobody there to pick her up from bloody police stations? It's not disruptive at all, Tony. It's just a little bit inconvenient and if you're so worried, then stop travelling all the time. Employ someone else to do it. Even when you're here, you're never here. Your head's in work!'

'You know darn well I've put heart and soul into the business,' said Tony, his voice rising, 'And it's not the right time for me to pull back. You know, I want you to have a job but just not one that takes you away all the time.'

'It's not a job. It's a career. I want my career back. Did you not hear me before, when I said I don't feel like me anymore? This is something for me. It's important to me. I've done all my looking after of you and April. Now I need to do my own thing.'

'Me, me, me,' said Tony, snippily. 'Well, if you get offered the job, I don't want you to take it.'

'What is this? Nineteen fifty fucking three? So, things are changing, Tony. Get over it. You don't back me up on how we deal with April, you never have. And you're not backing me up on doing something for myself now she's grown up. You expect me to just carry on as I was, meeting your needs, and you're unwilling to make any changes to meet mine. Well, fuck you, Tony. You can take your plate of biscuits and shove it where the sun don't shine.'

I stormed upstairs and flung myself on the bed. Well, that TONY talk went just as well as the driving one. Possibly worse. I couldn't believe that he wanted me to stay at home, like the good little wifey. All these years I thought we'd been a partnership, when all he wanted was a cleaner for life. Years of resentment over Tony's inability to stick to any agreements we had about April bubbled through me. Anger over his stubborn refusal to make any changes to accommodate me made me want to scream into the pillow. To think I'd been worried about being selfish. No more! I resolved to go to that darn interview and be brilliant. If they offered me the job, I'd take it. I'd also stay overnight in York on Thursday. It would get me away from my husband-from-another-era and, for once, I'd be the one leaving towels on the bathroom floor for someone else to pick up.

CHAPTER 5

The week went by in a blur of resentment. Tony kept to his corner, I stayed in mine. If April sensed the tension, she didn't say anything. On the Wednesday night, she went out with Janine and I switched my phone off. If there were any problems, Tony could deal with them. He was sleeping in the spare room, having claimed he was going to be working late every night due to the time differences between the UK and the States. We both knew that was a lie and he was avoiding me, but, rather than argue, I left him to it. I hadn't bothered going into the study and suspected that, by now, the bookshelves were the tidiest they'd ever been and, somewhere on his computer, was a neat spreadsheet listing all the pros and cons of "letting" me take the job. I'd put money on him not having included me nutting him in the balls again if he continued to resist. From my point of view, that would be a definite pro.

On Thursday morning I packed far too much into my suitcase, ready for the afternoon train to York. I should have been excited to pack all my lovely new things, but they seemed tarnished now, the gloss worn off by arguments and marital impasse. Around 2pm, I made a rather dismal, lonely departure. April was still in bed, nursing a hangover, and Tony had announced an urgent meeting, firmly closing the study door. We both knew that he could have scheduled this meeting for any other time and this was yet another excuse to avoid me. Only Archie was there to see me off as, eyes brimming with tears, I hefted my suitcase into the boot of the old jalopy. I gave Archie one last squeeze, prolonging the moment in the vain hope that someone would appear to wish me luck. Nobody came and, as I ushered Archie back into the house, all I could hear was the distant murmur of Tony droning on about budgets to some no-doubt-bored executive on the other side of the world. I quietly shut the front door, got in the car, prayed to the god of engines that the jalopy would start first time, thanked the god of engines and made my way to the station.

Tickets, check. Suitcase, check. Sunglasses, check. Purse, check. Charger, phone, good book, check, check, check. Passport to prove to interviewers that I am indeed Katie Frock and not some weirdo who randomly turns up to other people's interviews, check. By the time I'd finished all my checks, I concluded that I was equally equipped for a fortnight in the Caribbean as a job interview in York. Wouldn't that be wonderful? Disappearing off somewhere hot and beachy to drink pina coladas for a couple of weeks. The last time we were on holiday, a fourteen-year-old April managed to sneak out of the hotel room on the first night and we found her in a Greek hospital, recovering from alcohol poisoning, the next morning. She was out and unrepentant by day three and spent the next eleven days having tantrums about everything. 'Why is there no wifi?! The food is rubbish! I can't sleep! Why haven't you taken me out on any trips?! I don't like this trip! Why are you taking me out on shit trips?!' It was like being trapped in paradise with Lucifer (and not even the sexy telly Lucifer). By day fourteen, she had thrown an ice cream at her father, stamped on the TV remote in a fit of rage because she couldn't find her flip flops and reduced me to a state of seven gins by lunchtime. Having paid £3000 for two weeks of misery, Tony and I vowed to have no more holidays with April. Even Tony couldn't find an excuse for her behaviour and on day five, when I suggested drowning her in the hotel pool, I could see he was tempted. Here she was, twenty-one, and we still hadn't had a holiday because we couldn't trust her to be left in the house on her own for a fortnight. Seven years without so much as a grain of sand in my sun tan cream. Never mind the Caribbean, I'd kill for a week in a B&B in Blackpool.

With some time to go before my train, I took a gander around the station shop. I knew that station shops were ridiculously expensive, but I loved to look at the odd range of things that some buyer had decided would meet the needs of travellers. There was a shelf of self-help books, with 'Getting Up, Staying Up' being the number one seller. I assumed it was about erectile disfunction, but a glance at the rear cover told me it was for "managers who aspire to leadership". I decided that any man daft enough to read this on a packed train was signalling that he didn't really need a self-help book so much as a girlfriend. Ooh, stationery. I liked stationery. I gazed longingly at packets of overpriced pencils and little coloured sticky tabs for organising notebooks. I'd always had a yen for a label maker but Tony said it would be a waste of money. This was mainly because he knew I'd go around labelling everything in the house and one day he'd cross his legs in an important meeting and the word 'shoe' would be stuck to his sole for all to see. I spotted a little writing set with a Beagle on it. An Archie writing set! It was meant to be. I had no idea who I'd write to, but my heart yearned for this writing set. I picked it off the shelf and wandered back to the self-help books. The number three best seller was 'You Doing You', which I decided must be about Roberta Rabbit techniques. After all, the smiley lady on the front cover looked very satisfied. Roberta was safely tucked away in my suitcase, ready to provide some good vibes at the end of this lonely day and, really, one was never too old to learn new moves. I grabbed the book and went to pay for it and the Archie writing set.

Emerging back into the station, I could see on the board that my train was leaving from platform four. Bugger, I hated platform four. I'd have to lug my case up the stairs and over the bridge. Why couldn't they be considerate and park at platform two? It was right there, at the other side of the barrier! Did they not know I was a lazy sod who didn't like steps? I hastily stuffed my book and writing set in my handbag and pulled out my tickets. There appeared to be approximately one hundred tickets for one simple return journey. If I actually managed to put the right one in the automatic barrier machine first time, I'd be high fiving myself all the way across that damn bridge. In the end I got through the barriers with no problems at all, although this was courtesy of a very nice station person who, spotting my look of panic as I sorted through the tickets, opened the disabled barrier and waved me through. I turned back to thank him, but already he was dealing with some utter idiot who couldn't even manage to put the right ticket in the slot. Pah! People!

I clunked my suitcase up the stairs and hauled it over the bridge and down the other side. By the time I reached platform four, I'd completely forgotten my carriage and seat number, so had to sort through the tickets again. 'D32, D32, D32,' I muttered, as I made my way down the platform. 'D32, D32, D32,' I muttered as I made my way onto carriage D, past the toilet with its distinctive train-loo whiff of chemicals and wee. The train had come from Scotland and was going to Fancy London. If it smelled like this now, pity the poor people who got on at Peterborough. I blamed men with sprinkler penises. Thank goodness April was a girl and Tony was both fastidious in his bathroom habits and well brought up. I could go to the loo in my bare feet in our house, with no fear of slipping on anything revolting. With train loos, you practically needed one of those scene of crime suits, although that might defeat the point because all the ladies would have to remove the suit to have a wee. They had all these confusing electric buttons on train loos now. Maybe they should add a button that only lets the person out if they've cleaned the seat and floor.

32, 32, 32, ah, here it was, seat 32. I looked at the little screen above the seats and fervently prayed that the Doncaster bound passenger next to me would miss the train. Mean, I know, but I wanted to read my new book. I didn't want to spend the next hour imparting all my deepest secrets to a stranger. Because that's what I did on trains. I talked to my neighbour, instantly became train-BFFs and exchanged life stories. By the time we got off, we knew more about each other than our spouses and partners did. I popped my suitcase into the luggage rack by the toilets and settled down in seat 32, fingers crossed for a quiet journey. A few minutes later, the train pulled away from the station and I decided it was safe to learn all about doing myself.

. . .

Sadly, the book was not about masturbation at all. The author, Irma Ford-Tinklebecker (she of the satisfied smile on the front cover), was instead encouraging me to be my best self. Presumably, instead of the complete wanker that I intended to be, after a few gins from the mini-bar in my hotel room that night. The lovely Irma, psychology graduate, mom of three successful young adults and possessor of thirty-two perfect American teeth, was full of positive experiences and life-affirming bon mots. She told me that in order to be my best me, I needed to get in touch with my inner me. If I was happy with the inside, then the outside would shine too. Who was my inner me? On the outside I was the housekeeper and dogsbody, the pub cook and food shopper, the dog walker and pooper scooper. The clapped-out Cinderella who never went to the ball. On the inside I was the feisty lady who got excited about mini-bars, had deep thoughts about men's toilet habits and loved shoes and label machines. I was the lady who wanted to be respected for being good at something, to be valued for my achievements beyond scraping the pus from April's spots off the hall mirror. I didn't actually care about going to the ball, but I wouldn't mind putting on my dancing shoes once in a while. Changing things up a bit.

I leaned back in my seat and pondered the idea of changing things up. What would happen if I stayed on the train? Didn't get off at York and just stayed on all the way to London? Getting a job near home would be different, but, even though Tony was treating it as the most inconvenient thing in the whole world, in reality little would actually change. I'd still come home every night, Tony would still be away, April would still be a liability and I'd end up fitting in all the housework around my work hours. Tony and April would carry on as normal and still expect a pile of freshly laundered socks to appear. I'd worried about being selfish, but viewed objectively (and with a little help from my friend Irma) I was just going to be more busy. So, what *would* happen if I stayed on the train? Disappeared into Fancy London. How would they cope?

I imagined Tony and April six months from now, wondering why the bathroom sink had gone grey and why their feet kept sticking to the kitchen floor. They'd be three stone heavier and have dreadful teeth, because April only knew how to cook fatty pub food and it wouldn't have occurred to either of them to go for a dental check-up now and then. None of our extended family would have had Christmas or birthday presents, except possibly Tony's mother because her birth date was the code for the house alarm. I'd deliberately chosen it when the new alarm was installed as I reckoned it was a sequence he'd remember. He'd still spent the first few weeks, post installation, phoning me up at work to ask the code and more than once, our elderly neighbours, George and Mildred, had appeared in their pyjamas at 7pm to shout at him about the incessant blaring keeping them awake.

Of course, I couldn't really just disappear. I'd have to let Tony know I was okay, otherwise he'd be so worried that he might even run out of collections to organise. But maybe not phone him because he'd just get all shouty. Ooh, the Archie writing set. I could write a letter. You're a genius, Katie Frock, a flipping genius. Let's do a little experiment. What would I write?

I fished the writing set out of my handbag and broke open the plastic cover. There was a pen, writing paper and cute envelopes with little pawprints in the corners. I pulled out a sheet of paper and, after a moment's thought, began to write.

Dear Tony and April,

I'm sorry for not coming home but I wanted to let you know I'm okay. I've been very unhappy recently and I need to take some time by myself. I tried to tell you, Tony, that I have to do something for me. I never wanted to argue and I really do understand that me getting a full-time job and not being around as much feels like a big change for you. However, I suspect that nothing will really change for me. Everything will carry on as it was and I'll have to pack it all in around my career, a career which you'll regard as an inconvenience. This doesn't seem very fair.

April, both you and your father make excuses for your behaviour, but the bottom line is that unless both of you adjust your attitudes, again, everything will carry on as it was. And how it was is what's made me unhappy. Somewhere along the way, I lost who I am.

I realised today that it doesn't have to be that way, so I'm walking away for a while. I'll be in touch when I'm ready. I love you both very much. Give Archie a hug for me.

Katie xxx

I didn't have to actually post it. It felt good to write the letter, but that was as far as it went. Wasn't it? I couldn't seriously disappear to London. Where would I live? Who would remember to feed Archie? How would I support myself? Who would remember to clean the skirting boards and put salt in the dishwasher? What if I became a homeless person? Don't be silly, Katie, you have savings. But how much is a flat in London? And what if Tony and April forgot to change their bedsheets and there were bed bugs and the house had to be fumigated? Who would teach Basil that he's actually Baz? What about my job interview? What if I didn't get a job in Fancy London because I wasn't Fancy enough? Bloody hell, Katie. You coped with all the Fancy London stuff when you were twenty and had nothing. I'm fairly sure you can manage at forty-five with a few quid in your bank account. Anyway, I wasn't really going to post the letter, so there was no point in worrying about it.

I folded the letter neatly, tucked it into an envelope and stuck down the flap, just to store it safely, you know. Then I added Tony's name and our address on the front. And rummaged around in my purse for a stamp. All I could find was a crumpled, second-class stamp, lurking among the 'buy nine get one free' cards I seemed to randomly collect from car washes and coffee shops. I stuck the stamp on the front of the envelope. I mean, better safe than sorry. This way, if it fell out of my bag, a random stranger might find it and post it, then I could intercept it when I got home. Yes, this was definitely the sensible thing to do.

I put the letter and my purse into my handbag, sat back and pondered my next move. Clearly, I was being ridiculous. I should just go to the job interview and see what happened next. Tony was right, I might not even get the job. My life wasn't really that bad. Sure, it was unfulfilling and I felt taken for granted, but I had a lovely home and family.

The train was pulling into Darlington, half way to York. Pretty soon I'd be at the crunch point. What crunch point?! I was going to York, wasn't I? I pushed all the Fancy London thoughts out of my mind and picked up my book. I'd just reached an interesting part, where the lovely Irma was waxing lyrical about teaching you about you again, when a small, neat elderly woman in a smart, green raincoat sat down next to me. She rummaged around in a tartan shopping bag and extracted two oranges.

'Orange, dear?' she offered.

Oh, bugger. A train-BFF had arrived.

I took the proffered orange and thanked its owner.

'Betty, dear, and you are?'

'Katie,' I said, digging my fingernails into the orange peel and knowing in my bones that I could get the whole thing off in one piece. A little personal challenge to keep me amused.

'Where are you off to today, Katie?'

It was like she'd fired the starter gun on our transitory BFFship. Within ten minutes, Betty knew all about my job interview, my dissatisfaction at home and my adoration of Archie. I knew she was a widow who had been visiting a schoolfriend she hadn't seen in sixty years. Her granddaughter had traced the friend through social media and it had been wonderful to meet again. Betty told me that it was her birthday and, since her Tom had died, she'd been lonely and a bit aimless.

'I have the family, of course,' she said, 'But, after a while, our friends drifted off. They had their own lives and their own families. I see them now and again, but, really, they were mostly Tom's work friends. I didn't work and we moved to the area once our boys were grown up, so I never had the roots there like I did in our last place. Now I'm stuck. Can't move back because it's too far from the grandchildren. Listen to me, droning on. It was a tonic to see Morag, though. Now we know we're only half an hour away from each other, we've made plans to meet up again.'

My heart broke for her. Poor, lonely Betty. Stuck in some Yorkshire village with only the occasional visit from one of her sons to look forward to. My imagination took hold and I pictured Betty in a stone cottage, a blizzard raging outside, stoking the fire and silently weeping because she knew that the snow meant no visits from her sons.

'You'll never guess what the best thing about today was, though,' said Betty. She leaned in close and whispered, 'We went shopping and I got myself one of them Roberta Rabbits.' Then, with that bombshell delivered, Betty sat back in her seat, a satisfied Irma Ford-Tinklebecker-like smile on her face. My imagination, which a moment before had been conjuring up a picture of lonely Betty prodding the coals on a meagre fire to coax out that last bit of warmth, immediately let go. Betty was clearly stoking an entirely different kind of fire.

To distract my brain, I looked down the train carriage and saw the portly figure of the conductor making his way up the aisle. 'All tickets please.' A couple of young women had tickets for a different train company and I could hear the stress in their voices as they argued about having to pay the full fare. There was the obligatory drunk, snatching his four remaining beer cans back when the train slowed and they made an escape attempt across the table, towards the person opposite. Loudly and repeatedly calling the conductor 'mate' in an attempt to reassure him that he was a friendly drunk, who should definitely not be asked to leave the train. A little boy, excited to be on a train journey with his Dad, asked if he could stamp his own ticket with the conductor's machine. He was beyond delighted when the conductor also let him stamp the tickets of everyone nearby. A tiny, elderly Asian lady, who spoke little English, had a small suitcase on the seat next to her. The conductor conveyed that he was going to put it on the overhead luggage rack. She nodded enthusiastically. He checked her ticket and asked a passenger going to the same destination if he wouldn't mind getting the case down for the lady when they arrived. This was why I loved trains – they were so human and interesting.

Betty and I rummaged in our handbags for our tickets. We each emerged with a deck of small, cardboard rectangles and sorted through them to find the correct ones.

'Gin rummy?' I said, winking at the conductor as I fanned out my deck.

'Strip poker,' declared Betty, smiling sweetly up at him. Being able to mildly sexually harass people because you look like a nice old lady must be quite liberating, I decided. They probably assume you're a bit batty. But Betty and I knew differently. Both of us were perfectly aware that she was sharp as a tack and, given the contents of her handbag, if he showed willing, she'd probably drag the conductor to join the mile low club in the train loo in a heartbeat.

I held my ticket out to the conductor. He was just about to take it when I jerked it away from his fingers.

'Oops, sorry, I don't know why I did that.'

Again, he reached to take my ticket and, again, I jerked it away.

'Actually, can I have a ticket to London?"

What?! My brain hurriedly consulted my mouth to check that it was working properly. My mouth assured my brain that it was, indeed, fine and was only doing what my brain had subconsciously told it to do. My conscious brain checked with the subconscious department and received a memo confirming that, yes, it had been in direct communication with my mouth.

'It'll be expensive. Full fare,' warned the conductor. 'Do you want a return?'

'Just a single.'

What?! My mouth appeared to be fully committed to this venture, even if my brain was flashing red and screaming 'WTF!'

'Are you sure about this, dear?' asked Betty.

My brain took a moment to once more consult with my mouth.

'Yes,' they said in unison, 'I rather think I am.'

PART TWO
TONY & APRIL (& ARCHIE)

CHAPTER 6

Tony heard the front door close and immediately regretted that he hadn't said goodbye to Katie. He'd thought that arranging a meeting so that he didn't have to talk to her before she went would be a good idea. Take the heat out of things for both of them. Now, here he was, trapped in the darn meeting and there she was, off on her own.

Tony put further thoughts of Katie to the back of his mind and switched his focus to the conversation at hand.

'We're a luxury brand. That needs to be reflected in our campaign,' said the marketing executive, running a hand over his balding pate.

'Yes, I can definitely see why you're aiming high with this one. Jack has some ideas that could help us bring you nearer budget, without compromising on quality. Jack?'

JT productions had a lucrative contract to produce a series of videos for a high-end American clothing brand, which was about to go public. The meeting was just the usual management of expectations versus budgets. This time, the company wanted top models partying in exotic locations. Jack and Tony had worked out some figures around using a social media influencer, with a festival in Barcelona as the backdrop. Tony let Jack pitch the vision, then he came back to costs. The meeting droned on, eventually ending in an agreement that the marketing executive would consult with his boss and get back to them.

Jack stayed on the line after the marketing executive had gone.

'Tony, mate, remember Mia? Met her in Italy last month?'

'Yeah, the one with the big…necklace?'

'Ha ha, yes mate, the one with the cracking pair of diamonds. Well, we spent the whole time there together and I got a bit…you know… attached. Anyway, long story short, she came back to England with me and I'm thinking of asking her to marry me.'

There was a moment of stunned silence while Tony processed this news.

'Jack, mate, remember you? The one who sleeps around and swore he'd never get tied down?'

'Okay, fair point. But this one's different. Really different. I'm not going to get all soppy on you, but if Mia went back to Italy tomorrow, I'd chuck the whole lot in, work, home, everything, and go with her. It's that serious.'

Tony took a deep breath and let the air puff slowly out between his lips. This was indeed very serious. Things were going to change and Tony did not like change. He'd had enough of that from Katie recently and suspected that he may have ballsed things up a bit there, although he wasn't sure how. He quickly weighed up his options and concluded that supporting Jack was the right thing to do. Not just for the sake of their company. For the sake of their friendship.

'Congratulations, Jack. Good one. When are you going to ask her?'

'Tomorrow night. We're going down the Swan for some posh nosh and I thought I'd get them to tie the ring to the neck of a champagne bottle and ask her to pour.'

'Women love that sort of stuff. Let me know how it goes, eh?'

'Will do. Truth be told, *I* love that sort of stuff,' Jack laughed, half embarrassed to confess his romantic side. 'Speak to you after the weekend.'

Tony rang off and eyed his CD collection. Led Zeppelin was next to Bad Company. How had that happened? How had anything happened? Jack getting married, for goodness sake. Things had been fine for years and now the boat was being rocked. Katie was on a mission about wanting to find herself and about April needing to grow up. All this job stuff. He knew he was being completely unreasonable in expecting her to be at home all the time, but he liked things as they were. They worked as they were. It was probably just another one of Katie's notions anyway. She'd get turned down for the job and be upset for a bit, but she'd get over it and everything would be back to normal. Maybe he should phone her and try to smooth things over. He really did feel bad that he'd let her go without saying goodbye. His phone rang. It was Priti from the office.

'Hello. Tony? We need you to look over the proposal for Coles. I'm not sure the numbers are stacking up and…'

All thoughts of Katie instantly fled from his mind, as Tony switched into work mode and brought the Coles spreadsheet up on his screen.

April rolled over in bed. What time was it? She groped under her pillow, pulled out her phone and squinted at the numbers on the screen. 3pm, ugh. She was covering Mum's shift at the pub tonight and tomorrow, while she was off to York for something or other. April hadn't bothered to ask. Better get her sweet ass in gear and go to the pub. Maggie phoning Mum to complain she was late again would be too much hassle to deal with. Anyway, Maggie wasn't bad for an old bird, so she didn't want to let her down. April belly-crawled down her bed, scooped a handful of clothes off the floor and gave them an experimental sniff. They'd do.

Swinging her legs round and scooting off the bed backwards, April felt her feet touch something furry.

'Aw, Archie-boy. How's my baby,'

Archie obligingly rolled over and she gave his tummy a rub, before padding over to the large chest of drawers in the corner of her room. Opening the top drawer, April rummaged through the contents, looking for her favourite purple thong. Where the actual fuck was her thong? She was going to have to wear the crappy pink one that itched her bum. She pulled on the pink thong and her jeans from last night. Oh, last night. Last night had been lush. Janine snogged the face off Jez from Blue and disappeared round the back of the club with him. April drank six cocktails and danced her tits off. The new top did its magic and all the lads were paying attention. She wasn't that interested, though. Which was weird. Why wasn't she interested? Ooh, her nails were lovely. That woman in ManicYour did a good job, even if it was a shit name for a shop. Wonder how Janine was today?

April checked her phone. Sure enough, fifteen messages from Janine. April flicked through them. 'Omd what did I do last night?' Shagged Jez by the bins at the back door, you filthy slag. 'I am dying text me back.' 'WTF April. Desi D is sayin on fb he was with u last night. You're mince if his ex sees that.' April quickly opened Facebook and checked Desi's status. Above a pic of her, tits busting out of the new top, Desi had posted 'Next new relationship for the D man, watch this space.' As if! And who even put stuff on Facebook anymore? What a creep.

April went back to the drawers and pulled out a clean t-shirt. 'Janine's right, though,' she groaned at Archie, as she attempted to hook her arms through the spaghetti straps, 'If Chloe finds out, I am very finely ground mince.' She looked at herself in the mirror, her long hair tumbling to her tiny waist, and smirked. 'But only 5% fat.' She scraped her hair into a pony tail, wiped off last night's make-up and padded downstairs to gaze hopelessly into the fridge and despair of her parents ever buying food she liked.

While she slurped cereal at the kitchen table, Archie at her feet doing his 'you've got food, I want some, but I know I'm not allowed to beg' thing of looking but not looking, April responded to Janine's texts.

'Desi fckn creep. Would rather drink my own sick. What I'm gonna do about chloe?'

'Comment and call him out. Message chloe and tell her its shit'

'Kk. Will comment but not messaging chloe. She'll just start'

'Kk. Seeing Jez again tonight. Might come past Plough later'

'You'll have to keep it in your pants then. Plough bins locked away'

'Hahahahaha. Kept it in pants last night. Just chatted. Jez a nice guy. Nothing like he was at school. Tell u about it later x'

Scroll, scroll, Facebook app, Desi, scroll, scroll, jeez this guy posts every five minutes, scroll. Ah, here it is. Comment. 'Never did happen. Never gonna happen. Am already in a relationship.' Send.

Slight flaw in the plan, thought April. Am not in a relationship. Better find one quickly. Who do I know that wouldn't mind pretending to be in a relationship? She pulled Facebook back up again and scrolled through her list of friends. Aron – would want to be paid. Charlie – would want an actual relationship. Davey – sad sack…actually, Davey might be an idea. None of her friends knew him, he didn't have many Facebook friends, he'd only ever posted three things and he didn't have a profile photo.

On her first night in the job, Maggie had given her Davey's Mum's number. More than once, a gloriously drunk Davey had had to be escorted/carried home and it had long since been woven into the pub health and safety procedures that after six pints and six shots, you rang Davey's Mum to warn her to put a bucket, a large glass of water and two paracetamol by his bed within the next hour. She checked her contacts and found, to her relief, that she'd stored Davey's Mum's number.

'Hello, Mrs…erm,' she realised she didn't know Davey's Mum's name, '…Mrs Davey's Mum. It's April from the pub.'

'Oh goodness. I thought he was at work. Don't tell me he's in a state at this time of day.'

'No, it's okay, Mrs Davey's Mum. He's not at the pub. I just wanted to talk to him about something. Do you have a number for him?'

Davey's Mum gave April the number and she rang Davey.

'Hello, Davey Grant Joinery.'

'Hi. Davey? It's April from the pub.'

'Hello April. Is everything okay?'

'Yes, it's fine, but I was wondering if I could ask you a favour. It's a bit awkward to explain over the phone.' April was suddenly uncomfortably aware that asking a thirty-five year old man to pretend to be in a relationship with you on social media, so you wouldn't get beaten up by the ex-girlfriend of someone who was pretending to be in a relationship with you on social media, was slightly ridiculous and better done face to face.

'Okay, why don't you pop past the workshop now? I'm doing some bookcases and I could use a break.'

April looked at the oversized kitchen wall clock. 3.25pm. She'd be cutting it fine for work. Sod it, not being mince was more important than work. She ran upstairs to clean her teeth and have a quick wash, then set out for Davey's workshop.

. . .

Tony heard the front door go for the second time that day and reasoned that it was April going off to work. She was a quirky little thing, he smiled to himself, she never said goodbye. If Archie wasn't here to make a huge fuss of anyone who came through the front door, she probably wouldn't say hello either. Katie found it quite irritating that the only time April signalled her impending departure was when she wanted to borrow some cash. Katie seemed to find many things about April quite irritating and it made Tony want to leap to April's defence. He knew Katie loved April, but she was so hard on her all the time. Tony knew for a fact that both he and Katie had gotten into their own fair share of scrapes at April's age and, because they were off at uni or college, their parents lived in ignorant bliss. His mother, God love her, would have a fit if she knew that he'd once tried marijuana, then thrown up over a nice girl at a party. The first time he met Katie, she and her friends had just been arrested at a protest over the building of a new road. They came into the bar where he was working, full of bravado and the buzz you get after a near miss. As her friends found a table, Katie came bouncing up to the bar to order a round of drinks. It was 11am and she'd spent a night in cells, before being released without charge. Her long, dark hair was sticking out at about forty different angles, yesterday's mascara bruised her eyes and she stank like an old Labrador. She was the most beautiful thing he had ever seen in his life. He'd always played by the rules, done as he was told, been a well-mannered boy, a good boy, and here was this gorgeous creature with fire in her belly, operating on the adrenaline of disobedience and sticking two elegant fingers up at the world. He wasn't just enchanted, he was blown away.

Katie later told him that what attracted her to him was his 'properness'. She said she loved the fact that he was decent and did everything methodically. She could always count on him to hold her back when she was ready to launch herself headlong into something without thinking it through. He was her voice of reason. Together, they were perfectly balanced. However, Tony now realised that something had gone off kilter. Perhaps a night in York, doing her own thing, would sort Katie out. Yes, all she needed was to spread her wings, then she'd have a bit more perspective on the April situation and calm down. If she did get the job, he was sure they could all manage around her working again. April would just have to walk Archie more often, feed him once in a while. Problem sorted.

Tony went to the cupboard in the corner of the room and took out the model Taj Mahal he'd been secretly building for the past two weeks. He and Katie had visited the Taj Mahal on their honeymoon and he was looking forward to unveiling it on their twentieth wedding anniversary. She always complained he wasn't very romantic, but he reckoned she'd definitely love this. He extracted the manual from his desk drawer and began fixing the tiny monument to his marriage.

April arrived at Davey's workshop out of breath. Aware she was short of time, she had half jogged, half speed-walked her way there and now she was a Sweaty Betty, her hair stuck to her forehead and dark patches under her arms. Not exactly great fake relationship material, she thought, catching sight of her bedraggled reflection in the workshop window. However, Davey was no catch himself. She pushed open the door, the bell above giving a tiny warning tinkle, and peered into the workshop, her eyes slowly adjusting to the gloom after the bright sunshine outside. The slight breeze stirred dust motes, whisking a fine glitter into the air, and April, feeling a sneeze tickle her nose, quickly shut the door. Walking further into the room, she saw, to her astonishment, that it was an Aladdin's cave of beautiful furniture. There was a modern table that looked like it had been sculpted from a single tree trunk. There were intricately carved bookcases and chests of drawers. An enormous dresser dominated one wall, its wooden surface waxed to a deep, rich shine.

Davey appeared from the back of the workshop, his belly straining against his dusty, blue overalls. He was carrying a small chisel and the set of goggles on his head were like an oversized Alice band, pushing his blonde curls off his face.

'Hi April. You okay?'

April slowly turned in a circle, her arms raised towards the furniture. 'Wow, Davey. Just wow. Did you make these?'

'Yeah, well, I get a lot of commissions for bespoke pieces. Fitting floors and staircases and kitchens is my bread and butter, but these are my babies. See this one here,' he said, pointing to a small writing desk, 'Lady's mad on birds, so I carved these birds into the legs. I found the silver duck handles on the internet. And if you open the drawer, here, I added a little secret wren.'

April ran her fingers over the carvings, stunned by the level of detail.

'C'mon back here and I'll make you a cuppa, April. It's the nerve centre of the wood working world.' Davey grinned and beckoned her to another door at the back of the shop. Sure enough, there was a large room full of tools and machines, discarded pieces of wood and what appeared to be half finished kitchen cabinets.

'What are the machines for, Davey?'

'Well, this one here is a lathe. I use it to cut and shape the wood, like this spindle for a staircase. Coffee or tea?'

'I'm okay, thanks. I'm supposed to be at the pub by 4. Maggie's going to have my guts for garters. Can I explain what I was going to ask you about? Davey nodded and April ploughed on. 'Right, this is going to sound weird, but...'

April explained about Desi and how his ex, Chloe, was a no-holds-barred psycho who took the view that if she couldn't have Desi, nobody else could either.

'So, I thought if I pretend I'm in a relationship with someone else, then Desi will back off and she'll leave me alone.' April hadn't realised, but she'd barely drawn breath as her tale of woe tumbled out. She breathed in sharply and held it, waiting for Davey to respond.

After a moment's consideration, Davey shrugged and said, 'Sure. Do you need me to do anything?'

'Not really. Just take a few selfies with me, so I can post them on social media and, if anybody asks, just say we were talking for a few weeks then you asked me out.'

Davey obligingly removed his goggles and smoothed down his hair, as April took her phone out and opened the camera app. She put her head next to his and snapped a few photos, regretting her decision not to wear make-up. Normally, April was a full warpaint girl, but she had quickly learned that hot kitchen + foundation = massive zits. Oh well, she'd airbrush out the flaws later.

'Thanks, Davey. I really appreciate this. I'll buy you a few pints tomorrow night. Do you mind if I take a picture of that writing desk on the way out? I want to show it to Dad.'

'No problem. And when you see your Mum, tell her I'm asking for her.'

'She should be in on Saturday. That'll be me out of a job, but at least there's less chance of the customers being poisoned.'

'Nah, you've done a great job standing in for her. Best chips in town.'

'You've done a great job too, Davey. I can't believe this stuff. You're so talented. You should do a show or put it online or something.'

'Ha! It's just me pottering away here. Nobody would be interested in that. Anyway, I've more than enough work to keep me busy. No need to advertise. See you later, lass.'

Davey turned back to his lathe and April made her way back to the front of the workshop, taking a few photographs of the furniture as she went. Seeing Davey's work had made her view him in a new light. He'd always been the creepy drunk at the end of the bar. He was different when he was sober, more serious, the desperation and the dirty jokes gone. She liked sober Davey.

The door merrily tinkled again as she opened it and she emerged into the warm sunlight. The pub was only a few hundred yards down the road, so she used the short walk to update her Facebook status to 'In a relationship' and scrolled through her selfies to add a picture of herself and Davey. She selected the least rank photo of herself and noticed that Davey didn't look too bad in it either. Weird. When you cut off his body, he was actually quite good looking. Yuck, what was she thinking?

When April reached the pub, she found a little Scotswoman, with a face like thunder, zooming around the kitchen, stopping only to swear loudly at the teenager who washed dishes for pocket money.

'Leon, get your arse moving. There's a pile of plates there like Killymanajaroo,' shouted Maggie.

'Kilimanjaro,' said April.

'And where the hell have you been?' roared Maggie, rounding on her. 'Coach load of pensioners turned up, asking if they could have an early dinner and me like a feckin' eejit says yes, not realising that Princess April was working to her own clock today.'

'Sorry, Maggie. I had to run an errand,' said April, pulling a clean apron off the peg by the door and slipping it over her head.

Maggie was not mollified by the apology. Maggie had spent the last fifteen minutes turning up ovens and pulling random food items out of the freezer, in the vain hope of finding some of Katie's steak pies at the back. Maggie's hair, normally sprayed into a stiff, puffy bob, had wilted and her complexion, normally pale and powdery, was now red and blotchy. She was not a happy Maggie.

'Aye, I can see that.' Maggie held out Leon's phone, which was open at April's Facebook page, announcing her relationship with Davey. 'You had plenty time for this though, didn't you? Bad news travels fast. Davey? For goodness sake, April, your mother's going to have a fit when she hears about this. He's a waste of space, that one. Anyway, get your arse in gear. There's twenty sets of false teeth oot there, waiting to get stuck into a sticky toffee pudding.'

'He's not a waste of space, he's actually…'

'Aye, we'll hear all about your taste in losers later. Chop chop. Literally. Chop chop. They're wanting fourteen lamb chops and six steak pies for their main course.'

With that, Maggie swept out of the kitchen, fixed a smile on her face and went to offer the pensioners free lemonades to apologise for their wait. April opened the fridge and pulled out the pies she'd prepared yesterday. Honestly, Maggie made such a big deal out of everything. If she'd checked the fridge, she'd have seen the pies. It wasn't April's fault that Maggie didn't know her way around her own kitchen. April sneaked her phone out of her back pocket and looked at the photograph of the writing desk. Her friend, Becca, worked for the local newspaper. Wonder if she'd be interested in Davey's hidden talents? April uploaded the picture to a message, 'Somebody local makes these, they're amazing and nobody knows.' April briefly wondered whether she should have asked Davey first, then pressed send.

CHAPTER 7

Friday arrived, bringing with it one of those summer storms that, within seconds, turns your average cagoule into cold cling film. Up and down the land, Brits were confidently declaring, 'That'll clear the air.' From 11am onwards, the media became fixated on the number of centimetres of rain which had fallen, gleefully announcing that today's downpour could be the equivalent of a months' rainfall and might even beat the highest ever rainfall, recorded in Little-Felching-on-the-Wold in 1963. By 3pm, there were dire warnings of rivers bursting banks and the BBC website was awash with drone footage and viewers photographs of overflowing storm drains. Other things may have happened in the world today, but Britain's focus was firmly fixed on the lowering clouds. By teatime, the show was over and the sun had once more broken through, meaning a swift media shift to dire warnings of climate change.

Tony was oblivious to the rain, other than its effect on his decision on whether to take Archie for a walk or shove him out the back door to leave little brown landmines on the lawn. Not being a fan of any weather which risked the warmth of his bottom, Archie voted for landmines. Tony agreed and, business quickly concluded, they hunkered down in the study. Computer on, big mug of tea at the ready, Archie silently praying there would be biscuits soon, Tony ran through his plans for the day.

- 10am Budget meeting with Coles
- 11am Go over recruitment plans with Priti
- 11:30 Planning meeting with the video production team
- 1pm TwoStepz website launch virtual party
- 2pm Meeting with accountant

At some point, Tony expected to hear from the Americans. He was hoping to get this one in the bag before he flew to Dubai next week. He hadn't told Katie he was planning on a few days away to meet with some prospective clients. He and Jack liked to meet with clients face to face, so they could get a feel for the company and build relationships with the decision makers. He'd tell Katie when she got back this afternoon when, hopefully, she'd be so full of excitement after her interview that she wouldn't think to object. Oh no! Katie! Interview! He'd forgotten to phone her. Mind you, it was a bit odd that she hadn't phoned him. She was usually the one who did all the phoning and texting and he thought he'd have heard from her by now. Probably miffed that he didn't see her off yesterday. What time was the interview? He checked his calendar and mentally kicked himself for not making a note. Maybe she'd texted him. He took his phone from his left trouser pocket, where he always carried it. He'd lost count of the number of times Katie had wailed about losing her keys or her phone and he'd had to calmly remind her that if you always kept things in the same place, you never lost them. He checked his messages, but there was just a reminder from the garage that the old jalopy was due its annual service. He only had ten minutes until his budget meeting, so he decided to do the decent thing and send Katie a quick text to wish her luck, all the while hoping she burnt whatever they asked her to cook and didn't get the job. 'Yes, Archie, I'm a shameless traitor. Now, if you're a good boy and stay quiet during this meeting, I'll give you a human biscuit.' Not at all impressed by the long wait for biscuits, Archie let out a small fart, stared disbelievingly at his own bottom and stalked off on a doggy mission to find crumbs.

April woke to a persistent scratching sound at her bedroom door. Archie had decided that, as no biscuits were forthcoming, he would quite like a snooze. He had investigated his favourite human's bed and found her absent, so he was going to have to make do with second best. Third best was downstairs talking to the computer again and Archie despaired of him ever discovering its true purpose. His favourite human had told him many a time that computers were for online shopping and appealing parking tickets. Archie quite liked the online shopping computer because it made post arrive, and Archie was nothing if not diligent in his efforts to eat the postman. He wasn't even sure if he could manage a whole postman. He was, after all, quite a little dog. If Archie could talk, he would tell number three to do some online shopping. If Archie could talk, he could tell number three quite a lot of things that number one got up to, but he wouldn't because he loved his favourite human more than anything in the whole world and, right now, he was a little sad that she wasn't here. Perhaps, if he had a snooze, she would be back when he woke up. With biscuits to say sorry for going away. Scratch, scratch, scratch. Open up, number two.

April stumbled across the bedroom and opened the door to let Archie in. She knew he was a persistent little sod, so there was no point in hoping he'd bugger off and annoy someone else. He was probably missing Mum, poor little fella. Archie streaked into the bedroom, launched himself onto April's bed and buried himself under the duvet. April got in beside him and he pressed himself into her warm legs, burying his cold, wet nose into the lovely hot spot behind her knee. April gave his bottom a friendly pat. 'Well, Arch, you've properly woken me up now. What time is it? I suppose I better get ready for work. Those chips don't cook themselves thrice, you know.'

Although the snuggle was brief, the bed retained April's warmth, so Archie decided to stay put while she showered and got dressed. Leaving the door open in case he changed his mind, April went downstairs in search of sustenance and the loan of a fiver from Dad. She wasn't normally up this early and the house seemed oddly quiet. Usually, Fridays were for fun and fun required stocking up on sleep to prepare you for the night ahead. Since she'd been covering Mum's shifts, she'd missed out on boozy weekends, instead getting up early to work long hours. Early, for April, was 10am. These last few weekends, she'd got up to find Mum buzzing about the kitchen, making batches of bacon sandwiches and mugs of coffee. The kitchen felt very empty without Mum, and not particularly clean. Dad had left toast crumbs all over the counter and had forgotten to put the butter back in the fridge. Last night's dishes sat, unwashed, by the sink, waiting for the loser of the 'well, it's not my turn' game to put them in the dishwasher. Well, it definitely isn't my turn, April decided, reaching into the cupboard for a cereal bowl.

While she ate her breakfast, she checked her phone. Message from Janine.

'Coming to Plough tonight. Jez working so meeting Becca. What time you finish?'

'9ish. See you and Becs later'

'Will we meet the new man?'

'Eh?'

'You're in a relationship?'

'Soz forgot to tell you. Fake news. Davey said he'd be my pretend boyfriend in case Desi and Chloe kick off'

'Good one. Laters gawjus'

'Luvs ya hunnybuns'

The Jez thing is clearly a Thing, thought April, as she tipped the last drop of chocolatey milk into her mouth and dumped her bowl by the sink. She looked at the big clock. Thanks to Archie, the hairy alarm clock, she had plenty of time before work. If Davey was at the workshop, she could drop past on her way. She wouldn't mind another look at some of those carvings. She could even stop off at the bakery for some warm muffins for them both and...better ask Dad for a tenner.

Archie padded into the kitchen, sniffing the air hopefully, just in case bacon sandwiches had magically appeared. No bacon sandwiches, no favourite human, just number two, who hadn't even bothered leaving him her cereal bowl to lick. April went to the biscuit tin and picked out a custard cream, waggling it at Archie. Archie's heart leapt.

Maybe he would promote number two to number one and a half. The other one, however, would always be number three. Far too mean with the biscuits, that one.

Tony was deep in conversation about production costs when April popped her head around the study door. He waved her in, signalling he'd be done in a minute, and April flopped down in the old armchair, pulling out her phone to check her social media while she waited. Omd, she'd been tagged in a post by Chloe. 'Chloe Mains is with April Meadows and 15 others @ The Plough – bitches get stitches'. April felt a flush of heat in her face. Fuck-a-doodle-do, as Mum would say. If Chloe followed through, April was in big trouble.

Tony finished his call and turned to April.

'Morning, princess, are you off to work soon?'

'Yeah, but I was wondering if I could borrow a tenner. I wanted to get a coffee and muffin on the way. The weather's rank. Is there any chance of a lift as far as the bakers?'

'Sorry, pet, I'm snowed under here. I think your Mum has an umbrella in the cupboard under the stairs,' said Tony, getting his wallet out. 'Here, treat yourself.' He handed April a £20 note and turned back to his work.

'Dad, can I talk to you about something? There was a guy on Facebook that said he was going out with me and…' Tony's phone rang and he answered it, waving his hand at April to cut her off. April sighed and left the room, figuring that she was on her own with this one. She texted Janine to tell her about Chloe's threat and to have a good moan about her father. She was Daddy's princess, but sometimes he was as much use as an arsehole in a pissing competition.

Fifteen minutes later, a very wet April was standing at the bakery counter, trying to decide between spiced apple muffins and chocolate fudge brownies. She'd been coming here since she was a tot and the owners, Moira and Donald, knew her well.

'Why don't you get one of each, love? How's your Mum? She hasn't been in lately,' said Moira, bagging up the cakes before April had a chance to change her mind.

'She's okay. She was off work for a couple of weeks when she burst her lip and I've been standing in for her, but she should be back at the Plough tomorrow. Knowing her, she'll pop in for a cake and a catch up on the way.'

'Aw bless her. Tell her I'm asking for her, will you? Here's your coffees. That'll be £6.50 please.' April handed over the £20 note and, with a wink, Moira gave her £15 change. 'Don't tell Donald. He'll have my life if he catches me giving discounts.'

Sometimes April cursed the fact that, since she was a baby, she'd lived in this place where everybody knew everybody and they all felt entitled to meddle. But sometimes, like today, the familiarity was a warm blanket. She thanked Moira and, stowing the cakes safely in her handbag, once more braved the rain for the brief dash to Davey's workshop.

When she arrived at the workshop, all was in darkness inside and the door was locked. She stood for a moment, rain bouncing off the plastic lids of the coffee cups and soaking through the legs of her jeans, wondering what to do. Ducking under a small canopy over a door across the road, April fished her phone from her pocket and rang Davey. The call went to voicemail, so she rang again. Still no reply. Mentally kicking herself for not calling ahead to check he was there, April sent a quick text.

'Am at your workshop. Are you around?'

The reply came in seconds.

'Am in back. I'll come and let u in'

Sure enough, seconds later, Davey unlocked the door and ushered a sopping wet April into the dry gloom of the workshop.

'Sorry, I was working in the back and didn't hear the phone. Lucky I saw your text, otherwise you'd have drowned out there. Come on through. I'll pop the heater on so you can dry out a bit.'

They made their way through to the back room where April handed Davey the coffees while she peeled off her coat and hung it on the back of a chair in front of the heater. With the coat merrily steaming away, she took the cakes from her bag and asked, 'Spiced apple muffin or brownie?'

'That's the hardest decision of the day. Which do you fancy?'

'I can't decide either. How about we split them and have half of each?'

That settled, they sat in companiable silence, enjoying the sugar rush.

'Didn't expect to see you back,' commented Davey, wiping his sticky fingers on his overalls.

'I fancied another look at the furniture. Also, I may have accidentally told the local newspaper about it. Now, don't get annoyed. My friend Becca works on the Enquirer and I texted her a photo. She'll probably be in the pub tonight and I thought I could maybe introduce you?'

'I wasn't looking for any publicity. I've more than enough work as it is. I wish you'd asked me first.'

'I know, I know, I'm sorry. I texted her a photo of that writing desk on impulse, then only thought about it afterwards. But will you meet her?'

'Okay, I suppose.'

'Can you not have too much to drink, though? You get a bit lairy when you're drunk and it's a bit…well…,' April tried to think of an alternative word to creepy, '…off-putting.'

'Off-putting? How's that then?'

April squirmed. This was awkward. 'It's just that you make jokes and sometimes it comes across like you're hitting on people, but not in a funny way.'

'Hitting on people? Most of the time I'm bollocksed out of my mind and haven't a clue what I'm saying. It's the only thing that gets me through the week – looking forward to a weekend of oblivion. Is that how people see me? Sad, creepy guy?'

'No, no, Davey,' lied April, 'We feel a bit sorry for you when you're in the drink.'

'So, pathetic, sad, creepy guy, then?'

Aw fuck-a-fucking-doodle-do, this was not how this conversation was supposed to go. Stop digging, April.

'Look, do what you like. Just meet Becca. You're really talented and people should know about it. Also, there's a problem. Chloe might come to the pub tonight and start something. Please, if you could stick to the story about us…?'

'Don't worry, I'll be your fake boyfriend. A pathetic loser you can be proud of,' said Davey, bitterly.

'For fucks sake Davey, you're not a loser. You're just a bit lost. What's going on with you?'

'You sound just like your Mum. I'm a thirty-five-year-old man who lives with his mother. All my friends went off to uni or got married years ago and I'm still stuck in the same place doing the same thing day in day out. That's what's wrong with me. A lifetime of fitting kitchens and fixing floors, then death.'

'That's one way of looking at. Here's another. You're also a brilliant craftsman with strong ties to the local community.' Where had that come from, April wondered. She sounded like she'd had a dictionary for breakfast. 'Anyway, why d'you still live with your Mum?'

'Dunno. Just never moved out.'

'Well, you can either sit there feeling sorry for yourself or you can make something happen, it's up to you. How's about you meet Becca? Nothing might come of it anyway and if I introduce you early on, then you have the rest of the night to get as pissed as you like.'

'Whatever. It'll be a waste of time but since you brought cakes...' Davey gave her a weak smile.

'Right, it's a deal. I have to get to work but I'll see you later, yeah?'

'See you later,' Davey said, despondently. April pulled on her coat and left him sitting by the heater, head down, hunched over his tepid cup of take-away coffee.

The Plough was quiet that lunchtime, all the customers having decided to stay in their homes or offices and hide from the rain. April spent the afternoon preparing for tomorrow's lunches so that her Mum didn't have too much to do on her first day back. She went over the order for the butcher with Maggie and made Leon do a deep clean of the big fridge. Shame it was her last day. She'd really got the hang of this.

'Right, April,' said Maggie, 'Last suppers for you tonight. The rain's stopped and the punters will be through that door as fast as ye can say fish pie. Bob said he'd take over about 7 if you want to knock off a bit early.'

'Thanks, Maggie. I've a couple of friends coming over later and I wanted to introduce Davey to one of them.'

'Davey. Can't believe you hooked up with him of all people. He's a nice lad underneath it all but he's a…what do you young ones say?...a complete twat when he's drunk. How his mother puts up with it, I'll never know.'

'I'm not actually going out with him. Long story, but he said he'd fake being my boyfriend so this girl Chloe wouldn't start on me.'

'Oh aye? Sounds like there's a story there but I've no got time to hear it. There better not be any trouble, though.'

'There won't be,' April assured her, crossing her fingers that Chloe stayed away. She wondered if she should warn Maggie, but Maggie would just be straight on the phone to Mum and it was pointless worrying Mum when she wasn't here. What time would Mum be back, anyway? April didn't have a clue. She texted her Dad to ask.

Tony was deep in conversation with JT Productions' accountant when his phone buzzed. Finally, Katie had bothered to get in touch. He checked the screen. Nope, just April.

'What time Mum home?'

'Don't know. Have you heard from her?'

'No'

'Will text her'

'kk let me know'

'Katie what time you home? How did interview go?' Send.

Tony turned back to his screen, where the accountant was still droning on about input tax. The man spoke in a nasal monotone, barely lifting his eyes from the papers in front of him, and was so focused on the thrilling intricacies of VAT that he hadn't noticed Tony's momentary distraction. Tony decided that he could probably get away with having a quick forty winks. He was a numbers guy himself, but this bloke took things to another level. Tony let the accountant bore on some more before interjecting, 'So, bottom line, things are picking up after last year's disastrous slump?'

'Yes,' the accountant agreed, 'Things have definitely picked up. In fact, they're better than ever. Now, if we can deduct…'

'Let me stop you there, Geoff. I think I've got the picture. If you could send me those figures, I'll run through them with Jack on Monday, but I'm not hearing anything to worry me.'

Tony ended the call before the accountant could object. He checked his phone. Still no word from Katie. She was probably emptying their bank account into the shoe shops of York – although, after today's news, that wasn't such a worry any more. Tony hadn't told Katie just how narrowly the company had avoided going under during the pandemic last year. If it hadn't been for cash reserves, a bit of propping up by the government and some nifty, creative moves, they might not have made it. A large contract to produce a series of home-schooling videos and some work for a weight-loss company had at least meant they clung on to solvency. Never mind, things were bouncing back now and it looked like they'd end the year with a healthy profit.

Tony opened his browser and checked the train times. The last train got in at 10:12pm so, at the latest, Katie would be home well before midnight. He rang her, but it went straight to voicemail, so he tried another text.

'Sorry for not being there to say goodbye yesterday. Are you okay? Miss you'

Then he thought that perhaps she'd respond to something light-hearted.

'If you're hitting the shops, get some sexy underwear and I'll show you how much I miss you'

Oh lord, now he sounded like a pervert.

'Sorry. Just call me please'

He waited. And waited. Still no reply.

Archie was ensconced in the old armchair, happily polishing his balls to a satisfying shine. He looked up hopefully when he heard the creak of Tony's chair. Biscuits? No, it was just number three fiddling with his collection of little plastic music boxes again, muttering something about a Zeppelin being in the wrong place.

The Plough began filling up about 4pm and April found herself run off her feet. Time went by in a blur of pies, sausages, steaks, chips and chops. Leon washed dishes and mopped up spills and the wait staff flew in and out of the kitchen, delivering the fruits of her labours to the hungry hordes. During the week, she or Bob cooked on their own, but at weekends kitchen help arrived in the form of two friends of Maggie.

The small army was under the command of April, who buzzed around, checking timers and inspecting plates. Normally she was useless in stressful situations, quickly going to pieces, but in the kitchen, April exerted calm control. She didn't know why or how, but she could see the thousand tasks in her mind and knew exactly when each would need attention. She thought that this must be what it felt like to conduct an orchestra. By 7pm, the worst of the rush was over and Bob came into the kitchen to relieve her. With mock ceremony, April handed over the apron.

'You know we'll miss you in here, lass,' said Bob. 'You've done a grand job, stepping in for your Mum, and we're very grateful. Maggie's tough on the outside, but she's got a real soft spot for you and we'd hire you in an instant if we could afford it. If you ever need a reference, we're here for you.'

'Thanks, Bob. I've loved every minute of it. If you ever need a hand again, just shout.' April gave him a hug and went out to the bar to find Janine and Becca.

Standing at the door, scanning the tables, April spotted Davey at the bar and went over to him, slightly apprehensive that, after their talk this morning, he may have reverted to sad sack Davey and got sloshed at the earliest opportunity.

'Hiya, Davey. Alright?'

'Alright. Do you want a drink?'

'I'm owe you, remember. What are you having?'

'Just a lemonade, thanks.'

'Lemonade? Sure you don't want a whisky in there?'

'Nah, it's like you said this morning. I'm staying sober to meet your friend. After that, though, who knows.' He grinned at her and, for a moment, she could see how handsome he'd once been, before the booze and the misery got to him. Her stomach did a little flip. She ordered their drinks and, once more, scanned the tables for Janine and Becca. There they were, squashed together at a small table between two groups of rowdy lads she'd gone to school with. She passed Davey his lemonade, picked up her gin and beckoned for him to follow her. They squeezed past the tables of lads, shouts of, 'Oi, oi, April Meadows, come and sit with us,' following her. Smiling, she waved the lads off, shouting back, 'Aye, Ryan Mills, are you still looking up girls' skirts and telling your friends they have a big bottom at the back and a little bottom at the front?' Ryan's friends jeered and he coloured, but shouted back, good naturedly, 'I was single-handedly responsible for the introduction of girl's trousers to the school uniform back in year 2. It's on my CV and everything!'

April turned to the table beside her and smiled at her friends. 'Janine, Becca, this is my friend, Davey.'

'Come and sit down, Davey,' said Becca, gesturing to an empty chair next to her. Becca immediately started make small-talk with Davey, so April took the opportunity to have a quiet chat with Janine.

'Okay, tell me about the Jez thing,' April muttered, shuffling her chair a bit closer to her friend so they wouldn't be overheard. 'Is it an actual Thing, then?'

'I think it is. He hasn't officially asked me out yet, but we're talking and there's definitely something there.'

As Janine waxed lyrical about Jez, April strained above the noisy shouts of the lads to hear what Davey was saying to Becca. She caught snatches of their conversation.

'...messaged you a picture...'

'Oh, you're the mystery carpenter. I thought...'

'Ha ha. Yes, I told her she shouldn't have, but...'

'No. I showed it to the editor...have more...come round and see them.'

'Yeah, what time?'

Things were going good there, April surmised. She turned back to Janine, who appeared to be giving her chapter and verse on Jez' difficult childhood.

'So, when his mam left, there was just him and his Dad and his big brother. His Dad was never there and his big brother left the minute he turned sixteen. He practically brought himself up. When his brother came back last year, he bought the club and made Jez the bar manager.'

April thought back to a teenage Jez, remembering him hanging out with the tough crowd, the likes of Chloe and her friends. 'I didn't realise. I kept away from him at school because he was so angry all the time.'

'Yeah, he hated school. He found out the headmaster had an affair with his mam and he said something in him snapped. Social services got involved and he told me it was the making of him. He got some counselling and they helped him turn things around. Hasn't seen the inside of a police cell since. He never heard from his mam again, though. Reckons his Dad probably found out about the headmaster and buried her under the floorboards.' Janine laughed at the ridiculousness of it, then stopped, eyes like saucers, and gasped, 'Oh my, what if he did!'

'If he paid as much attention to her as he did to his kids, it's more likely she upped and left.'

'You're right, but still, it's weird. What sort of person disappears and never even contacts her kids?'

'I suppose things must've been really bad. Davey and Becca seem to be getting along.'

April and Janine watched their friends laughing together at something Davey had said. It was odd seeing Davey sober on a Friday night, when usually he'd be sitting alone at the end of the bar, slowly reaching the point where he fell of his barstool and they'd have to call his Mum.

As she smiled inwardly at the thought of Davey, there at the bar one minute, gone the next, no magic required, she looked over the heads of the rowdy lads and saw pub door open. Four familiar figures walked in, stopped and gazed around them, like gunslingers preparing for a shootout. Chloe and her three henchwomen, all of them tall and solid, wearing green crop tops and leggings – comfy casuals, the female equivalent of tooling up for a fight. April fervently wished she could pull off Davey's disappearing trick right now because this was definitely a major fuck-a-doodle-do situation. She elbowed Janine, causing her to spill good splash of vodka tonic down her top.

'Oi, April,' yelled Janine in surprise.

'Shh,' hissed April, 'Bogey at two o'clock.'

'Eh? What?'

'Chloe. Big green, slimy bogey bitch over there. Keep your voice down.'

But it was too late. Chloe had spotted April and came stalking towards her. She stopped at the table, hands on hips, and demanded, 'So, what the fuck do you think you're playing at?'

'Oh, hi Chloe. Haven't seen you in ages. Have you met Becca? And this is my boyfriend, Davey.' April gave Davey a sharp kick under the table and he yelped. Chloe eyed him suspiciously.

'Bit old for you, isn't he? Bit fat. Been on the bacon sarnies, mate?' Chloe sneered, leaning over and giving Davey a prod on the belly. 'If he's your boyfriend, then I'm the fucking queen of this pub.'

'No, you're not, because I'm the fucking queen of this pub and I think you better leave,' said a voice behind her. Maggie stood there, drawn up to her full five feet, two bright spots on her cheeks, her blonde helmet glittering in the warm light from the wall lamps. A wee Scots terrier, ready to bite the legs off anyone unwise enough to cause trouble in her pub. The groups of lads nearby went silent, waiting to see how this played out.

Chloe whipped round to face Maggie. 'Get lost old lady, this is between me and April.'

'I'm warning you, leave my pub now or I'll call the police,' said Maggie, well-practised in the pub landlady's art of being firm and staying cool in the face of potential trouble.

'Well, let's give you something to call them about then.'

Quick as a flash, Chloe slapped Maggie's face and shoved her backwards. The three henchwomen dodged out of the way and Maggie went tumbling to the floor. April stood up, tipping the table over and sending the drinks flying. If she noticed, she didn't care.

'That was low, even for you, Chloe. Do you go around hitting old ladies now? I bet you mug them too.'

'I'm not an old lady, you cheeky wee wench,' said a voice from the floor.

A space opened up around April and Chloe, as the lads stood up and moved back. Someone helped Maggie to her feet and took her over to the bar, where Bob was on the phone, presumably to the police.

'Think you've got a chance with Desi, do you? Little Miss Perfect, dancing around with your tits hanging out like a slag.'

'I wouldn't touch Desi with yours. And I wouldn't go near yours without rubber gloves and a hazmat suit.'

April was beyond angry. Nobody hit her Maggie and she was not going to let this bitch bully her. She had never been in a fight before. She'd seen plenty and once got swept up when the police swooped in and arrested everyone at a house party. Mum had been so angry at her for getting herself into that situation, lord knows what she was going to say about this.

Chloe's henchwomen started to crowd in on April, but Chloe waved them off. 'Leave it, girls. I've got this one.' And, with that, she launched herself at April.

Chloe was not a slim girl. It was like getting hit by a squidgy train. April fell back, but Chloe caught her by her hair and pulled April towards her. Despite the stinging in her head, April summoned her cool, kitchen self to the task and, instead of trying to get away from Chloe, she used the momentum to drive herself forward, knocking Chloe backwards. Chloe took April down with her, but April was prepared and landed a knee hard in Chloe's belly. She staggered to her feet and Chloe lay on the floor, winded.

'Get out, Chloe, before this gets any worse. I'm not interested in Desi. It's all in his head. It's all in your head.'

Chloe started to get up when, out of nowhere, a small blonde bombshell landed directly on her head. Maggie had rushed back into the fight and planted her backside firmly on Chloe's face, roaring, 'Think you can slap me and get away with it? Well, you can kiss my arse!'

Chloe bucked and lashed out, trying to dislodge Maggie, but it was pointless. Maggie had once hired a bucking bronco for a special event night and outlasted every customer in the pub. She grabbed a hank of Chloe's hair in each hand and prepared to beat her own record. The only way she was getting off was if Chloe turned blue.

April heard the sound of breaking glass and turned to see one of the henchwomen coming towards her, broken bottle in hand.

'Oh, no you don't,' she said, picking up a chair to use as a barrier between herself and the weapon. The henchwoman lashed out with the bottle and April dodged backwards, jabbing the legs of the chair towards her. Still, the woman came on. Being taller and stronger, she managed to reach past the chair and caught April with a swipe to her arm. Blood immediately welled up in the deep gash and April almost dropped the chair. She could see that the other two henchwomen were getting ready to step in and knew that if they started, she was a goner.

April sensed, rather than saw, Janine, Becca and Davey behind her. Janine suddenly stepped around April and delivered a hefty kick to the woman's crotch. Women may not have the sensitive dangly bits of boys, but a hard kick in the lady garden could still be effective. The henchwoman doubled over and dropped the bottle. Unfortunately, she also closed her legs, trapping Janine's foot, and the two of them went down in a tangled mass of bodies.

Distracted by the sight of Janine trying to drag her foot free of the woman's crotch, all the while fending off wild blows, April didn't see the other two henchwomen making their move. At the sound of a bellowed, 'Nooooo!' April turned just in time to see Davey whirl around and take them both out with a chair. For a nanosecond, she was amazed that the chair hadn't broken, then she realised that Davey hadn't stopped whirling and the chair was coming directly at her face. She started to duck but, in one massive own goal, Davey cracked the chair across her forehead and everything went black.

April woke to find a man with an impossibly long nose peering down at her. Wow, this was just like in the movies, when people woke up after being unconscious and were surrounded by blurry weirdos. Any minute now, someone would ask how many fingers they were holding up. Well, if they couldn't be bothered counting their own fingers, she didn't see why she should. Although, counting fingers might distract her from the motherfudging pain in her head.

'April, it's okay, I'm a paramedic and I'm here to help you. How many fingers am I holding up?'

There was a long pause. 'Eighteen,' she said, confidently. The paramedic looked slightly worried. April patted his arm and gave him an understanding look. Having eighteen fingers must be a nightmare when you're trying to put bandages on people. She could hear Davey in the background, howling something about a chair, and Janine appeared briefly to say she'd phone Dad. Why was Janine phoning her Dad? What was Janine's Dad going to do about this?

The paramedic did lots of fiddly things and asked her if she was diabetic, if she'd taken drugs and how much alcohol had she drank. Finally, he seemed happy that she was addled but not in any real danger.

'Right, I think we need to get you checked out. Let's get you to hospital.'

As she was being wheeled into the ambulance, April spotted two policemen talking to Chloe, who looked like she'd just gone ten rounds with Tyson Fury. She was covered in scratches and there were two bald patches either side of her head. Yesssss, there is a god. April was about to shout, 'Arrest the big bogey!' when the ambulancemen shunted her outside, the pub door swinging closed behind them. She contented herself with the thought that she'd found her purple thong that morning, so at least she was wearing clean knickers. Mum would be proud.

CHAPTER 8

Tony must have dropped off to sleep in his armchair because he was woken by a burst of loud music. His hand went straight to his left pocket, but it was empty. It took him a moment to realise that the Flight of the Valkyries was emanating from his bottom and he quickly scrabbled under his left cheek to retrieve his fallen phone.

'Hello?'

'Hi, Mr Meadows. It's Janine. Listen, don't panic or anything. There was a fight at the pub and April's been taken to hospital. She's okay, but she was knocked out and she has a cut on her arm.'

'What?! A fight? How did that happen? Never mind. Right, okay, erm, right, go to the hospital, right, thanks Janine.'

He hung up, took a deep breath and steadied himself. This was not the time to panic. Panic would only cause delay, he reasoned. He went into the hall and took his shoes off the rack, replacing them with his slippers. He tied his shoe laces, stood up and called for Archie. He let Archie out for a pee (no sense in coming home to a puddle on the kitchen floor later), locked the back door and took his coat off the hook. Back in the hall, he retrieved his car keys from the key cupboard, where he always hung them, switched the lights on so it would look like someone was home, set the alarm, went out and made sure he locked the front door behind him.

Tony drove to the hospital, obeying all the speed limits and keeping a sensible distance between his car and the one in front. He was not entirely immune to freaking out and had to suppress the urge to scream at a doddering pensioner in an ancient but perfectly preserved Skoda, who was 'racing' along at 20mph in a 40 zone. 'People like that should be arrested. Why don't the police do something about it?' he muttered to himself, completely forgetting that he had once been stopped by the police for having a faulty tail light and incurred the wrath of the officer (and a very stern lecture) when he had been unwise enough to ask, 'Why aren't you out there arresting real criminals?'

Tony pulled the ticket from the machine at the hospital car park entrance, ignoring the angry revs from the car behind while he carefully placed the ticket in his wallet, so that he knew exactly where to find it later. He drove to the furthest point of the car park, where lots of empty spaces meant there was minimal risk of his car being damaged by a sloppy parker, and parked neatly between the lines. No panic. Everything was as it should be.

In the hospital reception area, Tony spotted Janine, who was sitting on a row of plastic chairs, deep in conversation with a slightly overweight, blonde chap. Tony thought he might have seen the man before, but he couldn't place him. He walked towards the pair and Janine looked up.

'Hi, Mr Meadows. We were just waiting here for you. April's being checked over now but they said they'll probably be moving her to a ward later. They think she has concussion and they want to keep her in overnight. Have you met Davey?'

Tony proffered a hand and Davey shook it.

'So, what happened? You said there was a fight?'

Janine opened her mouth to explain but Davey got there first. 'It's my fault. I hit her over the head with a chair. No, no,' he protested, seeing Tony's brows furrow, 'It was an accident. These lasses were having a go at your April and I hit *them* with the chair. Only I kept going, see, couldn't stop the swing, and I took April out as well.

Whacked her on the forehead and she went out like a light. I feel really bad.'

Tony was slightly mollified by the confession. 'But why was there a fight in the first place?'

This time, Janine spoke first. 'This lad, Desi, put on his Facebook that he was seeing April and he has this horrible ex, real nasty pasty, Chloe, who doesn't want anyone else seeing Desi, but April wasn't seeing Desi, so she asked Davey to be her fake boyfriend so Chloe would know she wasn't with Desi, only Chloe didn't believe it and she came to the pub with her three friends looking for a fight, then she hit Maggie so April kneed her in the guts and Maggie sat on her face, then I kicked her friend in the fanny…sorry Mr M, the vagina…and Davey whacked everyone with a chair, then the police arrived.' Janine drew in a deep breath and shrugged, explanation clearly and cogently delivered. 'Becca videoed the whole thing on her phone, if you don't believe me.'

Tony took a moment to sort through the jumble of facts, before concluding that some girl had taken offence about something to do with a boyfriend and had hit his little girl. 'Why didn't April tell me about this? We could have gone to the police and they could have had a word with this Chloe before anything got out of hand.'

'She texted me that she tried to tell you this morning, but you were busy working,' Janine said, awkwardly. Tony recalled April saying something about someone on Facebook and felt a knot of guilt in the pit his stomach. However, no point in crying over spilt milk. He would sort this, he could fix this.

'I'm going to find out what's happening,' he said, abruptly, and strode off to interrogate the reception staff. Janine watched the straight-backed figure march purposefully towards the desk and called after him that she and Davey were going to head off now. Tony didn't look back, merely raising a hand to signal that he'd heard.

Tony spent the next few hours sitting on the bank of plastic chairs, waiting to hear news of April. He'd waved his BUPA card threateningly at an anxious looking receptionist, who assured him that someone would be out soon to give him an update. Nobody came. A procession of Friday night drinkers shuffled through, clutching bloody noses, scalp wounds and cauliflower ears. Girlfriends, boyfriends, best friends, all either aggrieved at the injustice of someone twatting their loved one or berating said loved one for being stupid enough to get twatted. 'I told you to leave it, Sandra, but you just couldn't. You kept winding her up and now you've ruined the night out. Well, you can eff off if you think I'm going out with you again!' 'I'm sooooorry. But she was bang out of order, you know that. Oh, Marie, I swear I'll never do that again. I'm sooooorry. Is my mascara okay?' 'C'mere you daft cow, stop crying. Your mascara's fine. What brand is that? Might get some myself.' One of the inebriated cauliflower ears sat next to him and gave Tony the benefit of his wisdom. 'What it is, pal. What. It. Is. Is the government don't understand the working man. We voted them in, but they've been caught red-handed with their pants down and their noses in the trough and now they're going to get their arses kicked at the next election.' Tony couldn't help but imagine a line of bare bottomed MPs bending over a rusting tub, their red hands clutching the rim, as a man in a flat cap and overalls made his way along the line, giving each white, pimply backside a kick in turn.

To distract himself from this disconcerting image, he called Katie for the fourth time that night, but once again it went straight to voicemail, so he texted her the news and asked her to let Archie out when she got home. He was surprised when she didn't call or text back, but assumed this was something to do with her letting April dig herself out of her own messes in future. Still, a bit cold not to even call to see how April was.

He couldn't get rid of the sense of guilt that he hadn't listened to April when she tried to tell him that something was wrong. Instead, he'd blithely got on with his day, while she was probably terrified of this Chloe girl. His head had been in work mode and he hadn't been thinking of anything else. He was such an idiot. Why hadn't he taken a few minutes to listen? He was so busy keeping everything on track at work, he'd taken his eye off the ball at home. What else had he missed? Maybe Katie had a point, even when he was here, he wasn't here.

Tony heard his name called and went to the reception desk. This time, he was met by a harassed looking nurse, who peered at a clip board and asked him for his details. 'Just popping you down as next of kin,' the nurse said. He saw Tony pale slightly and quickly reassured him, 'She's fine, a bit woozy, so we just want to make sure we have all the correct details.'

'Can I see her?'

'We're moving her up to a ward now. It's well past visiting hours but I'm sure they won't mind you paying a quick visit.'

The nurse directed Tony to the ward, where another nurse took him to April's room. She explained that they'd given April some strong painkillers to help with her headache and these might make her a bit sleepy. April had a concussion and some stitches in her arm. She'd be sore tomorrow, but would probably be well enough to go home.

'She took quite a nasty blow to the head. Don't worry if she doesn't seem quite herself. Apparently, the police tried to talk to her earlier and she kept going on about bogies. Between the painkillers and the concussion, she's quite sleepy and confused, but it usually resolves itself within a few days.'

Tony looked down at his sleeping daughter. She had a whopping great egg on her forehead and her arm was bandaged, but at least there was no permanent damage.

April stirred, opened an eye and said, 'Oh, hello. Who are you?' A look of pure angst came over Tony's face. 'Just joking, Dad. Sorry 'bout all this,' she spun a hand, gesturing at the room. 'It really wasn't my fault. They said I was knocked out. Funny, last thing I remember is Maggie sitting on Chloe's head.'

'It's okay, love. Janine and Davey explained what happened. Davey hit two girls with a chair and accidentally hit you as well.'

'Oh. Did you meet Davey, then? He's the nicest creepy pervert I know. I wish I could fall off my barstool like him.'

Tony wasn't quite sure how to respond to this, so resorted to, 'How are you feeling?'

'Very tired. Where's Mum?'

Good question. Where *was* Mum?

'She's probably home by now. Maybe she didn't get my message when she was on the train.'

'She hasn't been right lately, you know. I thought she was mad at me about the drugs thing, but it seemed like more than that.'

Tony settled himself down on the chair next to the bed. 'Don't worry about your Mum. She's been having a mid-life crisis. It'll all blow over. She's probably bought fifty pairs of shoes in York and is prancing about the bedroom, trying them on right now.'

'Yeah. I think we maybe take her for granted, though. I like shoes.' April yawned and closed her eyes.

Tony took his phone from his left pocket and checked the news. May as well catch up with the world while he waited for April to wake up.

Sometime in the wee hours, the nurse looked in on April. Smiling to herself, she quietly closed the door and went to the store then, silently creeping back into April's room, she gently laid a blanket over the sleeping figure of Tony.

The next morning saw an aching, dishevelled Tony lever himself slowly out of the chair, thank the nurses and wander off to find a toilet and a bacon butty, in that order. Afterwards, he went to the hospital shop and bought April some toiletries and clean knickers. He also spotted a t-shirt, which turned out to be surprisingly cheap for hospital stuff (he was considering a second mortgage to pay for the parking and the bacon sandwich). The elderly lady behind the counter explained that someone had donated a couple of hundred t-shirts and that the money from sales was being donated to a charity.

Feeling like father of the year for being so thoughtful towards April, as well as doing his bit for charity, he made his way back to the ward, where he handed over the bag of essentials, then stood outside the room while she dressed. He expected she would be pleased, so was most surprised when a loud wail of, 'WHAT THE ACTUAL FUUUU,' rent the air. Tony rushed in to find April, red-faced, sitting on the bed wearing her new t-shirt. 'FBI Female Body Inspector! Are you joking, Dad? Is this your idea of a wind up? I'm not wearing this. You're going to have to go back to the shop and get me another one.'

'But, sweetie.'

'No, Dad. Get me another t-shirt. I am not leaving the hospital with this on. It's like wearing sexual harassment.'

Tony didn't see the problem. Both he and the shop lady had thought the t-shirt was mildly amusing. Before they could argue any further, the doctor swept in, unannounced.

'Just doing the rounds. How are you feeling?' he asked, checking April's chart.

'I'm fine. Just tired and headachy.'

'That should go. We're going to discharge you, but you need to go home and rest for the next few days. Paracetamol or ibuprofen for the pain. Dad, you need to stay with her for at least 48 hours. The nurse will give you a leaflet, but if any of the symptoms get worse, see your GP or call 111. Funny t-shirt by the way. Where did you get it?'

'Hospital shop,' interjected Tony, before April could say something they'd all regret.

'Right, I might get one for my husband. He's a gynaecologist. He'll think it's hilarious. Better not wear it to work, though.' He winked at April and swept out of the room as suddenly as he'd arrived.

'The mind boggles,' muttered Tony. 'Put the t-shirt on outside-in and I'll lend you my coat to cover up.'

'Should that be outside-in or inside-out, Dad?' April knew how to push her Dad's buttons.

'Bugger, I'll have to Google that now. Just get your things together and let's go home.'

CHAPTER 9

Tony and April drew up to the house and an unsettling sense of things being out of kilter immediately descended upon them. The drive was empty and the lights that Tony had switched on when he left the night before were still glowing. Something was most definitely wrong, yet neither of them was quite willing to admit it. There was an unspoken hope that they would walk through that door, to be greeted by an ecstatic Archie and a Katie bearing presents from York.

They got out of the car and trudged across the drive, the crunching of stones beneath their feet loud in the silence. April felt an irrational urge to tiptoe. She couldn't explain why, but being quiet felt important. Tony unlocked the front door and Archie launched himself at them, wild with happiness, before dashing into the front garden for the longest, most satisfying pee of his life.

'Katie! Katie!'

'Mum!'

Nothing. The house was still and the only sound was Archie dashing around the garden, overcome by the utter joy that he was not, after all, an abandoned dog. His favourite human had once told him about dog shelters and he'd had a nightmare afterwards. He'd done so many unexpected woofs and leg twitches that he woke himself up!

Where was his favourite human? Her scent was getting fainter every hour and it made Archie sad. So sad that he stopped running and went back inside to press himself against the leg of his one and a half favourite human.

April reached down and gave Archie's ears a rub. 'I don't know what's happened, Archie. I'm worried too.'

Tony, who had been upstairs checking the bedroom, joined them in the hall. 'No suitcase and her passport's gone. She hasn't come back from York.' He could feel panic welling up inside him and pushed it down so as not to worry April. 'I'll try calling her again and if there's no reply, I think we'll have to call the police.'

April could hear the worry in her father's voice and knew he was trying to stay calm for her sake. She waited what felt like an age while he dialled. She could hear the muffled rings, followed by Mum's tinny voice, 'Sorry, I can't take your call. Please leave a message…bugger… how do you work these things…April, what do I press…oh, right… well, leave a message. Thanks.'

Tony's voice had a slight catch in it as he spoke. 'Katie, it's Tony and April. Are you okay? Please phone to let us know you're okay.'

He hung up and took a deep breath to steady himself. Come on, Tony. Crisis is what you're good at. In his best, capable-parent voice, he issued instructions to April. 'Can you ring Suzy and ask if she's heard from Mum? Try Maggie as well. And anyone else you can think of. But not your grandparents, I don't want to worry them.'

'No probs, Dad. Go and put the kettle on and feed Archie while I make the calls.' April was glad to have something to do because it kept her from totally freaking out. She went into the study and rummaged around in Dad's desk drawer. Mum was such an old person. Despite April telling her that all her contacts were on her phone, she said she didn't trust the thing and still kept an actual handwritten contacts book. April flicked through the pages until she found the entry for Suzy and Graham, then dialled the number.

In the kitchen, Tony was making a call of his own to York Hospital. He didn't want April there if there was bad news. He googled the number and pressed call.

'Hello, you're through to York Hospital, please pick from one of the following options…'

Tony wanted to scream with frustration. Fucking options. He wanted a human being. One who could tell him where his wife was. He glared at Archie, who was standing by his bowl, casting hopeful looks at the bag of dog food. 'In a minute,' Tony hissed at him, as he stabbed angrily at the number pad on his phone.

'Hello, York Hospital. You're speaking with Stacey today. How can I help you?'

'Hello. My name's Tony Meadows. I'm trying to find out if my wife has been admitted. She was in York and she hasn't come home and I'm worried something has happened to her. It's Katie Frock.'

'Do you have her date of birth?'

'Yes, it's 28th September 1975.'

'And is Katie short for anything?'

'Yes, she's quite short. Five foot four. Lies in wait for tall people in supermarkets so they can get things down from the top shelf for her.'

'No, her name, is it short for anything, like Katherine?'

'Oh, sorry. I thought you asked "is she short or anything?" No, it's just Katie.'

'I'm going to check for you. Please hold the line.'

While Tony waited, he fumbled one-handed with plastic clip on the bag of dog food. How did these bloody things work? He pulled on the end and pushed the sides together, but it refused to spring open. Eventually, he gave up, took some scissors from the drawer and cut the bag. Hundreds of brown pellets spilled forth and bounced onto the kitchen tiles, surprising Archie, who thought this was a wonderful new food game and set about tidying them up with his mouth.

'Hello? Mr Meadows, I've checked and I can't find any record of your wife being admitted. I'm sorry. Have you tried the police?'

'That's my next call. Thanks anyway.'

Tony opened the back door for Archie, figuring that, once he'd stuffed himself with a week's worth of food, there may be a minor explosion in the bottom department. That done, he filled the kettle, switched it on and went through to the study to find out how April was getting on.

April was not getting on. Suzy hadn't heard from Mum since they'd gone shopping the other day and offered to phone around their mutual friends. Maggie had no news either. She took the opportunity to tell Maggie that she'd have to draft in some help because they couldn't find Mum and April was under orders to rest for a few days.

'Don't you worry. Just focus on your Mum and getting better.'

'I'm really sorry about the fight, Maggie. Are you okay?'

'Aye, I'm fine. Wee bitch bit my backside and I had to get a tetanus jab. That new lad at the GP's saw a bit more than he bargained for this morning. There's so much cellulite down there, it looks like I sat on a bag of Rice Krispies. Now, off you go and make your phone calls. Let me know what's happening. Bob and I are here for you, love.'

April ended the call, opened Katie's book at A and started calling Katie's contacts. As she dialled the first number, she wondered at her mother's system. There were all sorts of names here and hardly any of them began with A. She flicked to B and saw the same random mix. She'd found Suzy under L! Back at A, she noticed an annotation in the top right-hand corner. Arseholes. She checked B. Bastards. L? Lovelies. R – Relatives, S – Sweetiepies, W – Wankers. April hung up before the A could answer and started again at L. She had just finished S, without success, when her Dad appeared.

'I didn't get replies from most of the numbers, but the ones I spoke to haven't heard from her.'

Tony sank into the old armchair and rubbed his forehead. 'I called the hospital in York. She's not there. I'll have to call the police, I suppose.'

The police arrived surprisingly quickly. Within half an hour of his call, Tony heard a car pull into the drive and stop. Glancing out of the window, he saw two policemen approaching the front door, and rushed to intercept them before they rang the doorbell and set Archie off. He ushered the policemen inside and took them into the living room, shouting to April not to let the dog out of the kitchen.

Looking rather bemused, the policemen introduced themselves. In his tired, worried state, Tony immediately forgot their names. He was usually very good with names. Katie, on the other hand, suffered with what she called 'Brain Fatigue About Remembering Trivial Stuff', or brainfarts for short, so she tended to privately give people nicknames. Their elderly neighbours had been christened George and Mildred shortly after moving in and their actual names were lost to the mists of time. Tony occasionally lingered by the garden fence, listening to his neighbours' conversations in the hope that he could learn their real names. He was fairly sure that George had noticed because he once overheard him saying something to Mildred about 'the damn nosey-parkers next door.' Rather than ask the policemen to repeat themselves, Tony decided to take a leaf out of Katie's book and think of them as Bobby 1 and Bobby 2.

'I'm glad you came so quickly,' he said. 'I'm going out of my mind with worry. She hasn't been answering her phone, but I thought it was just because she was in a mood with me. I even told her to get herself some sexy underwear so we could…erm…make up. Usually she'd laugh and do something daft like send me a picture of herself in big granny knickers. And then this morning I thought she'd be there with presents and she wasn't.' Tony realised he was babbling and abruptly stopped talking.

'And do you normally exchange sexual pictures, sir?' asked Bobby 1.

'Well, sometimes. Nothing illegal, but I go away a lot for work and, you know how it is.'

'No, I don't, sir.'

'Okay, uh, sometimes she sends me a topless one and I send back a pic of me in my boxers.'

'And you think this is okay?'

'Why wouldn't it be? We're both consenting adults.'

'We'll need to speak to your daughter to see what she has to say.'

'I'd rather you didn't speak to April about this. It's quite private and she doesn't need to know what me and her Mum get up to.'

Bobby 1 looked confused and turned to Bobby 2, who appeared to be on the verge of tears. His face had reddened and his shoulders were shaking. Bobby 1 frowned and turned back to Tony.

'Let's start again. I think we have some crossed wires. We're here to speak to April Meadows about a disturbance at the Plough last night.'

'Oh. I thought you were here about my wife. I just rang to report her missing.'

'I'm sorry, we didn't know about that. Hold on, I'll just call into the control room and find out what's going on.'

While Bobby 1 radioed control, Tony offered the officers tea and went to put the kettle on. The moment he opened the kitchen door, Archie bolted out and made a beeline for the living room so that he could give the exciting strangers a proper welcome. Reckoning that Archie would keep the Bobbies busy for a few minutes, Tony slumped into a chair and leaned forward, resting his head on the cool table. What a grade A prat. Pull yourself together, Tony, for goodness sake. You haven't been in this much of a state since April was born. If Katie were here, she'd find this hilarious. But she's not here. She's really not here. Tony could feel tears prick his eyes and tensed his jaw, biting his upper lip to stem the emotion. Action, that was what was needed. Keep moving, keep busy. He switched the kettle on and shouted to April to come downstairs.

April had heard the police arrive and had been sitting on her bed, unsure whether to go down and support Dad or stay out of the way. As soon as she heard him call her name, she sprang off the bed and thundered down the stairs. She could hear Archie in the living room, making a huge fuss and probably annoying the life out of everyone. She supposed she should rescue them before he licked them to death. Entering the living room, she saw two policemen, one of whom had Archie wrapped around his face. Bottom waggling vigorously, chest pressed into the officer's head, Archie's joy at having visitors was on full display.

'Put your lipstick away, Archie. Honestly! I'm so sorry about this,' said April, dragging the unrepentant Beagle off the object of his affection. She carried him into the dining room, then dashed out and shut the door before he could escape.

Back in the living room, the policeman was straightening his uniform and retrieving his notebook from the floor. April bent over to pick up his pen.

'Really sorry. He's not normally quite so…enthusiastic. I think he's missing Mum. Do you need any information from me about her? I mean, she hasn't been in touch or anything like that.'

'Not at the moment,' said the policeman. 'We actually came to talk to you about last night, then your Dad told us your Mum's missing. My colleague's just getting some details now. While we're waiting, we may as well have a chat. We'll need to speak more formally about the events at the Plough and we'd like you to come to the station. The hospital said you have concussion, so we'll give you an appointment to attend on Wednesday. Do you think you'll be well enough?'

April, already stressed, felt a twist in her guts and sat down on the sofa. 'Probably. They said I'd be okay in a few days. Am I under arrest?'

'No. You'll be interviewed under caution because we're investigating an affray, but you're not under arrest at this point.'

The policeman gave April an appointment card and an information sheet to explain her rights. His colleague came off his radio and sat next to April.

'I have the details your Dad gave when he rang us. When did you last see your Mum?'

'Wednesday. I went to a student's night at Blue and I went back to a friend's house afterwards. It was an all-nighter, so I didn't get home 'til about 5, then I slept in until late afternoon. Mum was gone when I woke up. I knew she was going to York for something and she was supposed to be back yesterday.'

'Was she in touch at all while she was away?'

'No, but I didn't think anything of it, really. I thought it was a bit weird she hadn't phoned Dad, though.'

Tony came in, carrying a tray with three mugs of tea.

'Sorry, I didn't know if anyone wanted sugar.'

'We'll take it as it comes,' Bobby 1 assured him. 'Now, if you could tell us a bit more about your wife's trip?'

Tony placed the tray on a side table and sat on a footstool, elbows on knees, his mug clutched so tightly in his hands that the bones of his knuckles pressed white against his flesh. Slowly, he recounted the events of the last few days. He explained about the job interview and what he knew of Katie's travel plans. He showed the officers his phone, with the times of his calls and texts. He told them about falling asleep at the hospital and not realising Katie was missing until that morning.

'Was there anything unusual about her behaviour at all?' asked Bobby 2.

'She was in a fettle about needing to crack down on April and she'd been talking about how, now that April was older, it was time for her to have a career again. I thought she was just going through a restless phase. I was annoyed because I'm away for work all the time and I thought if she ended up doing long hours then there'd be nobody here for April and the dog.'

Even as he said it, Tony realised it sounded ridiculous.

Bobby 2 checked his notes and turned to April. 'You're twenty-one, yes?'

Point made, thought Tony. 'Look, we'd always had this deal that I'd concentrate on the company and Katie would look after things at home. We didn't have much when April was born and I was starting a new business, so it made sense at the time. I suppose we got used to it and that was how it was.'

'Did you and your wife argue at all?'

'Not argue, as such. We had words and she was annoyed with me, but it wasn't a serious argument. We both knew she was going to get over this job idea. It was one of her impulses. She's quite an impulsive person and she takes notions. Then, the next week, she's moved onto something else. I set her straight and told her not to do it, but sometimes with Katie you have to wait for her to move on in her own time.'

Bobby 2 muttered to himself, as he wrote in his notebook, 'Argued, forbade his wife from getting a job so she could stay at home and look after adult daughter.'

Tony was starting to get the uncomfortable feeling that he was being judged and found wanting.

'What about you, April. Did you notice anything unusual about your Mum recently?'

'Not really, she seemed a bit down, but I just thought it was an age thing. You know, like menopause or something. We'd actually been getting on better. She was showing me how to cook and I was covering her shifts at the pub.'

'Oh? Why was that?'

'She had a really bad split lip.'

The Bobbies eyed Tony suspiciously. 'How did that happen?'

'Dad didn't hit her or anything. She bit her lip when she headbutted him in the balls.'

Tony groaned inwardly. This was going from bad to worse.

'We were having a canoodle in the shower and she slipped on the soap,' he interrupted.

'A canoodle,' April snorted. 'First time I've heard it called that.'

Tony put down his mug and sat upright. 'You're supposed to be resting, young lady. Do you need her for anything else? No? Right, off to bed with you. I'll wake you if there's any news.'

'But daaaad!' April reverted to her ten-year-old self, banished from the adults' conversation.

'Really, April. The hospital said you need to rest. I'm not being mean. None of this is easy and I just need you to get well.'

April realised that her Dad looked like he'd aged a hundred years in the past hour or two. She knew he was worried. She was worried too. But he only had to deal with missing Mum. How did he think she felt?! She was the one with a brain injury AND a missing Mum AND a police interview. Yet her head was sore and she was so darn tired. Okay, she'd go, but she was setting an alarm for two o'clock. Poor Dad. She felt sorry for him and she was annoyed with him at the same time. Even as these thoughts flashed through April's mind, she knew she was being irrational. Probably the concussion, she decided. They said she might have mood swings. She stifled her need to argue further, gave her Dad a quick hug and made her way back upstairs to her room.

Shortly afterwards, having taken some final details from Tony, the policemen left, promising that a family liaison officer would be with them shortly. Suddenly finding himself alone, Tony was at a loss as to what to do now. He tidied away the mugs and loaded the dishwasher. Scraping and whining at the dining room door alerted him to the fact that Archie was still locked away, so he released the hound and let him out for a pee. Then he made his way to the study and stood before his precious CD collection. Who even has CDs any more? It's all digital now. Maybe I should just bite the bullet and download all of these, then they'll always be in order. He stared at Dire Straits, which had mysteriously appeared next to Aretha Franklin, and he wept.

CHAPTER 10

The family liaison officer was a kind man, who made conversation when he was needed yet was able to fade into the background during private moments. He kept up a steady flow of tea and biscuits and became a firm favourite with Archie, possibly due to the odd custard cream finding its way under the coffee table, where Archie had set up his own doggy command post.

By Sunday morning, news had come in that Katie's car had been found at the train station. A phone call to the hotel revealed that she had never checked in and Duns told the police that she hadn't turned up for her job interview. The police were checking her bank account, tracing her movements at the train station and obtaining details of her journey after she boarded the train. At this point, all they could say was that she either didn't arrive in York or, if she did, she had gone missing between York train station and her hotel. With such a narrow timeline, the police were hopeful of being able to provide some answers soon.

Suzy arrived, having phoned ahead to say she was coming to help. She breezed in and placed her hands on Tony's shoulders, stepping back to inspect him in the light from the open front door.

'You look awful, my darling. Did you get any sleep at all last night? And when's the last time you ate a proper meal?'

Tony signalled to the half-eaten packet of custard creams on the coffee table and said, 'Lovely to see you Suzy. There's no real news. They say she got on the train and that's as much as we know right now. They're checking the CCTV at York station and on the train, so hopefully we'll hear more later.'

'Custard creams, and they're not even on a plate. Things really *are* bad. Well, you'll be no good to anyone if you don't get some sleep and decent food. And a shower. You smell worse than Archie. Go and take a shower and a nap.' She pulled a paper bag from her handbag and shook it at him. 'Moira sent round some pasties. She's as worried about Katie as the rest of us. Right, off you pop and set your alarm for an hour. If there's any news before then, I'll wake you up. Do you have baked beans and chips? Good old-fashioned stodge. Cures everything. Now, where's that April?'

Tony didn't argue. There was never any point in arguing with Suzy. She was like a benign bulldozer. Tall, big-boned and all jolly hockey sticks, he bet she was head girl back in her youth. He watched her bustle off in search of beans, chips and April, and was glad that she was here to take charge. Lord knows, he was in no fit state. An anxious twitch in his stomach had kept him awake last night and he'd eventually got up, intending to do his usual thing of organising something to calm himself. He'd joined a music service, meaning to download some of his favourite albums and create playlists, but instead, had found himself, like a lovesick teenager, playing pop songs that reminded him of Katie. A burst of Girls Aloud conjured up memories of a holiday in Cornwall when April was about four, all of them singing along to a hits of the summer tape as they sped through narrow country lanes in his old Fiat. Unable to listen any more, he had switched the music off and taken the model Taj Mahal from its hiding place. He'd tried to finish building that tricky little turret, minaret, whatever it was called, but had been unable to push from his mind the question of whether Katie would ever even see the model. In the end, he'd lain on the sofa in the living room, half-watching an old movie, in the vain hope that he'd eventually nod off. Suzy was right, he was no good to anyone if he was too tired to function. He lumbered up the stairs, took a clean towel from the airing cupboard and slumped onto the bed. Maybe he'd just rest his eyes for a minute before he took a shower.

. . .

Suzy found April in the study, slowly spinning around in Tony's large, leather desk chair, nose in phone. She glanced up as Suzy entered, clutching the edge of the desk to stop the chair.

'How are you holding up, April?' asked Suzy, her brows furrowed in concern.

'Okay, I s'pose. Not sure how I feel. I can't even take in that this is happening. I mean, it's Mum. Mum's always here. They said they don't know what happened to her after she got on the train. She could be hurt or anything. Suzy, do you think she's…' Tears welled up in April's eyes.

'Oh, no, love. Don't think that.' Suzy put an arm round April and hugged her tightly. Her customary brusque, capable tone softened to one of motherly reassurance, as she said, 'There's no point in trying to imagine anything like that, sweetie. We really don't know what's happened. Your Dad's expecting to hear more later. Now, come on through to the kitchen and I'll put the kettle on. Tea always helps. I nipped into the bakery on the way here and Moira told me there was some trouble at the Plough the other night. What was that all about?'

They went into the kitchen and April sat at the table, telling Suzy about the fight at the pub, while Suzy bustled about making tea. Suzy suppressed a smile when she reached the part about Maggie's tetanus injection. She leaned forward and brushed the hair back from April's forehead, peering closely at the dark blue patch below her hairline.

'Well, that explains the lump on your head. I imagine that awful Chloe won't be showing her face for a while. How is the concussion? Awful? Sick?'

'Much better today. I'm still very tired, although that might be as much to do with Mum being missing as anything else.'

'And Janine and Davey?'

'They're fine. Davey texted me earlier. My friend, Becca, works on the local paper and she's maybe going to write a story about his furniture.'

Suzy looked at her quizzically and April explained, 'He makes bespoke furniture. Amazing stuff with all these carvings on them. It's all word of mouth, you know, like, old ladies tell their friends and they ask Davey to make stuff for them. Only, everybody thinks he's this total loser drunk and nobody knows about all the amazing stuff.' April didn't think she'd explained this very well, so she added, 'And he's a really nice guy when he's sober.'

'It sounds like you've got lots to tell your Mum when she gets home. Right, look at the state of this kitchen. You and I have got some tidying up to do.' Suzy smiled kindly, handed April a pair of yellow gloves and, resuming her brusque tone, urged her to, 'Chop, chop. If you do the dishes, I'll do the floor.'

Twenty minutes of 'when did you last vacuum?!' and 'no don't put that in the dishwasher, you'll ruin it' later, all was to Suzy's satisfaction. April had to admit it looked a helluva lot better. She and Dad had definitely let things go a bit, although she hadn't really noticed the mess too much until Suzy pointed it out. She watched Suzy bustle about the kitchen, switching the oven on, pulling open drawers to find things and tutting about the state of the tins cupboard. 'There's some soup in here that's older than you,' she announced, her sturdy backside waving to and fro as she stuck her head into the depths of the shelves. 'Aha! Beans!' Suzy emerged triumphant, a tin of baked beans held aloft, and strode off to investigate the freezer for any trace of oven chips. April could hear her in the pantry, muttering something about, 'Fifty bags of broccoli in here and not much else.' April was exhausted and hoped Suzy wouldn't cajole her into any more helping. She'd have to say yes because this was Mum's friend, but all she wanted to do was sit quietly in the study and play some music. Maybe if she pretended to be busy on her phone, Suzy would take the hint. Suzy, mother of six, did indeed take the hint and busied herself finding baking trays and pans.

Lunch was an eclectic mix of pasties, baked beans, broccoli and cabbage, with tinned custard and a spoonful of raspberry jam for afters. All served on Santa paper plates, along with the posh cutlery normally reserved for high days and holidays, because nearly every plate and fork they owned was currently in the dishwasher. The family liaison officer declined to join them, declaring that his wife had made him some corned beef sandwiches. Although, if nobody minded, he wouldn't say no to a couple more custard creams. He went back to the living room, trailed by Archie, who knew a soft touch when he saw one. April hoped that Mrs Family-Liaison-Officer had made double helpings because Archie was quite partial to a bit of corned beef.

Just as the oven timer pinged, Tony had appeared, freshly showered and shaved. He still looked tired, but the hot meal soon brought some colour back to his cheeks. The three of them roundly agreed that Suzy had whipped up the best school dinner they'd ever had and, leaving the washing up until later, they repaired to the living room, where the family liaison officer was on the phone.

Tony, April and Suzy sat on the edge of the sofa, listening to the one-sided conversation.

'Uh-huh…yes…and that was where? Okay…what time?…I see… And you have the CCTV…'

This went on for some time, the three of them scrutinising the man's face for any hint of whether it was good news or bad. It took all of Tony's self-control not to grab the phone and scream, 'Just tell me!' Eventually, the family liaison officer hung up and, seeing the three anxious faces before him, quickly explained, 'It's not bad news. Well, at least, we think she's fine.'

In unison, the trio sagged back on the sofa and breathed a sigh of relief.

The officer continued, 'We checked the CCTV on the train and spoke to the conductor and another witness. That's why it's taken so long, the CCTV was very poor and we had trouble getting hold of people. Long story, never mind. It looks like, while she was on the train, she bought a ticket to London. Having spoken to the other witness, a passenger on the train, it appears she changed her mind about going to York and decided to carry on to the end of the line. Now, we checked the CCTV at Kings Cross and there was nothing to indicate she was under any duress. There has been some activity on her personal bank account and we've viewed footage from a cash machine in London. We're as certain as we can be that she was alone and well. Her mobile phone has been mostly switched off since the day she travelled, but has been briefly switched on a few times, suggesting that she's seeing messages and choosing not to respond.'

There was a stunned silence as Tony, April and Suzy digested the news. Tony was the first to speak.

'So, you're saying she just left? Upped and left of her own free will?'

'It appears that way. I know this isn't exactly the news you hoped for, but it's positive that she's unharmed. As you know, we had concerns about her state of mind and the fact that this was so uncharacteristic, but we're no longer treating her as a missing person.'

'Where is she, then?' Tony could hear his voice starting to rise and made a conscious effort to suppress his anger. 'She could be anywhere. She could be in France by now. Have you made any effort to find out exactly where she is?'

The officer adopted a more formal tone. 'As I say, she seems to have made a decision to go to London. There are no factors, such as vulnerability, medical or mental health issues, which would indicate she was impaired in any way. There is nothing to indicate she was coerced. In the circumstances, we won't be investigating further.'

Tony realised there was little point in taking his frustration out on the officer. The man was just doing his job, after all. He was hurt, and angry with Katie, not the police. He couldn't believe she had walked out on him! Walked out on April!

The family liaison officer handed Tony a card, telling him that if he had any new information which raised concerns, he should call. Otherwise, the police intended to take no further action. Tony thanked him for his help and, with Archie, April and Suzy forming a procession behind him, saw the officer to the door.

As soon as they were alone, Tony turned to April and Suzy. Holding on tightly to his emotions, lest he cry in front of them, he said through gritted teeth, 'I need some time to think. I'll be in the study if you need me.' With that, he strode stiffly down the hall to his sanctuary.

As soon as the study door clicked closed, April, who had been silent all this time, said, 'I don't fucking believe it. Sorry for swearing, Suzy. I just don't fucking believe it.' Tears welled up her eyes. 'Why would she leave us? Does she not love us anymore? How could she not love me? I'm fucking great.'

Suzy didn't have an easy answer, but privately thought that Katie had clearly been a lot more unhappy than any of them ever realised. She was an emotional, impulsive, little firecracker but this was off the charts, even for her. Suzy reflected that, with Tony being as much use as a paper canoe right now, the best thing she could do was to sit with April and listen.

'Come on,' she said, 'I'll put the kettle on and make us a nice cup of tea.'

CHAPTER 11

Over the next few days, Tony emerged from his study only to sleep and grab a bite to eat. April had spent Sunday afternoon and evening with Suzy, hashing and rehashing everything Katie said and did before her disappearance, examining every nuance for clues as to her intention to leave. Suzy had listened patiently as April came up with new reasons for her mother's abrupt departure, before eventually circling back to old reasons she had already explored, reiterating the details as though they might contain some heretofore undiscovered nugget. They discussed that Katie had felt taken for granted and wanted to carve out a piece of life for herself, although Suzy didn't feel it was her place to tell April that Katie had had enough of her antics. She decided that it was perhaps just as well that Katie wasn't around for the pub fight. She also held back on telling April how unsupportive her father had been of Katie's efforts to restart her career. She'd leave that one to Tony, if he ever got his head out of his own backside for long enough to realise how unequal their so-called equal partnership had become, and that his resistance to change and fair-weather father approach to April had left Katie feeling powerless and unappreciated. April clearly sensed that there was more to the story, so Suzy suggested she speak to her Dad.

'Speak to Dad? There's no way he'll tell me what went on between them. Dad doesn't do "sharing".' April made air quotes to emphasise her point. 'Dad does "bottling up", "stiff upper lip" and "making things neat and tidy to distract oneself".'

'Well, you need to talk it through, even if he doesn't. Get your friends round. Pinch a bottle of your Mum's good wine. Have a good chinwag. Actually, probably better skip the wine. Not good for the concussion.'

'I'll do that. Thanks for being here, Suzy, you've made all the difference. Can I ask you a favour? Would you come with me to the police station on Wednesday? They want to interview me about the fight.'

Suzy thought for a moment then said, 'No. You're twenty-one years old and perfectly capable of dealing with this yourself. You got into the fight and you'll have to sort it out yourself.'

'But it wasn't my fault! I tried to tell Dad and he wouldn't listen!'

'Telling your Dad wasn't your only solution. You could have told the police or warned Maggie. So, there's no point in blaming Tony. Put your big girl pants on and deal with it.'

'I can't deal with it on top of Mum leaving. It's too much.'

Suzy softened. 'You're hurt, but life goes on, my darling. I'm not trivialising how painful this is for you. However, the police interview isn't going to go away because you're hurt.'

Suzy left shortly afterwards, hoping that she hadn't been too harsh. She reckoned that sorting out her own problems, without Mum or Dad there to catch her every time she fell, would do April no harm, even if it was coming hard on the heels of Katie's disappearance.

Having waved goodbye until Suzy's taillights disappeared beyond the end of the drive, April fetched the post from the mailbox, placed it on the table by the front door and went to see her Dad in the study. She found Tony sitting at his desk, grim faced and stoic.

'Hi, Dad. I'm making myself a sandwich. Do you want anything?'

'No, I'm fine.'

'Listen…Mum…do you want to talk about it?'

'No, I'm fine.'

'Because I'm here for you, you know? Why do you think she left us, Dad?'

Tony turned in his chair to face her. He looked worn out, with deep lines fracturing his forehead and dark patches under his eyes. 'Because I didn't listen. Because I held her back and expected her to just always be there, the glue holding us all together. Because she asked for support and I didn't give it. I don't want to talk about it, April. I just need some time to think.'

He'd given her more than she expected, so April decided not to push it further. She knew Dad would brood and do jobs, maybe throw himself into his work, anything to avoid dealing with other people who might, God forbid, ask how he was…ugh…*feeling*. Eventually, having thrashed things out in his own mind, he would become all practical and come up with solutions. This was how Dad dealt with things. Unfortunately, it made him very bad at coping with other people's emotions. If he found himself cornered into a conversation about someone's problems, his first instinct was to tell them how to fix things, when all they really needed was someone to listen. Mum was the empathetic one, Dad was the one who awkwardly offered a bunch of flowers or a box of chocolates to cheer you up and considered the problem dealt with. Granny and Grandad were practical people too, who expressed their love through kind deeds rather than words, and April guessed that's where Dad got it from. She closed the study door and went off to make a sandwich, let Archie out for a pee and set up an 'April's Almost An Orphan' WhatsApp group chat. Not that she was being melodramatic or anything.

Tony turned back to his computer and reopened the spreadsheet he had hastily closed when he'd heard April's feet coming down the hall. The spreadsheet contained four columns; what Katie said, what I did, what I could have done better and what I will do now. He had spent hours thinking about things Katie had said over the past few weeks. Hints of trouble to come. He had broken down the other day's argument into key points and analysed his own responses. The policeman's comment about him making his wife stay at home to look after their adult daughter had stayed with him, making him realise that what had seemed perfectly reasonable to him at the time, was perhaps entirely *un*reasonable.

His ruminations were disturbed by a sudden burst of Flight of the Valkyries and he reached into his left-hand trouser pocket for his phone. The name 'Jack' flashed on the screen and Tony debated whether to answer. He didn't want to explain things to Jack. However, Jack would somehow hear anyway and ring him up to talk. He may as well get it over and done with now.

'Tony, mate.' Jack's voice was full of bonhomie, so he clearly hadn't heard. 'She said yes!'

'Eh? Who said yes?'

'Mia. Double diamonds. She said she'd marry me.' Jack lowered his voice and confided, 'We've been shagging all weekend. My cock's like a boiled lobster, mate. If this is what it's like getting engaged, don't know how I'll cope with the honeymoon. Might have to borrow yours, ha ha. Listen, we're coming round to yours tomorrow night, with some champagne to celebrate. I know we have the Dubai thing on Wednesday but it'll be a dry couple of days. Thought I'd celebrate with my oldest pals first. How does that sound?'

Tony was going to have to burst Jack's bubble. No way of avoiding it.

'Sorry, Jack. I'm really pleased for you both, but I'm not up to it at the moment. I'm going to have to give Dubai a miss as well. Can you take Mo? He's done a lot of the prep work on the finance side and is pretty much up to speed on the rest.'

'Aw, mate. Are you ill? Katie been busting your balls again, has she?'

'No, she's left me.'

There was silence on the other end of the line, while Jack took in the news.

'Why? I mean, what happened?'

Tony explained about Katie's disappearance and the fact that, on her way to York, it looked like she'd just decided to cut off all contact and go to London.

'And is she still in London?' Jack asked.

'I don't know, mate. She had her passport for ID for her interview, so she could have gone anywhere. I've texted her and called her about a dozen times in the past couple of hours alone, but she's not answering. The ring tone sounds like it's still the UK.'

'How are you and April holding up? How are you feeling?'

Tony cringed inwardly. 'You know, we'll manage.'

Jack told Tony to take whatever time he needed and he'd get Mo and Priti to cover Tony's work. Before ringing off, he promised to visit when he got back from Dubai and keep Tony updated. For the first time in his adult life, Tony couldn't care less about work. Funny, he reflected, it took Katie leaving him to make him take the time off he should have taken when she was here.

By Tuesday, April was running out of clean knickers. She lay on her bed, idly stroking Archie's silky ears, and grumbled, 'Dad may be upset about Mum, but if he doesn't do some washing soon, I'm going to be knickerless. Something must be done about this!' Resolved to give her father a piece of her mind, she quickly got up and thumped downstairs. Archie did not like the sound of ladies with no knickers. Ladies' knickers were one of his favourite salty snacks. He did not think he could cope with the disappearance of both his favourite human AND ladies' knickers. Archie agreed with number one and a half, something must be done about this! He padded downstairs after her, giving a little woof to assure her of his full support.

April strode into the study, fully expecting Dad to be sitting at his desk, glumly typing away at something on the computer. Except he wasn't there. With some of the wind taken out of her sails, she went off in search of Tony and found him in the kitchen, loading the dishwasher.

'Dad, you're out! I mean, we need to talk.'

'I told you, April, I don't want to talk about Mum. You know I'm no good at that sort of thing.'

'No, we need to talk about knickers. Not just knickers, washing in general. I'm running out of clean clothes, so you need to do some washing.'

Tony plonked a fork in the basket, where it sat surrounded by its fellow forks. All the spoons were in the spoon section and the knives were neatly corralled at the back. 'Was it you or Suzy who loaded this last time? There were knives in the fork section and the plates had been shoved in willy nilly. Big plate, little plate, big plate, no regard for ease of unloading!'

'Dad, washing, clothes washing?'

'Oh yes,' said Tony, sitting down at the table and waving a piece of paper at her. 'Come here and take a look at this.'

April sat next to him and took the piece of paper. It appeared to be a spreadsheet listing household chores.

'With your Mum gone,' said Tony, 'we are slowly descending into chaos. The house hasn't been vacuumed in a week, Archie hasn't been walked in days and we can't keep eating takeaway pizza. So, I've made a rota. I've worked out how long each task takes and divided them fairly between us, so that in any four week period we each get a fair spread of tasks, taking an equal amount of time.'

April was quite impressed. Her father had taken 'avoiding dealing with your feelings' to a whole other level. 'When you calculated how long it would take to mop the floors, did you add in extra time for cleaning the skirting? Mum always mops the skirting.'

'Bugger. No, I didn't. Anything else I've missed?'

'Clearing cobwebs, cleaning doors, vacuuming down the back of radiators, cleaning windows, dusting rooms that aren't the living room?' Jeez, thought April, how do I know all this stuff?

'Bugger. It's back to the drawing board with this, then. Fortunately, it doesn't affect the washing situation. Starting from now, we each take care of washing, drying and ironing our own clothes.' Tony slapped his spreadsheet down on the table and stood up. 'Right, any idea how to work the washing machine?'

A minute later, Tony and April stood before the washing machine, gazing uncomprehendingly at its array of mysterious buttons. Tony pulled open a little drawer, which contained three compartments. ' You must put a big scoop of washing powder in here at the beginning, a smaller scoop in this one at the half way point, then a tiny scoop in here near the end,' he declared.

'It has settings for cotton, delicates and other stuff,' said April. 'Look, it says cotton 90. You must have to put all the things that are made of the same material together. So if I take all these cotton things -' she pulled a navy pillowcase, some white sheets and a yellow towel from the basket and shoved them in the machine - 'and I turn this dial to 90 degrees, then you put the washing powder into the big bit…yes, that's right Dad…voila!' Triumphantly, she slammed the washing machine door shut and pressed the on button.

Tony and April high-fived each other. Archie sighed and put his head on his paws. He had helped his favourite human do this job a thousand times and she was not going to be happy to come home to green sheets.

On Wednesday, April attended the police interview alone. All her friends were at work and Dad was holed up in his study again, so she hadn't had much choice. She'd lost the piece of paper the policeman gave her the other day, so she had no idea what to expect. Truth be told, she was absolutely bloody terrified. Still, big girl pants and all that jazz.

The interview was much easier than expected. Becca had already been spoken to as a witness and had provided the video she took on her phone. A rather good-looking constable explained that they were treating April as the victim of an assault and asked her to give a witness statement. April wondered if you were allowed to ask handsome police constables for their Snapchat. Sitting up straight in her chair and flicking her hair, she decided that giving this witness statement might take quite some time.

An hour later, a very relieved April emerged from the interview room and found Davey waiting for her in the reception area. He was in his usual overalls, but he'd made an effort to brush his blonde curls and they stood proud of his scalp, in a fine frizz. She felt an unexpected flutter in her belly at the sight of him. What was that all about? It was Davey FFS! Oh, what the hell, let's just see how this new friendship panned out.

'I thought you were working!' she squealed, rushing over to give him a hug.

'Yeah, well, I couldn't leave you on your own, could I? Not after I whacked you over the head. Thought I'd give you a lift home.' Davey grinned sheepishly. 'How is the head, by the way?'

'Much better, thanks. What about you? How did it go with Becca? I've been so obsessed with Mum, I forgot to ask.'

'She came over to the workshop on Monday and took some photos. She's going to write something up and give it to her editor. Something along the lines of The Undercover Craftsman. She suggested I get a website, but I haven't got a clue about making websites.'

April tucked her good arm into his and steered him towards the door. 'It's just as well I know someone does, then. He's currently underemployed and going through a bad break up, so he could do with a project to take his mind off things.'

PART THREE
KATIE

CHAPTER 12

Holy guacamole and fuck-a-doodle-do, what had I done? Betty stood on York station platform, tartan shopping bag in hand, giving me a big thumbs up and a cheery wave through the window, as the train door hissed shut. Point of no return passed. Well, not exactly. Every station between York and Kings Cross was an opportunity to change my mind. All I needed to do was get off the train and get on another going back North. Between stations I was fine, Irma had my back with all her cheerleading about me being my best me, but as soon as we pulled into a platform, a wave of stress swept over me. Have you ever been so filled with dread that your fanny goes prickly? It was like that. I swear my vagina was having a stroke. I wondered if I should go to the stinky toilet and get my compact mirror out to have a look, just in case it had gone droopy on one side. I paid for an hour of wi-fi so I could google vaginoplasty, then accidentally clicked on images and thanked my lucky stars that nobody was sitting next to me.

I was leaving my family. LEAVING, Katie, LEAVING. I had to do some inner shouting at myself to try to come to terms with the enormity of what I'd done. It broke my heart that Tony and April were at home, blissfully unaware that I'd just dropped a bombshell on them. Tony would be chuntering on to someone on the other side of the world about money and April would be at work. Archie, bless his hairy little behind, would be wondering why nobody was keeping up a steady supply of biscuits. I'd given the letter to Betty to post, just in case I chickened out, so by tomorrow they'd know. Where would I be tomorrow? I had no idea. I opened Irma at a random page, like she was a magic 8-ball with all the answers. "Be confident in your decisions. They may not always be right, but they will be made for the best of reasons." Really, Irma, confident, REALLY?

After what felt like a month of yoyoing between sheer panic and the benign urgings of Irma to have the courage of my convictions, I finally looked up to see London flashing by. There really was no going back now and, as the train pulled into Kings Cross station, I mentally put on a pair of Suzy's big girl pants and dismantled the suitcase Jenga in the luggage rack outside the toilet. I'd been right about the toilet smell – welcome to London, now breathe through your mouth and try not to think about the air being full of pee particles.

Swept along by the crowd, I bustled down the platform to the ticket barrier, my pull along suitcase swaying drunkenly on its wheels as it caught unwary toes. This was London, nobody cared about toe safety. Everyone was on a mission. Everyone had somewhere to go. Except me. I had no plan, no people waiting for me, no comfortable sofa on which to eat ice cream. For the last couple of hours, I'd blocked out thoughts of what I was going to do when I arrived because it was almost inconceivable that I'd actually arrive. So, I decided that the situation called for wine…possibly several wines…and maybe a nice hotel with a minibar.

I navigated the ticket barrier like a true non-Londoner, by which I mean that I put my ticket into the machine, got my suitcase trapped behind me, finally freed the suitcase and turned around to find the barrier closed and my ticket swallowed. A short lady with an incongruously loud voice and a yellow tabard came to my rescue, with the kind words, 'You're in the way, love. You can't block the exit.' A hundred pairs of Londoner eyes glared at me for daring to impede their progress and I shamefacedly pushed my way against the crowd, tears threatening to ruin the mascara I'd so carefully applied at home that morning. I stood at the edge of the ticket barriers, my inner twenty year old self rather appalled at this forty-five year old mouse, who was trying not to cry because the people weren't nice to her. Twenty year old me would have told the loud lady that if she wanted me to move then she should come and open the bloody barrier. However, twenty year old me didn't care if loud lady called security and sometimes there are advantages to being a forty-five year old mouse, especially when a nice barrier man eventually takes pity on you and helps you through, without requiring a sobbed explanation that the bastard machine ate your ticket.

To avoid having to deal with texts or calls from Tony and April, I'd switched off my phone, but I realised that if I was to find a decent pub and a bed for the night, I'd need Google. As per, Google provided lots of options and, as per, I thanked her very much, proceeded in roughly the direction indicated and went into the first vaguely nice-looking pub I came to. It was packed with what appeared to be half the population of Australia, all of whom were glowing with the buzz that comes from being in your twenties and full of alcohol and hormones. Standing at the entrance, I looked around at the smooth, tanned faces and assured myself that, even if my lady bits were of the transient ischaemic persuasion, I still had hormones. I pushed through the crowd to the bar, tucking my suitcase in close to my leg, lest some minion of Fagin bugger off with it. Unfortunately, Roberta Rabbit chose this moment to agree that I did, indeed, have hormones. To my horror, I felt my suitcase begin to vibrate against my knee, a merry buzzing somehow managing to rise above the shouts and laughter of my fellow patrons. Oh, fudgecakes, all the jolting around must have set her off. Could I ignore her until her batteries ran out and hope no one noticed? But I didn't have any spares and she was my only friend in London! I was going to have to discreetly open my case, reach in and switch her off. Yes, that was the ticket. Discretion.

I felt a nudge on my arm and I turned to find a very tall, blonde woman grinning at me. 'S'cuse me mate, but your bag's buzzing?'

Was she asking me or telling me? I considered my options. I could pray to be struck down by a bolt of lightning immediately, I could smile politely and ignore her or I could brazen it out. There were probably other options, but it had been a very stressful day and quite frankly I was becoming bored of worrying about everything. If I was going to have a mid-life crisis, I may as well do it properly and take advantage of the one good thing about being middle-aged – the decreasing number of fucks given about what other people think. Stick that in your pipe, Irma, and vape it.

I smiled back at the Aussie giantess and shook my head ruefully. 'That's Roberta. She's such an attention seeker.' I opened the zip at the top of my suitcase, bent down and shouted through the crack, 'Any more nonsense out of you, young lady, and there'll be no batteries for a month.'

I reached in and switched Roberta off, then stood up to find the giantess staring at me. 'It's okay,' I reassured her. 'We both know it's an empty threat. I could never go a month without Roberta.' And, with that, I turned back to the bar and ordered a very large wine. Twenty-year-old me gave forty-five-year-old me a silent round of applause.

The giantess turned out to be called Rachel and I later felt quite guilty about thinking of her as a giantess when I first met her, as she was very self-conscious about her height. However, she was also funny and friendly, and without her taking me under her wing, my first days in London would have been far less fun. That evening, she congratulated me on my Pommy balls and bought me a second glass, as she put it, 'To make sure the first one went down properly.' Rachel told me she'd been seeing some friends off on their travels at the station and had popped into the pub to say hello to another friend who worked here. In her thirties, she was bit older than your average backpacker and I wondered what had brought her to London.

'Office work, boyfriend blah, blah, blah. It was boring as. Needed a change and thought I'd do the London thing.'

'So, you left your boyfriend. How did he take it?' I asked, with just a hint of self-interest.

'No idea. Dick was one of *those* types. Always wanting to know where I was and who I was with. Tried to stop me doing things, but I did them anyway and lied about it. Loved the bloke, but being with him was getting to be like too much hard work. In the end, he phoned me for the fourth time that day to ask where I was and I told him I was on my way to the airport. No sense in dragging these things out.' Rachel shrugged, as if to say 'it is what it is.'

I told Rachel about Tony and April, although I wasn't nearly as sanguine about my departure as she had been about hers. We managed to find a table and, as we got to the stage where we agreed that it would be both economical and practical to share a bottle of wine rather than keep making trips to the bar, we traded war stories. She laughed like a drain when I told her about my mother-in-law who, on the rare occasions she stayed with us, always insisted on kissing Tony goodnight. Not a peck on the cheek before he went upstairs. Nooooooo, she'd come into our bedroom and, with me lying there, kiss him on the forehead. As it was practically the only physical contact Tony ever had with his mother, it seemed rude to object, but on the inside, I was quietly freaking out. Rachel told me about how, when Dick once went to visit his mother, she'd sneaked off to a concert with friends, had a few too many tinnies and asked the lead singer to autograph her boobs. Unfortunately, she'd used permanent ink, so spent the next week undressing in the dark and feigning a headache if Dick so much as looked hopefully in her direction.

We were having such a good time that it came as a shock when I looked at the clock above the bar and realised it was 9pm. I hadn't booked a hotel and I was starving. 'Rachel, it has been brilliant meeting you, but I have to go and find a hotel and some food.'

'There's a spare room at mine if you want. The guys I was seeing off? My flatmate and his girlfriend.'

'Really? That would be –'

'No worries. You alright to change the sheets? Steve and Em, stinky blighters. C'mon, we can get some tucker on the way.'

I stood up and immediately felt the effects of the wine on my empty stomach. Rachel saw me sway and, laughing, grabbed my suitcase in one hand, my arm in the other and gently steered me towards the door.

Her flat was just under an hour away, in Putney. I'm not sure what I expected, perhaps a 1960's box above a row of shops, so I was pleasantly surprised when we stopped outside a large Edwardian house in a pretty street about a ten minute walk from the tube station. Rachel unlocked the front door and we made our way upstairs, suitcase bumping, to the top floor.

'It's not much,' Rachel said, as we entered the flat door and I found myself in a cluttered living room, 'but it's home.'

It really was a home. Clean, yet gloriously untidy, with fairy lights strung across the divide between living area and kitchen. An old-fashioned fireplace was filled with candles and a pile of magazines acted as a very unstable support for a pot plant by the window. Quite literally, a pot plant. Rachel saw me staring and said, 'No worries. It's Steve's and he's not coming back, so I'll get rid.'

Rachel showed me to my room, a small double, littered with the detritus of the recently departed Steve and Em. Receipts, clothing tags, dust bunnies and a mysterious cable lay scattered on the wooden floor. As Rachel went off to find some clean sheets, I checked drawers and the wardrobe, wondering what else Steve and Em had left behind. The drawers only contained a couple of buttons and one of those silicon sachets you find in new handbags. Expecting to find more of the same, I opened the wardrobe. Yep, not much here, just something at the back. I stretched an arm into the wardrobe and felt around, my hand meeting a small, furry object. What on earth could it be? I closed my fingers around it.

'Aaaaaaaargh!' They must have heard me scream in Stepney. The thing was moving. Oh fuck, a rat! I let go, slammed the wardrobe door and stumbled away, falling onto the bed. My first thought as I faceplanted onto the duvet - Rachel was right, Steve *was* stinky. My second thought – why didn't I book a nice, rodent-free hotel?

Rachel came running through to see what all the fuss was about.

'Rat,' I gasped, pointing at the wardrobe.

She opened the wardrobe door and I could hear a faint scrabbling as she reached inside. 'Fat Bastard!' she exclaimed. 'I've been looking everywhere for you, mate.'

Rachel emerged from the depths of the wardrobe, holding the fattest hamster I'd ever seen. She held him up and kissed the top of his furry head. 'Fat Bastard, meet Katie. Katie, Fat Bastard. FB's a crafty little mucker. Must've got in there last night when Steve was packing, didn't you, mummy's lovely boy.' FB sat still in her hands, like a hairy, orange Buddha, looking vaguely nonplussed, as she once more covered his head in kisses.

I followed Rachel into the living room, where she gently placed FB into a large cage behind the sofa. FB immediately scrambled onto his wheel and assumed a slow trot. 'I inherited him from the guy who lived here before me,' she explained. 'No idea how old he is. A teenager, I reckon. Sleeps all day, comes out at night and eats anything he can get his chubby little paws on.'

We watched for a moment, as FB lumbered around on his wheel, seemingly going for a steady speed-walk rather than a sprint. My only experience with hamsters was when April had brought the school hamsters home for the summer holidays, without checking with us first. This was when we discovered Tony's kryptonite. It turned out he was absolutely terrified of all rodents and I only just managed to catch the outraged email to the headmistress before he pressed send. April and I were united in our determination to keep the hamsters and Tony eventually gave in, on condition that they came nowhere near him. Hamsters or husband? Quite the dilemma. Tony spent the next six weeks confined to his study, as the hamsters had free reign of the living room. Despite my limited experience, I figured that FB was probably quite an old boy.

Rachel and I went back through to the bedroom. She briefly disappeared and returned with some clean bedding. Between the two of us, we made short work of changing the bed, before returning to the living room for a well-earned glass of wine. Rachel reached under her chair cushion and pulled out a squashed leaflet. Flattening out the wrinkles, she asked, 'Pizza?'

'It's a bit late, isn't it? Will anywhere be open?'

'London, mate! You're in the land of 24-hour delivery now. The world of convenience is at your feet.' She dialled and ordered a large pepperoni.

'What are your plans after this?' she asked.

'I don't know. Get a job? Find somewhere to live? I have some savings but they won't go far with London prices. I'll definitely need a job.'

'I'll be looking for a new flatmate anyway, so...'

'Maybe give it a few days, see how we get on?'

'No worries.'

As if in agreement, FB picked up the pace on his wheel and a series of happy squeaks came from behind the sofa. Rachel and I grinned at each other and clinked glasses, problem solved.

The arrival of Friday morning was marked by a shaft of sunlight lasering through the gap in the curtains and piercing my brain. I rolled over in bed, groaning, as a wave of nausea made its way to my mouth before retreating in the face of saliva glands that refused to work. My head was pounding and my whole body felt greasy on the inside. Too much wine, Katie. Must never drink again. Oh, lordy, stomach cramps. Bad stomach cramps.

I shot out of bed and ran to the bathroom, where the stress and booze of yesterday signalled their intention to make a swift appearance from my rear end by sending a substantial watery advance guard into my knickers. 'Just a small taster of what's to come,' said my bottom. 'Aaaany second now.' 5…4…3…For the love of flannel, why has my nightie become impossible to pull up?…2…Where? Just where have the sides of my knickers gone and why can't I pull them down?!…1… What sort of psychopath leaves the toilet lid down?…Blast off. It was the Niagara Falls of diarrhoea. Diagara Falls.

As I whipped my knickers off and aimed my bottom at the porcelain, the contents of my gusset splattered in a projectile spray across the bathroom door. I sat there, nightie around my neck, knickers sagging at my ankles, shitting like my life depended on it, all the while staring aghast at my impromptu door artwork. The wave of nausea chose this moment to come back to check if my mouth was working yet. I hastily looked around, calculating the distance to the sink, and decided that, even with liquids projecting at speed from both ends, there was no way for me to hit the sink and the toilet bowl at the same time. I took my only option. I leaned over and threw up in the bath, chunks of pepperoni hitting the taps, and the retching sending another high-pressure jet of fluid gushing from the ring of fire down below.

Eventually, I sat there, shaky and empty, using my nightie to wipe the sweat and vomit from my face. There was a tap at the door and

Rachel's muffled voice came from the other side. 'Are you going to be long in there, Katie? I need to get ready for work.'

I surveyed the carnage. Aw, jeez, first day sharing a flat and…this. Where did I even begin? 'Can you hold on for ten minutes, Rachel? Bit of a dicky tummy from last night. Sorry.'

'Right-o. Is there enough toilet roll or can I chuck you in some more?'

I checked the toilet roll. Three sheets left. I looked around. No more to be seen. Bugger, bugger, bugger. I absolutely could not let Rachel see this.

'Erm…it's fine. I'll be okay.'

Fuck-a-doodle-do, Katie's in a stew, she's gone and shit all over the door, and knows not what to do.

Step one – un-poop Katie and un-vomit bath. I used the remaining toilet paper and my nightie to clean myself off, then sprayed the bath down with the shower nozzle, frantically pushing chunks of pepperoni down the plug hole.

Step two – un-poop nightie and door. I got into the bath, stood under the shower and quickly washed both myself and my nightie, before using the nightie to clean the door.

Step three – hide the evidence. I wrapped myself in a bath towel and, with my nightie and knickers rolled inside a hand towel, strolled nonchalantly out of the bathroom. Carry on. Nothing to see here. Rachel, fresh toilet roll at the ready, made a beeline straight for the bathroom and, as soon as she closed that door, I dashed to the kitchen to throw towels, knickers and nightie into the washing machine. I took a moment to reflect that it was probably just as well I hadn't taken to a life of crime, because I was far too good at covering up dastardly deeds, then I ran back to my bedroom before Rachel could catch me standing naked in her kitchen.

I peered out of my bedroom window at the unfamiliar view of trees and houses. The rain was barrelling down and I switched on my phone to check the weather back home. Every media outlet gleefully informed me that a ridiculous amount of rain was expected today, but they had run out of things to say about it for now, so here was every rain statistic they could think of. I wondered how Archie was coping. He did not like adverse bum weather conditions.

Half an hour later, Rachel and I sat at the small table next to the pot plant, sharing a coffee and talking about our plans for the day. Rachel worked for a recruitment agency in the finance sector, but she had a lot of contacts and promised to keep an eye out for anything 'cheffy'. I asked if she'd mind me printing out some copies of my CV, so I could hand them out to local restaurants. With a breezy 'no worries' she gave me her printer password and told me to 'go get 'em, tiger.'

Before she left for work, Rachel asked if I'd mind ringing the landlord. 'The bath seems to be draining quite slowly, there's a dreadful smell and I'm worried it's the drains again. Card's in the kitchen drawer.'

Step four – call a plumber!

CHAPTER 13

Over the following weeks, I tramped miles across Putney, Wimbledon and Wandsworth, handing my CV in to restaurants, bars and upmarket cafés. I bought a laptop and a new phone, then scoured websites for job search tips, seeking ways to make myself stand out from the crowd. I signed up for a chef's course with a highly reputable cookery school, praying that the cachet of the certificate would turn out to be worth the hefty chunk of my savings.

Bored of sitting in the flat, I got into the habit of taking my laptop to a small café off the high street. Café Deniz was run by a Turkish couple, Meryem and Mehmet, who treated their customers like family. Having reluctantly succumbed to the London way of avoiding eye contact and never talking to strangers at bus stops, their friendliness felt like home to me. It made me think of popping into the bakers on the way to work and Moira slipping me an extra sticky bun, with a whispered, 'Don't tell Donald. He'll have my guts for garters if he catches me giving out free buns.' It made me recall the ninety-four-year-old man who went to the local shop and bought milk, bread and a lottery ticket every Friday morning. He said he couldn't bear not to live in hope of something. It made me think of Graham, who came round to fix our boiler on Boxing Day, even though his father was ill and he and Suzy were having the worst Christmas ever. All these connections that I shared with my family and friends, these things that brought warmth and colour to my life. I realised how very much I missed them.

By September, the heat and humidity of the summer had given way to fresh mornings and cool evenings. Ladies' handbags bulged with umbrellas and emergency cardigans. Late summer storms swept across the country and the constant yo-yoing between sunshine and torrential rain reflected my mood.

At first, I'd been quite reserved around Meryem and Mehmet's easy familiarity. At their happy cries of, 'Katie, my darling, come in, here, I will clean you a table,' I would just smile politely and thank them. By now, though, I'd become used to the garrulous welcome and responded in kind. As Meryem bustled over to clear her best table, the one by the window, Mehmet approached me, arms outstretched. He did his usual thing of looking like he was about to hug me, before quickly clapping his hands then clasping them beneath his chin, telling me, 'Katie, my darling, you are too thin. Today we shall fatten you up.'

No sooner had I taken my seat than Meryem appeared with a tuna sandwich and a small mountain of pistachio baklava. Meryem and Mehmet rarely bothered their customers with such mundane items as a menu and price list. Mehmet would scrutinise his patrons, head tilted to one side and hands clasped under his chin, then he would scuttle off to the kitchen, reappearing a short while later with whatever he had decided they needed. What they got, often as not, was an eclectic mix of British and Turkish staples at whatever price Mehmet decided they could afford.

I had just begun tucking into the baklava, when Mehmet came over and sat opposite me.

'Katie, every day you're here, click-click-clicking on the computer. Meryem says you are writing a book but I told her, no, Katie is changing the world.'

'Sadly, not changing the world, Mehmet. Or writing a book,' I reassured him. 'I'm looking for a job, but I'm not having much luck.'

'It is a tough world out there, indeed it is,' said Mehmet, sighing. 'What job are you looking for, Katie?'

'Chef's jobs, but I think I'm going to have to start again at the bottom. The pay is pretty poor and there's a lot of competition out there.'

'Ah, you can cook. Meryem! Meryem!' He beckoned his wife over. 'Katie is looking for jobs. She is a cook.'

'Oh, Katie, that's wonderful. What do you like to cook?' asked Meryem.

I gestured towards the baklava. 'Nothing as marvellous as this. Did you make it?'

Meryem's round face beamed with pride. 'Yes. It is my family's recipe. Our tradition.'

'I don't suppose you could…'

'Of course I will share it with you. Here, put the computer away and come with me to the kitchen. I will show you how it is done.'

I followed Meryem to the kitchen. She was a small, slightly stout woman, but in the kitchen she was nimble as a ballet dancer, stretching high into cupboards to snatch at jars and bending gracefully to pull a tub of nuts from a low shelf.

She plugged in a food processor and inserted a blade. 'Traditional Turkish food processor,' she announced. She pulled an iPad from a drawer. 'Traditional Turkish iPad.' She winked at me, opened Safari and scrolled. 'Ah, here we are, traditional Turkish BBC Good Food recipe.'

'So, it's not a family recipe?' I asked, confused.

'Yes, it is a family recipe. My mother googled it too and passed it down to me. Neither of us could cook for shit, so thank you BBC. But don't tell Mehmet. He thinks I'm a bloody genius.' She produced a bottle of raki and a couple of glasses. 'Here, Katie, this will put the bloody hairs on your chest.'

Meryem wasn't quite telling the truth. She could cook for shit, she just preferred to try new things, rather than go with tradition. Most days, she would hustle me into the kitchen and ask me to taste something to which she'd added her own twist. Often, we would cook together, coming up with new takes on traditional Turkish food and trying them out on Mehmet. He would either announce to all who would listen that there were angels in his kitchen, or he would march out, crying, 'They are devils trying to bloody poison me.' Good or bad,

Meryem and I would emerge, laughing, from the kitchen and offer the customers free samples of our culinary efforts. Mehmet delighted in conducting straw polls and, if popular opinion was on his side about something he deemed 'bloody poison', he would chase us back to the kitchen, happily roaring, 'Away, devils, away!'

Where Meryem and Mehmet were my London family by day, Rachel and FB were my night family. FB would wake up in the evenings and loved to come out of his cage to play. Rachel and I would lie on the floor, talking about our day, as FB ran around with his little exercise ball, cheerfully knocking over unattended wine glasses and pooping on magazines. We would cuddle him and stroke his little head and he would make the happiest of happy noises.

There was never any question of me staying for just a few days. Rachel and I both knew I was definitely in it for the long haul when, a few weeks in, I bought FB a little hamster playpen. 'To keep the wine safe and stop his escape attempts via the fireplace,' I told her. We filled it with toys and, as we watched FB scuttle over a little wooden bridge, I told her about my very weird job interview that day.

'So, you know that posh place by the river, the white building? Have you ever been?'

'Yeah, I went there for someone's birthday, oh, about six months ago.'

'Well, don't go back. I went there for an interview today. Brian the head chef was really nice, but the manager...ugh. Brian took me into his office to introduce me and he was sitting there clipping his toenails and putting the clippings in a box. He stood up, no shoes on, and held out his hand for me to shake it. Didn't even wipe his hands.'

'Ew,' said Rachel, scrunching her nose in disgust.

'That's not the worst bit. I shook his hand, said some nice things then made a quick exit to the ladies to scrub my hand. When I came out, Brian asked if I would mind making an omelette. No problem! I went to the fridge for some ingredients and there it was. A full tub of toenails.'

'Ew ew ew ew ew!' Rachel howled with laughter and asked, 'What did you do?'

'I told Brian that the manager was such a lovely man, would he mind if I made an omelette for the manager as well. He said that sounded like a great idea. So, I did two.' I gave her my best evil grin. 'While Brian was tucking into his basil and tomato, I whipped up a nice cheese and toenail for the manager.'

'Oh my god! That's so brilliantly disgusting!' Rachel laughed until, as they say, the tears ran down her legs.

The next day was my birthday, the 28th of September. Forty-six, Katie, crappy birthday to me. I missed Tony and April more than ever and couldn't help wondering what we'd be doing if I were at home. I'd be lounging around, eating chocolate for breakfast and insisting everyone make a fuss of me. April would buy me some ridiculously expensive perfume, that I knew she couldn't afford, and I'd be torn between telling her off for spending too much and being delighted to own such a luxury. Tony would buy me something practical that I'd never use, like slippers, even though I had pointed out six pairs of earrings and directed him to my 'Presents for Meeee!!' Pinterest board. Archie would adopt one of the slippers as his love interest and slope off to hide it in his bed, ready for some special Archie-time later. I wondered how they were coping without me. Had they remembered to pay the milkman and get the chimneys swept before winter? Were they humanely removing spiders with my spider-catcher thingy or were they running around screaming and whacking the poor little buggers? Had anyone thought to wash Archie's beds? Had anyone thought to wash Archie? Suzy would keep them right. I could imagine her delivering military-style training on floor mopping, bathroom hygiene and emptying the vacuum cleaner. I didn't want to get in touch with Tony or April, but perhaps I could ring Suzy? Check if everyone was okay? No, leaning on Suzy like that and asking her to keep it a secret wouldn't be fair.

I made my way to Café Deniz, thinking that scrambled egg and sucuk might be in order. However, as soon as I entered, I could tell something was wrong. Mehmet and Meryem were nowhere to be seen and, other than a shabbily dressed, elderly lady in the corner, the place was empty.

'They're in the back, love,' said the lady, spotting me lurking by the door. 'Lawd knows what's going on. She gets a phone call and rushes off, then he goes after her. I could hear all this wailing - not sure if it was him or her. Mind you, these foreign ones, they don't half make a fuss about things.' She sat back, clearly content that she'd imparted her quota of casual racism for the day, and picked up her knitting.

I hurried through to the kitchen and found Mehmet comforting a sobbing Meryem. 'What's wrong?' I asked. I knew they had an adult son who worked in the City and thought perhaps something had happened to him.

'It's Meryem's mother,' said Mehmet. 'Her sister has called to say Meryem's mother is gravely ill and that she should come right away.'

'Oh, Meryem, I'm so sorry. Is there anything I can do to help?'

'Katie, you are truly an angel. Could you look after the customers please? We need to call the family to find out what is going on. Please, just give us an hour.'

I told Mehmet and Meryem to take as long as they needed and returned to front of house. The shabby knitting lady still sat there in her dirty, black raincoat, a headscarf tied tightly under her chin and green wellingtons leaving patches of mud on the floor under her table. Even her face was grimy, although her hands, gripping those clacking needles, looked clean.

'What's going on, love? Are they alright in there?' she asked.

'They're okay. Family emergency. Can I get you anything?'

'Can I get you anything? That's a turn up for the books. Usually I just does what I'm told in 'ere,' she laughed.

'Okay,' I said, grinning, 'that's a challenge, then.' I adopted Mehmet's thinking pose, hands under my chin. 'I've got just the thing for you...'

'Judy.'

'Katie. Prepare to be wowed.'

I went back to the kitchen and checked the cupboards and fridges. Meryem had made a batch of fresh flatbread buns. Excellent. Bacon buttie, Turkish style. Although Meryem and Mehmet didn't eat pork themselves, they were business people and knew the value of a good English breakfast for getting customers through the door. I cooked some bacon and stuffed it into a couple of buns, adding tomatoes, onion and lettuce. A side dollop of scrambled eggs mixed with peppers and chilli, et voila, a vaguely Turkish English breakfast. Well done, Katie Frock.

I took two plates and two large mugs of tea through to the front and set them on the table. 'Mind if I join you, Judy?'

I watched as Judy took her first bite of the hybrid bacon roll. Her face remained set. She had a slurp of tea then tried a forkful of the scrambled eggs. Her face went red. She swallowed, took another slurp of her tea and said, 'The bacon sarnie's lovely, but, flamin' hell, them scrumpled eggs is a bit hot.'

I must have looked a bit hurt because she leaned over and patted my arm. 'Sorry, lovey, I'm eighty-three. I don't do well with foreign muck.'

What the heck was she doing in a Turkish café then? And where's the effing tub of toenails when you need them? Deep breath, Katie. She's one of Mehmet's customers. Be nice. 'Can I get you anything else?'

'Oh, no. The bacon sarnie will do me fine. I'm just glad of the seat and the company. I do the old folks' gardens of a morning then I like to come in here for me breakfast. I've seen you in here before, tapping away at that computer. Wotcha doing?'

'Applying for jobs. Not having much luck. What about you though? Gardens?'

'Yeah, I just tidy 'em up a bit. Gives the old folk something nice to see from the window. Cheery like. Though the best of it's gone. I'll be sweeping leaves off their steps soon.'

Maybe Judy wasn't that bad, I decided.

'How much am I owe you, Katie, love?' she asked as she finished her 'bacon sarnie'.

I guesstimated the cost of the ingredients and added a pound. '£4?'

'Flamin' hell. I am a pensioner, you know.'

'£3?'

'That's more like it.' She extracted three pound coins from her purse and made a big show of adding 20p. 'Seeing as you're unemployed, love.'

. . .

Over the course of the day there was a steady stream of customers. Local builders came by for their lunch (I knew this one, having seen Mehmet serve them before – köfte and chips with gravy), office workers bought salads and fresh pitas stuffed with whatever I could find in the fridge (at one point, a microwave chicken tikka, which was quite possibly Mehmet's lunch) and various shelterers from the rain came dripping through the door, seeking a warm bowl of scotch broth and a simit. Mehmet dropped by late morning to ask if I could stay on for the rest of the day and I sent him away with strict instructions not to return before locking up. However, it wasn't easy, looking after everything on my own. Thank goodness for Mehmet's rather lax approach to menus and Meryem's batch baking, which meant I could cheerfully raid the fridges and cupboards for whatever I could find and fill in the blanks with a bit of imagination.

The afternoon brought school mummies and their sticky offspring, chasing each other, shrieking, around the tables (the offspring, not the mummies). Weirdly, there were no daddies. They had wisely stayed away, presumably because daddies are less tolerant than their female counterparts of small screaming humans, who smell faintly of wee, in enclosed spaces. While the mummies sipped lattes, I served the children salep with a generous dusting of cinnamon. The mummies declared this to be 'delightfully traditional' so I charged them £4 each. Little did they know that I'd unearthed a tin of powdered stuff from the back of the cupboard. It didn't have a sell-by date and was probably packed with E numbers, which may explain why the little blighters went mad for it.

At exactly 4pm, one of the regulars, Scott, arrived. He was a tall, thin lad of around eighteen and tended to keep himself to himself. The only person he really opened up to was Bill, an elderly gentleman with the most beautiful voice I'd ever heard; a low, rich baritone sound with a Jamaican lilt. I'd never spoken to Bill before, but my visits had regularly coincided with his and I could have listened to him all day. I don't know if it was the voice or if it was just Bill's easy-going nature, but something made Scott relax around him. Scott would tell Bill at length about his latest interest and Bill would patiently listen, before suggesting a game of chess or cards. The two of them would while away an hour or two, happily arguing about the game and putting the world to rights, as they drank mugs of tea and uncomplainingly ate whatever was put in front of them.

Scott sat at his usual table and I brought him his tea. He looked at me as if to say, 'Who are you and what are you doing here?' then stared down at the table, fiddling nervously with the handle of his mug.

'Hi, Scott, I'm Katie. Meryem's had a family emergency, so I'm helping out today. I don't know what Mehmet normally gets you, but I was thinking maybe a pita stuffed with lamb and some salad?'

'Has Bill been in?' Scott asked, ignoring my question.

'Not yet.'

'I don't eat until Bill's here.'

'Okay, just let me know when you're ready.'

'When Bill's here, obviously. Please.'

Rude and polite in the same sentence. Scott was a nice lad, although definitely quirky. Lord knows how he could afford to eat in here practically every day, but he was one of Mehmet's best customers, so I didn't argue and just left him alone until the door eventually opened and a gust of chilly early autumn wind blew in, bringing with it Bill's dulcet tones. He shook raindrops off his jacket and peeled his sodden trouser legs away from his calves, saying, 'Boy, summer sure is over. Can I have a tea please, Mehmet?'

'Katie,' I told him, coming over to take his coat. 'Here, I'll hang this up by the radiator for you. Mehmet and Meryem have a domestic emergency, so I'm standing in for them today.'

'Ah, Katie, nice to meet you. I've seen you in here before. Is Mehmet okay?'

I explained about Meryem's mother and we started to settle into a good chinwag, but, out of the corner of my eye, I could see Scott beginning to look agitated.

'Scott said he'd wait for you before eating,' I told Bill, 'so just let me know when you're ready.'

Bill went over to sit with Scott, who immediately began a monologue on a movie he'd watched the night before. Suddenly very tired and reckoning I had a good twenty minutes before Bill managed to get a word in edgewise, I sank gratefully into one of the weird, brown plastic chairs that Mehmet must have bought from some clearance sale when he time-travelled back to the 1970s. They did not match the blue laminate tables (presumably a job lot from his jaunt back to the 1950s), but together the furniture had a kitsch, retro feel. Knowing Mehmet and Meryem, I suspected that this was by accident, rather than design, yet it gave the place charm and was another reason I loved coming here. I took the opportunity of the unexpected break to get my phone out and check my e-mails. Ooh, one from the posh toenail place. Steeling myself for another 'unfortunately you didn't get the job' letter, I clicked on the message.

Dear Miss Frock,

Thank you for your recent application. We are pleased to inform you blah, blah, blah and the manager said it was the best omelette he'd ever had blah, blah, blah.

Sincerely,

Brian.

Hang on, this didn't sound like a rejection. Read it again, Katie! Read it again! "We are pleased…start Monday…please bring lots of stuff… we'll pay you loads of money…don't fuck it up because it's taken you ages to find this job." Or words to that effect. Okay, maybe I was reading between the lines a bit, putting my own spin on things, as usual. I mean, I'd once read an entire BBC article on the astonishing number of calories in ice cream, only for Tony to tell me it was an article on childhood obesity. I read the e-mail a third time, just to be sure. Definitely got the job. Woo hoo! Happy birthday to me! I did a little sitting down dance (my feet were far too tired for a standing up dance) and took a celebratory sip of coffee. This called for a bottle of proper wine, as opposed to the cheap stuff Rachel and I had been drinking in an attempt to economise rather than cut down on the booze. I'd pop past the supermarket on the way home. I could even get a treat for FB. He'd been looking a little peaky recently, so one of his favourite dog biscuits might cheer him up.

At 6pm, Mehmet returned with the news that Meryem was leaving for Turkey the next day to look after her mother.

'Who knows how long she'll be needed there, Katie, darling,' he told me, 'it's a bloody bugger and no mistake. So, when can you start?'

I had clearly missed a step in the conversation. 'Start?'

'Meryem told me to tell you 010138 for the traditional family recipes. Said you'd understand.'

'Rewind a bit here, Mehmet. Are you asking me to fill in for Meryem while she's gone?'

'Meryem is asking. I told her you are looking for a fancy pants cooking job. You wouldn't be wanting our boring pants.'

I thought about the well-paid job at Toenail Palace, with its career opportunities and the chance to work in its sister restaurants around the world. I considered that I'd be working under some of the best chefs and, if Tony and April would have me back, I'd return to Northumberland with some of my dreams in the bag.

'No problem, Mehmet, I'll stay for as long as you need me.'

CHAPTER 14

Thank goodness Meryem left me the code to her iPad, otherwise I'd have sunk. It was packed with notes, folders and browser favourites full of recipes, tips and shortcuts. Mehmet drafted in their son, Ozzy, to help over the weekend, while I brought myself up to speed. Although I'd learned a lot about Turkish food, I was no Meryem, so I batch cooked and froze as much as possible. I quickly realised that I wasn't going to be able to cook according to Mehmet's whims and that I needed a set list of dishes to get me started. Mehmet wasn't overjoyed at this cramping of his creative customer service style and I had to persuade him that if he memorised the list, then he could still give the appearance of being creative whilst not giving me a nervous breakdown in the process.

Mehmet dug his heels in. 'Meryem tried the same thing. I told her no bloody way. I tell people what they will like, Katie, it's why they bloody come here.'

'But you and Meryem grew up with Turkish food and I didn't. There's no point in you telling customers what they like, me cooking it badly and them not bloody liking it.'

'No swearing from you, young lady!' he exclaimed, marching off in a fit of pique.

I turned to Ozzy, who was supposed to be helping bake bread but was in fact lounging around in his designer suit, nose deep in his phone. 'Ozzy, can you talk to him?'

Ozzy looked up, seemingly irritated by the interruption, and muttered 'No point. You know what he's like. He'll come back when he's calmed down.'

Sure enough, ten minutes later, Mehmet was back. He sat down opposite Ozzy at the small kitchen table and said, 'Okay, okay with the bloody list. *And* we will have room to wiggle. Ozzy, you must take time off work to help in the kitchen.' He held a finger up to stem Ozzy's protests. 'No, no. We can't throw Katie out of the frying pan and into the deep end of the swimming pool.'

There was a brief exchange in Turkish, which ended with Ozzy marching off, shouting back at me in English, 'I am not washing the fucking dishes.'

Mehmet gave me a sly grin and winked. 'That boy is all Meryem. Nothing like me at all. Don't worry. You know what he's like. He'll come back when he's calmed down.'

Ozzy did come back. In fact, he stayed for a couple of weeks and, afterwards, still came in at weekends. Mehmet declared himself to have two tails like a dog, so happy was he that his son was finally involved in the family business. He greeted customers with renewed enthusiasm, introducing Ozzy to his regulars, and regularly threw cats among pigeons by promising our patrons culinary delights that weren't on the list. Ozzy took over the financial side of things, saying it was something he could do even when he was back at work. This left Mehmet free to zoom around in his little blue van, stocking up at the cash and carry of an evening. Mehmet loved the cash and carry. With no Meryem there to supervise, he was free to buy glorious nonsense. Thus, by November, the café was fully decked out in Christmas lights, with a huge glittery lamppost taking the place of the coat stand. I thoroughly approved, with the possible exception of a motion activated Santa Claus who said, 'Ho, ho, ho. Merry Christmas,' every time the café door opened or closed. I resolved this by "borrowing" Santa's batteries for Roberta, although I told Mehmet it was for one of FB's toys.

Rachel and I were quite worried about FB. He'd lost some weight and was a little quieter than usual, so we took him to the vet. There we met Lulu, a Springer Spaniel who appeared inordinately pleased with herself for having scoffed an entire chocolate cheesecake, and we cooed over Doug and Hilda, two gorgeous little girl kittens who were there for their vaccines. Their owner confided that Doug was a bit of a late bloomer and by the time they discovered that he was actually a she, the name had stuck. We also commiserated with Boris, a small, scruffy mongrel who had done himself an injury while attempting to make love to a reluctant Staffy. The teenage girl who was anxiously clutching the amorous mutt, started to tell us what had happened, but her father spoke over her, loudly informing the entire waiting room, 'He's never done it before. Didn't have a clue what to do, so he decided that the head was definitely the place to start. Didn't reckon with her teeth though, did you, Boris? Just a little nip, but it hurt, didn't it, Boris? Going to get your bits chopped off if you do that again, aren't you, Boris.' Everyone stared at Boris, who looked very sorry for himself, as though he knew his bonking days were numbered.

Eventually, it was FB's turn to see the vet. We'd agreed to tell the receptionist his name was FB because we suspected that making the vet stand in the middle of a crowded waiting room shouting, 'Fat Bastard!' might be inappropriate. I slightly regretted this because the vet was one of those busy, efficient people, who had no time at all to listen to tales of how wonderful FB was and how he had a little playpen and how he liked knocking wine glasses over and hiding behind the candles in the fireplace. She was, as April would say, a proper grumpy cow. I thought, bitterly, that it would have felt like karma to make her shout swear words. She checked FB's bum, said he felt a bit warm and perfunctorily told us it was probably a cold. We protested that he hadn't been himself for ages, but she said she couldn't find anything obviously wrong and further tests would cost the equivalent of the GDP of Luxembourg. 'Not cost effective for an older hamster,' she snapped.

All the way home on the bus, Rachel and I peered into the pet carrier, keeping up a steady stream of comforting noises and songs to reassure FB that, even though he wasn't in his lovely cage, we were with him and we loved him. A little girl and her mother joined in with singing and, before long, everyone else had joined in too. Somewhere on social media there is a video of the entire top deck of a London bus raucously singing 'The Wheels on the Bus', before the vehicle grinds to a halt and an angry driver pokes his head above the stairs to find out 'What the bleedin' 'ell's going on up 'ere?'. It probably didn't do poor FB much good, but it cheered Rachel and I up.

We arrived home and gently put FB back in his cage. 'My mum used to make us warm milk and honey when we were under the weather,' I told Rachel. 'Do you think you can do that with a hamster?'

Rachel took out her phone and checked with doctor Google, who said this sounded like a marvellous idea. FB thought it was marvellous too and the little bowl was soon empty. Belly full of the good stuff, FB settled down for a snooze. Rachel, who had been sitting on the floor, anxiously watching over our poorly furball, suddenly stood up and announced, 'I'm bored. Can't do much for the crook one. Fancy going clubbing?'

'Aren't we a bit old for clubbing?'

Rachel stretched out one long leg and pointed her toes at me. 'Don't worry, mate, we'll find you one that lets grannies in.' Then she executed a neat pirouette and went off to get ready.

I wasn't too sure about clubbing. What did people wear to clubs these days? A quick canter through the internet gave me the answer; as little as possible. Jeez, I didn't even own anything clubby and I couldn't borrow something from Rachel, she was a size smaller and a foot taller than me. She'd be all glam and I'd look like her dowdy mother. Oh, bugger it. I looked down at my ample chest. If the fashion was tits out, then I'd make the most of what I had. I had the shiny push-up bra that Rachel had bought me for my birthday, on the basis that she was sick of seeing my greying Marks and Spencer stalwart drying on the bathroom radiator, and I had a see-through floaty top to blur the lines a bit. I grabbed the smart black skirt I'd been wearing to job interviews and chopped six inches off the bottom. Some of that spider's web hem gluey stuff and a once over with an iron…et voila! A mini skirt. All those years making effing World Book Day costumes for April were not wasted. Although, if motherhood had taught me anything, it was that World Book Day ought to be banned. It had absolutely eff all to do with books and everything to do with parental playground rivalry.

That first year, when April was five, I'd made the mistake of assuming that throwing together something home made about an hour before school would do. I duly wrapped her in toilet paper, told her she was an Egyptian mummy and popped her into the car. All the way to school she howled, 'But what book am I from?' At first, I patiently explained, 'There are lots of books with mummies in them.' Buggered if I could think of any, though. By the time we reached school, thoroughly exasperated, I roared, 'I don't flipping know. You're a mummy. They can't talk, so just be quiet!' Mother of the Year award winning stuff, I know. April cried so hard that her little face turned into tear and snot papier-mâché. Then I hugged her so hard to say sorry that I ripped the toilet roll on her arms. It was a very bedraggled, despondent mummy who shuffled through the school gates that morning. In the meantime, Tabitha's mother triumphantly paraded her precious little Cinderella, complete with Tabitha's twin older brothers dressed as footmen, around the school yard. Tabitha's mother either had a PhD in sewing or she knew a designer, so elaborate were the costumes.

That day was also my first encounter with Suzy, who was ushering a Mr Potato Head and a Buzz Lightyear, both embroiled in a fierce argument over an Alice band, through the gates. She nudged me with her elbow and snorted in the direction of Tabitha's mum. 'Don't worry about her. She does this every year. "Look at me, I'm the best mummy." Overcompensating, if you ask me.'

'What for?'

'Husband left her for the au-pair when Tabitha was a baby. Spent six months drinking wine. Culminated in her crashing her car through the butcher's window, with the kids inside. Nearly lost the kids and ended up in rehab. Been trying to show the world she's a great mum ever since. Poor, silly cow. Absolute pain in the backside in PTA meetings, but I feel sorry for her.'

I immediately warmed to this pragmatic, compassionate stranger and asked whether she fancied going for a coffee.

'Can't. Meal on wheels,' she declared. 'But take my number and ask me again soon.'

Now, I looked at myself in the hallway mirror, all tarted up, and imagined Suzy firmly pronouncing me, 'Marvellous mutton dressed as lovely lamb, my darling.' Rachel came through, a tanned antipodean goddess in a figure hugging white dress, and stood behind me to take a mirror selfie of the two of us. Soon, all the people on insta would be wondering, 'Who are these sexy ladies?'

It was still quite early, so we stopped by the café to give Mehmet an FB update. Judy was there, chatting to Bill, and I introduced them to Rachel.

'Oh my,' said Bill, admiring our glamour. 'It's Strictly Come Dancing meets Putney.' He stood up, pulled me towards him and foxtrotted me around the tables, laughing uproariously and shouting, 'Judy, marks out of ten?'

'Well,' said Judy, 'Nifty footwork but a bit too much tit for my liking.'

'Oh, Judy. This is what the girls wear to go dancing these days. You must be kinder!'

'I wasn't talking about her, Bill. I was talking about you!' Judy cackled at her own joke and, letting go of me, Bill joined in the laughter.

'You're a bad woman, Judy, but I like you.'

Mehmet came through from the kitchen, wiping his hands on a tea towel, and greeted me like he hadn't seen me in a year, as opposed to that morning, when I'd cooked an enormous batch of food so that I could have a rare afternoon off.

'All my favourite people are here,' he beamed. 'Rachel, darling, so good to see you.'

'G'day Mehmet. Just came in to tell you the vet thinks FB has a cold.'

'Oh, little FB. Katie has been so worried.' Mehmet frowned for a moment, then gave himself a little shake. 'Okay, you girls are going out to cover London in red paint, yes? Then you will need food first.'

As Mehmet disappeared into the kitchen, the café door opened and Scott came in. He stood for a moment, eyeing the little gathering uncomfortably, before sitting down alone at his usual table. Bill shouted over to him, 'Hey Scott, can we join you?'

Scott did not look happy. 'Too many people,' he mumbled.

'Good people. Nice people, Scott. How about we sit at the table next to you?'

Scott grunted what we took to be assent and there was much scraping of chairs and shuffling around as we all moved to the table next to his.

'Scott, have you met Rachel before?' I asked.

'Seen you in here a few times.' Scott briefly smiled at Rachel then looked at Bill. 'Can we play chess now?'

Before Bill could reply, Rachel interjected. 'I wouldn't mind a game. I'm not very good, though. Haven't played in a while.'

'Okay, you can play.'

Rachel moved over to sit opposite Scott and they started laying the pieces out. Bill and Judy were chatting again, so I took the opportunity to do a little social media stalking on my phone. I'd missed Tony and April terribly and had taken to monitoring their social media accounts. Tony had a Facebook page, but he rarely posted anything. He was more of a lurker. April, on the other hand, was like a social media queen. Every movement documented for the world to see. Here she was on insta, dancing with Janine and some fresh-faced lad I didn't know. Here she was on Facebook, playing tug of war with Archie. I checked the JT Productions website for any news. Odd. Usually there was a blog with updates of their latest projects but nothing had been posted for two weeks. I checked Twitter. No updates there either. Oh well, at least I knew April was alright. If there was anything wrong with Tony, she'd have plastered it all over the place.

I turned my attention back to the conversation, which had moved on to reasons why Scott didn't have a girlfriend. A red-faced Scott was mumbling that he was too awkward to ask girls out and Rachel was assuring him, 'You're a good-looking bloke, mate.'

Judy chimed in with, 'You need to get out more, ducky. Ain't you got no mates to go out with?'

Scott protested that he did have friends, but he always worried about meeting new people in case they didn't like him. It was at this point that Judy did something most unjudy-like. She leaned towards him and said, 'Just be yourself, lovely boy. When you're comfortable with what's on the inside, then the outside shines too.'

We all looked at her in surprise. Judy normally said things like, 'I ain't touching no food that comes from foreign,' and, 'I told Jeanie that she needed to get them bleedin' bunions seen to and now she's gone and got piles and all. Can't stand, can't sit. What's the world coming to? I blame the Tories.' For a moment there, she had sounded…wise.

'What you all looking at?' she said, adjusting her head scarf and sniffing. 'I may be seventy-nine, but I ain't ga-ga yet. There's so much goin' on in 'ere,' she tapped her head, 'I could write a bleedin' book, I could.'

That was debatable. For a start, I was fairly sure she'd told me she was eighty-something.

Mehmet came back with mugs of tea and a selection of the Turkish street food I'd been practicing earlier. As the early evening rush happened around us, all six of us munched and chatted companionably, Mehmet sporadically bustling off to see to customers. Bill and Judy seemed very relaxed around each other and I wondered if there was a little spark there. I'd noticed that they'd been getting on rather well recently and Scott had even started to accept Judy into his inner circle, presumably as some sort of mildly irritating extension of Bill. What was Scott's home life like, that he sought the comfort and familiarity of the café every day? One day I would catch him alone and ask him. However, for now, it was 7pm and Mehmet was jangling the door keys at us, loudly asking whether we all had bloody homes to go to, so we took the hint and left.

Stepping outside, I was hit by the chill autumn air and wished I'd worn a coat. Never mind, a few wines would soon make me impervious to the weather. Shivering, Rachel and I hopped on a bus headed for Clapham. She refused to tell me where we were going, merely assuring me that I'd love it. I had my doubts. Rachel was young enough to enjoy all the dance music, but I was a grand old dame of forty-six now and the relentless thud would probably send me into perimenopausal shock, if such a thing existed. Menopause – the last taboo. Companies had plans in place for stress, mental health, illness, disability and so on. Yet, despite the fact that half the working population would spend years of their lives going through it, nobody spoke openly about the menopause. Millions of itchy women with foggy brains, sweating into their polyester uniforms and wondering why they felt happy five minutes ago, yet were now contemplating a raid on the milk club money to buy chocolate, it being the only thing that would get them through the rest of the day. Shh. Don't mention the menopause, it's very personal. I decided that, when it came to my turn, I would own the menopause. I'd proudly declare that my ovaries were now overies. My libido was now libidon't. My oestrogen had gone westrogen. Rachel asked what I was thinking about.

'Just contemplating the future of my ovaries,' I replied. 'Are we nearly there yet?'

We were, indeed, nearly there. Five minutes later we alighted onto Clapham High Street and Rachel, towering over me in her high heels, held my hand to cross the road. It always made me feel like a toddler when she did this. She was like a mother, gathering waifs and strays to her, whether that be me, FB or Stinky Steve, who she had found living in a hostel in Amsterdam. I would never be able to thank her enough for nursing me through those first weeks without Tony and April; the long nights spent listening to me ramble on about my problems, followed by the weeks of cheering me on from the sidelines as dozens of 'dream job' applications were rejected. Now, here she was, enthusiastically pulling me into a bar for pre-drinks, ploughing a path through the crowds to land us a spot right in front of the barman.

'Freddo!' she exclaimed. The barman's face broke into a wide smile and he leaned forward to kiss her cheek. 'Katie, this is Freddo. We went out a couple of years ago. I told you, remember? Name's Tenpe but all you Brits think a Freddo should be ten pee so…?'

Ah, yes. I did remember. She'd told me an awful lot more than that and, if she were to be believed, he really should have been nicknamed Giant Toblerone.

'Nice to meet you, Freddo,' I said, pushing aside all lewd thoughts about which chocolate bar would best suit Freddo's rumoured anatomical gifts. I accepted a glass of wine and we stayed there awhile, chatting and drinking, with Freddo providing the odd free top up, before Rachel eventually announced that it was time to hit the club. Oh, lordy, could my poor, old wine-sodden brain handle the dunt, dunt music and flashing lights?

I didn't have to wait long to find out. The club was only a few metres away and, with the pubs not yet closed, there was no line of women in tiny dresses, huddled together against the cold, and swaggering groups of men trying to impress the ladies with their age-old mating ritual of who can belch the loudest, before sending forth the least pissed of their number to brave the giggling female herd. We were able to walk straight past the bouncers, into a cavernous space that thrummed to the beat of...the Eurythmics! Oh, Queen Annie of Lennox, how I worship thee.

'Welcome to Cheezees. Tonight, we're going granny,' said Rachel, grinning at me as we settled ourselves at a table by the dance floor. 'Give it an hour, this place will be full. Let's get the drinks in now?'

It's fair to say that we made substantial inroads into the cocktail menu. We'd just started on the pina coladas when I spotted a familiar face in the crowd. 'Ozzy!' I shouted, waving frantically.

Ozzy and a couple of his friends sauntered over to our table. Oz was looking sharp tonight, I thought. Rachel didn't like Ozzy very much and had often voiced her mistrust of him, saying, 'He's a handsome slime-bag. Trust me, Katie, I know the type.' She hadn't seen him in an apron, balancing a carrot on the end of his nose or playing a game of cabbage keepie uppie to amuse me. Yes, he was handsome. Yes, he wore fancy suits and considered himself a bit of a ladies' man. But he was also fun, charming and had stepped in to take the load off Mehmet and Meryem when they needed him. We'd formed a pretty good team in the café and if I were ten years younger and single, well, let's just say I wouldn't turn him down. I think Ozzy sensed this because he was definitely not averse to the occasional flirtation.

Ozzy slung an arm casually across my shoulders and introduced myself and Rachel to his friends, Cam and Gary. They both said a polite, 'Hi,' to me, but it was clear that, of the two of us, they regarded Rachel as the star of the show. Fair enough. I was short, middle-aged and wed, whereas Rachel was willowy, glamorous and, quite possibly, available. In their perfectly polished Oxford brogues, I'd have done the same thing.

All night we danced, drank and danced some more to the music of my youth. There was a glorious moment when the dancefloor came together in a spontaneous, coordinated hoedown to 'Blame It On The

Boogie.' That one was before even my time, but I could still do sunshine, moonlight and good times with the best of them.

The wee hours found us at a table in the smokers' area outside, puffing guiltily on Ozzy's cigarettes. I couldn't help thinking of the last time I'd had a sneaky smoke, round the back of the Plough with Maggie, but before I could get too maudlin, Ozzy squeezed in next to me for a quiet chat.

'Hey, Katie. You look good enough to eat. If we served Katies for lunch, Dad would be a millionaire by now.'

'Get away with you Ozzy. How much have you had to drink?' I laughed.

'Far too much but that is not the point.' He did a silent belch and continued, 'Can I ask you a favour Katie?'

'Sure.'

'I've sold a house in Turkey and need to put the money somewhere Dad won't find it. My bank account still has Mum and Dad's address and he opens my mail. I want to buy him a new van for Christmas. Can I put the money into your account for a few weeks?'

'I don't know. This sounds a bit dodgy, Ozzy,' I said.

'No, no, it's only £20,000 until I get the van sorted. Honestly, Katie, I didn't know who to ask. You know what he's like. If he sees the money, he won't shut up about it. I thought you'd understand.'

I couldn't help feeling uneasy about it, but I reasoned that this was Ozzy. He wouldn't be mixed up in anything illegal. He wouldn't hurt Mehmet and Meryem by doing anything stupid. Against my better judgement and with the full support of my cocktail-sodden cerebrum, I agreed and gave him my bank account details.

Ozzy gave a little whoop and kissed my cheek. 'Thank you, Katie. Now, let's get you a Screaming Orgasm.'

Yes, let's, I thought.

CHAPTER 15

November trundled along, boring as ever. My least favourite months of the year were November and February. They were the boring months. Unless you counted the forced romance of Valentines Day as an event (which I didn't – I liked my romance spontaneous, preferably topped off with ice cream and a bubble bath), February was a nothing month. Four weeks of dark, cold tedium before we hopped into March and started talking about Spring and Easter eggs. Ditto November – four weeks of dark, cold tedium where everyone moaned that shops shouldn't be allowed to put their Christmas decorations up before December, utter bastards were setting off fireworks and frightening all the dogs and, for a few hours, we stood in public parks, praying that some bugger would light the big fire before our nipples froze off and fell into our wellies. I liked the rich colours of autumn, the hope of spring, the lazy heat of summer and the glitter of December. I only coped with January because I'd had my fill of going out and was glad of the break. If I ruled the world, November and February would be banned, along with sodding World Book Day.

Scott surprised us all by arriving in the café one evening with a date. And not just any date. As Judy later put it, the girl was 'like a flippin' supermodel!' It seemed that the wise words of Judy had had an impact and his social life was starting to branch out beyond the café. Much to Scott's disgust (he was a teenager – all adult kind intentions were interference), myself, Bill and Judy rushed to introduce ourselves to the new girl.

'Aviana,' she said, leaning over to offer a slender, pale hand. I wasn't sure whether to kiss it or shake it, so perfect was this icon to the 21st century notion of beauty. I myself would have gone down a storm in the 17th century, when Rubens was at his peak, I thought, sniffily.

Scott scowled at Bill and Judy as, like a pair of overbearing grandparents, they interrogated Aviana. Where was she from? Chelsea. What did she do? Model (yes, I rolled my eyes). And then the clincher. How did she and Scott meet? I really should have been cooking everyone's food, but I was staying to hear the answer to this one.

'We've known each other since we were kids. We lost touch a bit when Scott went to Eton, but we hooked up again in the summer. It's good that we've known each other so long. We're comfortable with each other.'

Everyone turned to Scott, who had gone pink and seemed quite the opposite of comfortable. In fact, he appeared to be highly interested in the surface of the table.

'Ooh, posh boy,' Judy teased. She nudged Bill. 'Did you know 'e was a posh boy?'

Scott's face turned a deeper shade of red.

'Judy,' warned Bill, 'Be kind. Scott, it makes no difference. I came here from Jamaica in 1950. We had nothing and my parents worked hard. Same as yours. Eton or Hackney, it doesn't matter - we both got the best our parents could give us and that's something to be proud of. Now, how about a game of whist instead of chess today? Judy, Aviana, whist?'

Scott relaxed and, as Bill took a deck of cards from his pocket, Judy and Aviana shuffled their chairs closer. I marvelled at the changes that friendship had wrought. A couple of months ago, Scott could barely bring himself to look at anyone but Bill, never mind actually share a table with *shudder* *other people*. Now, here he was, still a funny young soul, but surrounded by an odd collection of people who cared. I realised that this was why Scott came to the café. Nobody minded his insistence on the same table every day (I'd even taken to putting a reserved sign on it), or his monosyllabic answers, or his preference for eye contact with the table. He could be himself here and we all liked him for it. Taking a date to Café Deniz might seem an odd choice, but from Scott's perspective, it made sense. It was his happy place.

I left them to their game and went back to the kitchen to make what I called Turkish street food tapas, but what was actually a hybrid mix of food from the region with a British twist. I'd been slowly building up a repertoire and trying it out on my friends. Bill and Judy, being on pensioners' budgets, were always happy to act as my guinea pigs and, even when I'd made something that I considered fit to add to Mehmet's dreaded list, I gave them a discount. Despite her alleged aversion to foreign muck, Judy had never been known to turn down a tantuni.

I appeared with a tray of food just as world war three was breaking out. Judy was refusing to speak to Bill, Aviana was accusing Scott of cheating and Scott was protesting loudly, 'You're allowed to memorise which cards have been played!' Children are much better behaved once they're fed, I reasoned, plonking the plates down on the table.

The others were used to the lack of menu and the eclectic offering of Café Deniz, but Aviana was delighted by the novelty of it all. She insisted that no one eat until she had taken photographs of everything, then she missed out on half of it because she was so busy Instagramming. This is clearly how you stay thin, I told myself. The Insta diet.

Aviana asked if she could take a selfie with the chef but, what with me being on the lam and all, I politely declined. 'In fact, if you wouldn't mind, I'd rather you didn't mention me in your posts,' I told her.

'The food is sooooo amaaaazing! I simply have to give you credit,' she cooed.

'Alright. But call me KT, like the initials K and T. Oh, and make me a man.'

'How comes you don't want nobody finding out who you are? You on the run or somefing?' That was Judy. Think the worst and come straight to the point about it.

Four pairs of eyes fixed on me. I thought for a moment then sighed. May as well tell them. 'I left...well, not exactly left...took a break from my husband and daughter. I'd been unhappy for a while. Desperate to get my career back now April was grown up but Tony, that's my husband, wanted me to stay at home and didn't really support me going back to full-time work. It disrupted his life, see. He travels all the time for work and relies on me being there. Then April was always needing something or getting into trouble and was long overdue a good kick up the arse to make her grow up. Only Tony thought I was being too hard on her. Don't get me wrong, I love them both. But in all the running around after them, I'd lost me. So, I was on a train one day, reading this self-help book about being yourself, when I thought, "What would happen if I didn't get off? Just carried on to the end of the line?" Well, I didn't get off. I just carried on and here I am. Having an adventure.'

'Bloomin' Nora!' exclaimed Judy.

'Oh my word,' said Bill.

'Wow, that's just, like, soooo courageous,' trilled Aviana.

'I'd like a mug of tea now, please,' announced Scott.

Aviana, Bill and Judy were full of questions. Had I been in touch with my family? No. When would I go back? I didn't know, probably when Meryem returned and I found myself unemployed again. Did I miss my family? Yes, oh, yes. I told them about Archie, Suzy and Graham, Maggie and Bob, Jack and even poor, sad Davey. All the things I'd kept locked inside came tumbling out. How we'd worked so hard on the house, how Tony had sacrificed so much for the business, how I loved my kitchen and how I…oh, just everything. I missed everything. Oh no, I was going to cry. My brain sent urgent 'don't cry' signals. Quick, Katie. Flap your hands. Because flappy hands definitely stop crying. My brain was wrong.

'So, that's why I can't appear on social media,' I sobbed. 'If Tony finds out I'm here, he'll come and I'm not ready for that. When I do go back, it has to be done gently. They might not even want me back, because I've done such a terrible thing.'

Judy adjusted her ubiquitous headscarf and patted me gently on the arm. 'You had your reasons, love. Sounds to me like nobody was listening.'

'It wasn't a bad life, though. Nobody did anything terrible. If it hadn't been for that bloody Irma Ford-Tinklewhatsit, I'd never have had the courage to do it. I read her book all the way here on the train and it all made sense. But now I'm saying it out loud, with a bit of distance, I'm wondering if I've made the biggest mistake of my life.'

A look of concern crossed Judy's wrinkled face. 'Them self-help books ain't all they're cracked up to be. You gotta go with what feels right inside. Do you want to go back?'

'Not yet. I'll stay as long as Mehmet needs me, then I'll decide. I actually love it here too.' I looked at the four anxious faces in front of me and gave a weak smile. 'You're like my London family. I love you guys.'

'Can I please have my tea now?' asked Scott.

One evening, a couple of weeks later, Mehmet and Ozzy appeared at the flat, carrying an enormous Christmas tree between them.

'Katie and Rachel, my beautiful angels. It is early, I know, but I was loving the cash and carry so much today that I bought one for the shop and one for you. Ozzy says he has done the books and the café is doing very well. Profit is up and we are rolling in green stuff. This tree is a thanks to you.'

We looked around the small living room, wondering where we were going to put the thing. Undeterred, Mehmet set about moving the pot plant from its space by the window and Ozzy nipped back to the van to get the stand. We put FB's cage in front of the fireplace and moved the sofa to one side, pushing it so close to the door that when Ozzy returned, he had to squeeze through the narrow gap in the doorway and climb over the sofa arm, before triumphantly presenting the stand to Mehmet. Together, they hauled the tree into place and stood back to admire their handiwork.

Mehmet adjusted a couple of branches, but they immediately sprang back into place. 'Who needs to watch TV anyway?' he declared. 'Now, how is little FB today?'

As I fetched coffee and biscuits, I overheard Rachel explaining that FB seemed no better. He wasn't even eating his dog biscuits anymore. We were going to take him back to the vet but we didn't hold out much hope. The vet hadn't seemed interested last time.

Ozzy came into the kitchen area. 'Need any help?' he asked.

'No, I'm almost done.' I picked up a jar of coffee. 'It's just instant, I'm afraid. Jaffa cakes or digestives?'

'Jaffa cakes.'

'Good choice,' I told him, putting the boring digestives back in the cupboard.

He lowered his voice. 'Katie, I wanted to thank you for looking after my money. My mate was going to take some as well, but he's split up with his missus and doesn't want it coming up if the child maintenance people get involved. Do you think I could put another forty grand in your account?'

'I don't know, Ozzy. You still haven't got your dad the van with the first lot and you moved that money out of my account last week.'

'Yeah, I found one but the deal fell through. Gutted, I was. If you could just hold on, I'll get all the money shifted before Christmas. I promise.'

'Why can't you just keep it in your own account. The van thing, I get. But the rest? If your Dad sees it, tell him you're saving for a flat or something.'

'You know what he's like, Katie. Questions, questions, questions. He won't let it go, then he'll tell Mum and worry her, like she doesn't have enough on her plate already. Nana is so ill, they think she might not have long.'

Feeling guilty, I reluctantly agreed, telling him that this was the last time, though, and he really must move the money before Christmas. Once again, he exuberantly kissed my cheek and, grabbing the Jaffa cakes, he climbed over the back of the sofa to join his father and Rachel, who were sitting on the floor in front of the fireplace, cooing over a rather bedraggled and sleepy FB. I passed the coffees over and joined them in the now rather shrunken living area.

'What is all the kissing for? I saw you,' chided Mehmet. 'You cannot make Katie an honest woman. She is already taken.'

Ozzy laughed off the suggestion that we were up to something, telling his father, 'No, no, Dad. We're good friends only. I was just thanking Katie for all she has done while Mum is away.'

'Good. Because there will be no sexy goings on here. You can keep the shenanigans for the girls you are too ashamed to take home to meet your mother.' Ozzy started to protest but Mehmet held up a finger to stop him. 'You think I don't know about all these women. I keep my ears wide open to the ground and I hear things. You are too old for shenanigans. You need to settle down.'

'This isn't the time or the place for this conversation, Dad.'

They lapsed into heated Turkish, voices rising as the argument wore on. Rachel placed FB back in his cage and I moved the coffee cups onto the hearth, out of harm's way of what was turning into a lively debate; a debate which finally ended with Ozzy shouting, 'I don't even want a fucking kettle!' and storming off. Well, climbing off. It's a bit difficult to do a full flounce when you have to clamber over a sofa first.

'It's buy one get one free on kettles at the cash and carry. BOGOFF!' Mehmet cried after him.

We heard the front door slam and Mehmet sank onto the sofa, rubbing his hands over his face. 'I'm very sorry, Katie and Rachel. I don't know what is going on with that boy. He is so angry these days.'

'He's probably worried about his Nana, Mehmet,' I said, handing him his cup of coffee.

'I don't know why. She is getting better.'

'But he just told me-'

'What?'

'Nothing. Never mind. How's Meryem?'

We distracted Mehmet from his troubles by asking him about his family in Turkey and, by the time he stood up to leave, his usual good cheer seemed to have returned.

Once Mehmet had scaled the sofa and squeezed his way out, Rachel gazed thoughtfully at me for a moment, before asking, 'What were you going to say?'

'What do you mean?'

'Back there, when Mehmet said Nana was better, you said "but he just told me" and then you stopped.'

'Ozzy told me in the kitchen that his Nana was dying.'

'Mehmet said she's improving. Why would Ozzy tell you that?'

Exactly what I'd been asking myself. Why would Ozzy lie? We'd grown quite close over the past couple of months and he knew how much I loved his parents. This wasn't just a lie, it was a really stupid lie. I was bound to find out.

'To guilt me into doing something I didn't want to do,' I admitted.

'Katie, mate, what have you done?'

'I let him put some money in my bank account. He said he wanted to buy his dad a van and it would be gone in a few weeks. He moved the money out, but he hasn't bought the van. Said the deal fell through.'

'Moved the money out? How?'

'I gave him the password for my online banking.'

Rachel stared at me, aghast. 'Sweetie, this does not sound good. How much money are we talking about?'

'Well, it was £20,000 the first time.'

'The first time?'

'He's putting another £40,000 in. That's what we were talking about in the kitchen.'

'Where's he getting this money from?'

'He said he'd sold a house in Turkey. All his bank statements go to Mehmet's house and he didn't want his dad opening them and finding out.'

'He could have just opened another bank account or changed his address with his bank. Sorry, Katie, I don't know what's going on, but it doesn't add up.'

'I was really drunk when I agreed. I wasn't thinking straight. Then, just now, he made me feel like I'd be putting extra pressure on Mehmet and Meryem.'

'I've always said he was a slimeball. There's something too smooth about him. He's Mr Charmypants with you but he ignores me. Because he knows I'm on to him, that's why. It's up to you what you do, Katie, but I say change your password and don't let him use your account again.'

I opened the banking app on my phone and logged in. Too late. The money was already there.

'I'll talk to him, Rachel. Find out what's going on and tell him to move the money out now. You're right. I've been a complete idiot. Just don't say anything to Mehmet, please. We don't even know for sure if Ozzy *is* mixed up in something dodgy. I mean, he works in the City, so it's probably shares or something. It's not like he's a drug dealer.'

'No worries. My lips are sealed. Want to hear some good news?'

'Definitely.'

'My parents have offered to pay for me to fly home for Christmas.'

'That's brilliant news!' I exclaimed, genuinely happy for Rachel. She'd been saving up for a trip home for ages and now she could enjoy some time with her family without dipping into her overdraft.'

'The bad news for you is that you're in charge of the monster tree and FB. Work has agreed that I can take six weeks off from the start of December.'

'Oh, wow. You're going so soon?'

'No point in hanging about. I'll leave you the rent money for December and January. Or would you like me to just put it straight into your bank account?'

'Ha, ha, very funny.'

CHAPTER 16

Back at work. I really didn't want to be there. For the first time since I'd worked at Café Deniz, I'd contemplated chucking a sickie. Not only did I have to talk to Ozzy, but I also had to babysit Carly. Custom had picked up so much recently that Mehmet had hired Carly to waitress after school and at weekends. It was Carly's first job and she was about as much use as a meat wetsuit in a shark tank. On her first day she'd incurred the wrath of Judy when she tipped a mug of tea over her coat. At the outraged squawks of 'Oh, my giddy aunt!' I came rushing through, to find Judy brandishing her oldest, filthiest mac at the girl, all the while asserting, 'This is my best bleedin' coat.'

'No, it isn't, Judy. It's your old gardening coat. Carly, take Judy's coat, give it a wipe and hang it on the radiator. It'll probably end up cleaner than it was when she came in.'

Judy drew herself up to her full five foot two. 'I didn't come in 'ere to be insulted.'

'All part of the service. Now, sit yourself down and I'll get you another tea. On the house.'

Never one to turn down free food or drink, Judy sat down, crossed her arms and glared at me like an unrepentant child who had just received an unwarranted telling off. I sighed and wished Bill were here. 'It's Carly's first day. She's only a kid.'

'I know. "Be kind, Judy."'

I smiled. She did quite a reasonable impression of Bill.

My glum mood was not improved by a prank call that morning.

'Hello,' said an American voice. 'May I book a table please?'

'We don't do bookings.'

'You don't understand. I'm calling for Jake Mallory.'

'Well, that's very kind of you to help Jake out, but, sorry, I can't reserve a table.'

The voice became rather haughty. 'Do you know who you're talking to?'

'Obviously not,' I replied, sarcastically, 'seeing as you failed to introduce yourself.'

'Jake will be there at one. Make sure there's a table,' the voice instructed, before abruptly hanging up.

This wasn't the first weird call I'd taken recently. A couple of weeks ago, a woman had phoned, asking to speak to the person in charge. I had supposed that would be me.

'I'd like to book the entire café for tomorrow afternoon,' she told me, in a clipped, plummy tone.

'I'm sorry, we don't take bookings.'

'You'll take this one. She's a VIP and privacy is paramount. I'll be sending someone ahead today to check security.'

'I think you have the wrong number. This is Café Deniz.'

'I know perfectly well what it is.'

'I'm not clearing out all the customers for one person. Whoever she is, she'll just have to slum it with the rest of us.'

'That's simply not possible-'

'Look, is this the Quilted Tea Cosy?' I interrupted. 'Because, if it is, you're not getting Mehmet to shut up shop on a weekend. Yes, we've heard that you've been trying to poach our customers. Well, it's not going to work. Now, bugger off.' That day, it was me who'd hung up abruptly.

'Bloody Quilted Tea Cosy playing silly beggars,' I'd harumphed to myself, as I clattered around the kitchen. It was a cut-throat business, running a café. They'd undercut each other on prices, pinch ideas from menus, snipe about each other at local business group meetings and, the ultimate weapon, anonymously report each other to Environmental Health. Mehmet had so far managed to dodge most of the bullets. His was a rather unique offering and the majority of Turkish food outlets in the area were restaurants catering to the dinner clientele. Mehmet generally closed around six, didn't serve alcohol and relied on local people, office workers and school mums for the majority of his trade. However, lately, the Turkish street food had become surprisingly popular, so much so that queues had started to form outside the café, and it was entirely conceivable that the nearby cafés were jealously sizing up the competition. I'd made a mental note to tell Mehmet to watch his back and thought no more of it.

When the next prank call came, a few days ago, I was in no mood to be messed with.

'Hello, I'm calling on behalf of Daniella Dankworth,' said a different American voice.

'We don't do reservations. Now, off you fuck,' I'd barked, hanging up.

And now, here was someone pretending to book a table for some Mallory bloke. Jeez, do these people never give up? Mind you, if that *had* been Daniella Dankworth the other day, I'd have done a little pee in my pants. Daniella was a TV chef known for her imaginative, yet easy to follow, recipes. All the mums loved her because she used cheap, readily available ingredients. All the dads loved her because she had a large bottom and big boobs, and licked a spoon like it was a stiff...

'Do you have the order for table three, only they're getting arsey?' asked Carly, interrupting my ruminations.

'No.' I frowned and looked through the stack of meal slips. 'There's nothing here. Where did you leave it?'

Carly looked around the counter and the floor, before stopping abruptly, brows raised and eyes wide. I could practically see the light-bulb go on above her head. She pulled her order pad from her pocket and riffled through the pages.

'Bugger,' she said, handing me table three's order, tears beginning to form in her eyes.

'Go back out, offer them free drinks and tell them there's been a short delay. Stay behind after work tonight and you and I will do some practice. Don't worry, a week from now and you'll wonder what you were fretting about,' I reassured her.

Carly was all cute dimples and pigtails, I mused as I readied table three's order. Add some self-confidence and she'd have the customers eating out of the palm of her hand. Well, not literally. Because then the Quilted Tea Cosy really would have cause to call Environmental Health.

With all orders out and the Sunday hangover breakfast rush slowing, I had time for a quick break. Ozzy hadn't shown his face yet, although he'd likely be in later, and Mehmet was out front providing his usual garrulous welcome to all and sundry. I sat at the table, trying to think why the name Jake Mallory seemed familiar. Must be a previous customer, I reckoned. Right-o, if it wasn't a hoax call and it was just some idiot trying to jump the lunchtime queue for a table, let's give him a table. The horrible one by the toilet. I took a yellow box from the shelf, emptied out its contents and, using Meryem's good scissors, cut out a large, neat star. A quick search of what Mehmet called the 'sods and odds drawer' unearthed a marker pen and I scrawled 'RESERVED' across one side of the star and, on impulse, 'FOR A BIG TWAT' on the other.

'What are you doing?' asked Mehmet suspiciously when, a few moments later, he caught me placing the star on the toilet table.

I explained about the call that morning, telling him, 'It's probably the place up the street playing silly beggars. We hardly ever use this table anyway, so if the guy does show up, just put him here. Only, you'll want to remove the star. I was annoyed and got a bit carried away.'

Mehmet looked at the back of the star, raised his eyebrows, grinned and placed it, reserved side up, on the table.

'Katie, you are a very naughty girl.'

It is just as well that Mehmet was enjoying the joke now because around half past one, he was definitely not smiling. He came into the kitchen, wide-eyed and wheezing.

'What's wrong, Mehmet?' I asked, hurrying to his side.

'Bloody…bloody…bloody.' He looked like he was about to explode. I made him sit down at the table and fetched a glass of water. Gratefully, he drank it, then tried to speak again. 'The toilet table. Carly took him to the bloody toilet table. He saw the bloody star. I am ruined! I will have no reputation and it will be everywhere that you don't go to Café Deniz because they are rude!' he wailed.

'Let me get this straight. The guy turned up and Carly took him to the toilet table, but she didn't remove the star. It's no big deal, Mehmet. Just some chancer.'

'Chancer! Not a bloody chancer. Go and see for yourself, you and your bloody big twat.'

I made my way front of house. Mehmet was clearly having a breakdown. All this family stuff must be getting to him. Maybe the fact that his cash and carry purchases were getting ever more outrageous was a cry for help. The front of the café was decked out in so many lights that people were taking their children to see it. The astronauts on the International Space Station had probably emailed NASA to complain that a bright spot in the south east of England was lasering through the ISS net curtains and keeping them awake at night. I'd just set off on a train of thought about why on earth they'd need net curtains in space, when I stopped dead in my tracks.

'Fuck-a-doodle-do.'

The occupant of the toilet table looked up at me and removed his sunglasses.

'Yes, fuck-a-doodle-do,' said Jake Mallory, four times Oscar winner and darling of the British media. He waved the star at me, the words 'FOR A BIG TWAT' emblazoned in bold black marker. 'Is anyone coming to take my order?'

'Bugger.' I died a little on the inside and looked around, helpless, for Carly. She was nowhere to be seen. She'd probably taken one look at Mehmet's apoplectic expression and fled to the ladies for a good cry. I suspected that my own face was approximately three shades pinker than normal. However, I tried to assume a nonchalant air as I approached this…this…absolute movie god…lordy, he was so handsome…there'd be no need for Roberta tonight, controls to manual, Katie…Jake Mallory aaaaaaaargh…so nervous…right, calm down… drinks, order drinks. 'Sorry 'bout that. I thought the table reservation was a wind up. What can I get you to drink? Key, toffee, slackcurrant bosh?'

'Slackcurrant bosh?'

'It's what we serve movie stars. Everyone else just gets plain old blackcurrant squash.'

'Coffee, please. Do you have a menu?'

'Nope. We bring you food, you eat it and, if you don't like it, we don't give it to you next time. Don't worry, Mehmet hardly ever gets it wrong. He's like the Food Whisperer. I'll send him out to take a look at you and he'll decide what you're having.'

Jake thanked me and I scarpered to the ladies loos to evict Carly. I pointed her in the direction of the coffee machine, issued a stern warning not to mess this up and went back to the kitchen, where I slumped down into the chair next to Mehmet.

'Bugger me, Mehmet, that's Jake Mallory.'

'That's what I bloody told you. And no bloody swearing in my kitchen.'

'You know you've got to go back out there and do your looky thing? He's expecting the Food Whisperer.'

'I know,' groaned Mehmet, 'and I can't look at him. He makes me think of those poor, bloody children in the jungle.'

'What are you on about?'

'What is the world coming to, that they let children go into a jungle? I look at that man and I do not see food. I see four lives and a villain!'

'Do you mean Jumanji?'

'Bloody scary movie! My heart could not take the tension. That man is a bloody bastard. Get him out of my café!'

'You know he wasn't in that movie. Also, it was a movie. It wasn't real.'

Mehmet thought about this for a moment, then hastily stood up. 'Okay, I will go out and do my magic. But first, do the google.'

'What am I googling?'

'The movies he has been in. Quick. It will be my talking point with him.'

I thought back to the horror film that won Jake Mallory his Oscar in

2019. Absolutely no way was I telling Mehmet about that. He'd have Jake out on his ear.

'I'm not googling anything, Mehmet,' I said firmly. 'Just go do your thing, then tell me what to cook.'

Mehmet straightened his waistcoat and stalked off, muttering something about me being bossier than bloody Meryem.

For the next few hours I cooked and cooked. I had no time to wonder what Jake Mallory thought of his meal or why Ozzy hadn't appeared yet. I'd pushed the Ozzy worries to the back of my mind because there really wasn't anything to be done until I talked to him. By 4pm, I was exhausted. The lunchtime crowd had given way to the afternoon coffee and cake people, leaving me free to emerge for a chat with Scott and Aviana, who were sitting at Scott's usual table, picking at some Baklava.

'Weird day,' I told them. 'Guess who was here? Jake Mallory! *The* Jake Mallory!'

'Yeah, he said he was coming.' Aviana examined her perfectly manicured fingernails. 'Do you think this red is too strong? Should I go for a dark pink?'

'You know Jake Mallory?' I squealed.

Aviana looked up from her nails. 'Well, yes.' She frowned. 'I know everybody.'

'Everybody? Like, loads of famous people?'

'Hmm, it sort of goes with the territory.'

'What territory?' Ye gods, this conversation was beginning to feel like pulling teeth.

'Do you know who I am?' she asked.

'Scott's girlfriend. Aviana.' I shook my head in puzzlement.

Aviana raked through her Hermès Birkin and extracted her phone. A few clicks later, she turned the screen towards me. There she was on Instagram, dressed in a clingy, midnight blue scrap of material that perfectly set off her carefully coiffured, blonde locks. Hang on. Twenty-eight million followers! WTactualF, as April would say. Aviana scrolled through her posts until she came to the photographs she had taken at the café. Over three million likes. 'Ah, so, when someone phoned a couple of weeks ago saying somebody important was coming, I probably shouldn't have told them to bugger off.'

'Probably not.'

'And telling Daniella Dankworth's assistant to off you fuck?'

'I'll call Daniella and smooth things over. Have you not seen the newspapers recently?'

'I check the BBC headlines, but that's about it.'

Aviana stabbed at her phone screen a few times and turned it towards me again. There was a Daily Mail article – Who is KT? 'You've gone viral, Katie. Everyone's mad for your food. You're like the Banksy of the food world.'

I gawped as she scrolled through headline after headline. Apparently, journalists and celebrities had been visiting the café and none of us had noticed. Well, it was Putney, wasn't it? You didn't expect Madonna rocking up and asking for a kebab. 'Holy guacamole. Why didn't you tell me?'

'We thought you knew.'

'I better tell Mehmet and Carly. At least it explains why we've been so busy recently.'

I pushed back my chair and Aviana put a hand on my arm to stop me leaving. 'You need to stay out of sight in the kitchen, if you don't want people to know about you. Take it from someone who gets papped all the time.' She smiled her perfect model smile. 'By the way, did Jake enjoy his meal?'

I shrugged. 'I accidentally called him a twat and offered him slackcurrant bosh, Carly hid in the loos and Mehmet nearly had a heart attack because he thought he was in Jumanji. I'd say he got the authentic Café Deniz experience.'

That evening, after closing, there was a 'family' conference in the café. Mehmet summoned Ozzy, I summoned Rachel and Carly asked Scott and Aviana to stay behind.

'We are gathered here today to mourn the passing of Katie and celebrate the birth of KT, cool and mysterious chef,' I intoned.

Rachel threw a packet of crisps at my head and told me to get on with it.

'Okay, to summarise, Aviana here is famous. She tweeted about my food, but I wouldn't let her tweet about me because, as you all know, I can't be on social media right now.'

'I didn't know that,' said Ozzy and Carly in stereo.

'I left my family a few months ago and I don't want them to see me all over social media or in the newspapers. That's all you need to know. Anyway, I told Aviana to make me a man and call me KT. None of us realised, but it went viral and that's why we've been packed out recently. Now the press is on the hunt. They want to unmask KT and I don't want to be unmasked. I need your help.'

'Why did you leave your family?' asked Ozzy and Carly in stereo.

'I was unhappy. It doesn't matter. I want to go back, but if I'm all over the news it'll be a nightmare. Imagine finding out from a newspaper that the wife who buggered off,' I held up a hand to apologise to Mehmet before he could shout at me for bloody swearing, 'and left you, out of the blue, is cooking up a storm in London. When Meryem gets back, I want to quietly go home and hope they forgive me. How am I going to avoid being outed?'

There was a long silence, punctuated only by slurps of tea, as we all gave some thought to the situation.

'Right,' said Rachel, 'here's a plan. They all think KT's a bloke. We'll stick to that. From now on, our Katie's called Sarah. We all call her Sarah. Nobody gives interviews or even mentions KT. If you're asked about him, no comment. Any other advice, Aviana?'

'Yes, there will be paparazzi hanging about. Katie, sorry...Sarah, you'll need to stay in the kitchen as much as possible in case you're accidentally photographed.'

Mehmet, who had been uncharacteristically quiet, finally piped up. 'This is a fine mess. Sarah Katie, I will smuggle you out in the van every night. Take you to my house. I will park in the garage and you can leave when the coast is transparent.'

Everyone agreed that this was a fine plan and went their separate ways. Except Ozzy. I asked Ozzy to stay back for a few minutes and, once Mehmet was out of earshot, ushering Scott, Aviana, Rachel and Carly out into the cold night, I brought up the awkward subject of the money.

'Look, Ozzy, I'm not comfortable with you keeping money in my account. I understand the reasons you've given, yet I really don't feel okay with this.'

'Come on, Katie, it's only for a few weeks. I'm getting Dad's van next week, honest. A bloke I know says he's found me a good deal. The rest of the money's a deposit on a flat. I was going to surprise Dad and take him round to see it.'

'None of it makes sense. You needed to hide twenty grand to buy your dad a van, yet no van and you somehow manage to find somewhere else to move it to. Then you need to hide forty grand and suddenly it's for a deposit on a flat. Wouldn't it have been easier to change the address on your own bank account or set up a new one?'

'No point if I'm moving, is there? Honestly, Katie darling, you're worrying about nothing.' He reached out and stroked my cheek. 'You're so beautiful. I can't believe there's a man out there who didn't hold on to you for dear life.'

I turned my head away and he withdrew his hand. I crossed my arms over my chest, prepared to stand my ground, and firmly told him, 'I'm not falling for that, Ozzy. I want the money moved out of my account tonight.'

He took a step closer and, again, reached out to stroke my cheek.

'Pity,' he whispered. 'Beautiful things can so easily get damaged.'

I didn't turn away this time. Heart hammering, I looked straight into the eyes of the man with whom I'd shared a kitchen, childhood tales, laughs and jokes, and I saw a hard, black anger. This was a different Ozzy, a dangerous Ozzy.

A surge of adrenaline ran through me as the threat hit home, and I tensed my jaw to hide what would surely be a tremble in my voice. 'Midnight. Then I'm changing the password.'

'What is going on in my bloody kitchen?' shouted Mehmet, from the doorway.

Ozzy casually stepped back. 'Nothing, Dad. Katie had a smudge on her face and I was wiping it off.'

'I have told you before. She is off bounds and out of limits. You need to find a nice girl to settle down with.'

This set the two of them off into another Turkish argument and I managed to slip out, unnoticed. I found Rachel waiting for me outside.

'What kept you?' she asked.

'I had a word with Ozzy. It didn't go well.'

She tucked her arm in mine and steered us in the direction of the flat. 'You're shaking all over. What happened?'

I told her about Ozzy's threat and, shocked, she said, 'You have to tell Mehmet.'

'I can't. It would break his heart and we don't even know that Ozzy is up to something.'

'Of course he's up to something. You don't go about threatening people if you're not up to something!'

'I'll think about it. I really will. This whole KT thing has my head in a spin. I can't cope with Ozzy being a twat as well. Let's just get home, saw the branch off the Christmas tree and watch some telly.'

CHAPTER 17

The following week saw Rachel bidding us a cheery farewell, as she set off back to Australia. Mehmet insisted on driving her to Heathrow in his van, which was just as well because she'd packed so much stuff, I don't think she'd have been able to haul it all on the underground. Mehmet declared himself delighted to drive to the outskirts of West London as he had heard of a cash and carry near Hounslow, which stocked inflatable snowmen.

'I thought you Muslims didn't believe in Christmas,' said Judy, blunt as ever, when he returned that evening with a van load of lights and an enormous silver snowflake.

'I do love the shiny things,' said Mehmet, who was perched on a chair, attempting to string some lights over the counter. 'Oh, Christmas isn't just a day, it's a frame of mind.'

'That sounds very wise,' said Bill. 'Shakespeare? Churchill?'

'Kris Kringle, Miracle on 34th Street.'

'But you ain't allowed Christmas,' said Judy.

Mehmet gave up on the lights and climbed down from the chair. 'It is not a religious holiday for me, but I do the same things as you. We have a big lunch with all the family, we argue, we watch the Queen's speech, we wish all the nosy aunties would bugger off. I don't have all this at home.' He gestured at the decorations. 'So, it is fun to have it here. This year it will be very quiet at home. Meryem is staying in Turkey, Ozzy has put me in Coventry and I have told the nosy aunties that I am going to visit other nosy aunties.'

'You've got other family, though. I mean, you foreign ones always have big, close families.'

'Judy!' exclaimed Bill.

'Oh, I didn't mean nothing by it, Mehmet, love,' said Judy, blithely. 'I was just thinking that if you've got nothing on and I've got nothing on, then maybe you'd like to come round mine for lunch.'

'Judy, you are a bad woman and a good woman,' Mehmet scolded her.

'She is indeed,' laughed Bill. 'Hey, I'm on my own too. And what about…,' he looked around to check the café was empty, '…Katie?'

I'd been standing by the kitchen door, listening to them chat, while I enjoyed a cup of tea at the end of another long day. I emerged from the kitchen and joined Judy and Bill at their table. 'It's just me and FB. And the way FB's going, it might only be me. We took him to a different vet and he said it's probably old age. He gave me some painkillers to see if they make a difference. They haven't, so I'll have to take him back.'

'Comes to us all,' said Judy, patting my hand. I gave her a weak smile, then gazed gloomily into my tea. It wasn't just FB. I felt responsible for Ozzy and his father arguing and, to top it off, there would be no Rachel there tonight to pour the wine and tell me, 'You'll be alright, mate.' I liked it when she called me mate. It reminded me of Jack and Tony, who had known each other since university and habitually called each other mate. I'd never heard Tony call anyone else mate. I mentally added Rachel to the list of people I missed.

'How about we spend Christmas Day here, in the café?' I suggested. 'I could cook. Mehmet could hook up his telly and we could watch some rubbish Christmas movies.'

'That would be nice. It has been a long time since I spent Christmas with anyone,' said Bill. 'My family are all passed away or back home in Jamaica.'

'It was the afternoon of Christmas Eve and Scrooge was conscious of a thousand odours, each one connected with a thousand thoughts and hopes and joys and cares long, long forgotten.' Everyone turned to stare at Mehmet, surprised by the eloquence of the man who had once, during a heated debate, announced that he was playing the devil's artichoke.

'Dickens,' said Bill, nodding sagely.

'The Muppet Christmas Carol,' beamed Mehmet.

With Christmas around the corner and the media announcing themselves as being on the scent of the elusive KT, the café was busier than it had ever been. Often, there were queues for tables and it was becoming more difficult for me to sneak in and out. It was only a matter of time before someone cottoned on. Carly, bless her little heart, brought me some of her mum's wigs.

'Doesn't she need them?' I asked.

'Nah. She had them during chemo a couple of years ago, but she's fine now.'

Wow. This gave me pause for thought. Carly seemed quite matter-of-fact about it, but that must have been a helluva lot for a teenager to cope with. I knew her dad wasn't in the picture, so she had probably missed out on a lot of teenage adventures while she cared for her mum. It might explain why, despite being a sensitive, timid wee poppet, she was mature beyond her years in so many ways. Nevertheless, each day, she emerged further from her shell.

Carly's confidence had soared once I took her under my wing. We'd done some practice after hours and Judy had kindly agreed to play the difficult customer. It wasn't a stretch. She gleefully sent back dish after dish, accompanied by a litany of complaints ranging from 'I do believe I might have caught botcherlism' to the fish being 'too fishy.' She pronounced herself 'allergic to triangles' and claimed 'the window seat plays havoc with me indigestion, love.' Finally, to a chorus of cheers and whoops from Scott, Aviana and Bill, Carly snapped and told Judy that if she truly believed the wet burgers looked like period fannies, then perhaps she should eat elsewhere. Mehmet's rather miffed declaration that, 'We do not sell bloody period fannies!' only served to prompt a fresh round of hilarity and we left the café that night in high spirits.

On the way home, I made a short detour to the postbox. I'd been undecided about whether to post this particular card. The message inside read:

Dear Tony and April,

I miss you both so much, especially with Christmas coming. I'm in London and I'm okay. I've been cooking in a Turkish café in Putney and have made some lovely friends. The owners, Mehmet and Meryem, have been so kind to me. Meryem has had to go back to Turkey to look after her mother, so I want to stay to help Mehmet until she gets back. I expect you'll be very hurt and angry with me, but I'd like to come home in the New Year. I completely understand if that's not what you want. My address is on the back of this card. Please don't come. Just write. I can't really explain, but I want to do this slowly and writing letters feels right. I love you very much. Give Archie a hug for me.

Katie xxx

On December 23rd, as had become our habit, Mehmet drove me to his house and parked in the garage. Normally, at this point, I would slip out into the street and go home. However, tonight, Mehmet invited me in for coffee, saying he had something to show me. It was the first time I'd been in Mehmet and Meryem's house and, whatever I'd expected, it certainly wasn't modern minimalism. On the outside, the 1930s semi was much like its neighbours, with a neatly trimmed hedge surrounding a small square of lawn and a paved drive. The front of the house was the standard mix of white paint above red brick, with curved bay windows to the right of a blue front door set into a patterned brickwork arch. So far, so normal. However, the interior was anything but traditional. The ground floor had been opened up and an extension added, to create a clean, open-plan living space. The stairs had been replaced with a wood and glass feat of engineering and the kitchen was an expanse of glossy white and grey. Before today, if someone had asked me what I thought Mehmet's house would look like, I'd have bet the farm on it being a hoarder's paradise.

'Mehmet, your home is beautiful!'

'Ah yes, this is Meryem's doing. She is not a lover of the cash and carry. And the car boot sales. How I love your English car boot sales. The café is my dream place and this,' he swept his arm around to take in the room, 'is Meryem's.'

Mehmet busied himself at a coffee machine that would be the envy of most baristas. Eventually, he slid two cappuccinos across the breakfast bar and, gathering a pile of paperwork from the table, came round to join me at the counter.

'I wanted to ask you what you think of this. It's the books from the café. Ozzy has been taking care of them for me. We have been very busy, but the turnover is I think too high. Most of it is coming from cash sales and there are large payments to suppliers I haven't used.' Mehmet handed me the print-outs and pointed to some of the transactions. 'You see here. There is a payment to GR Commercial Catering Equipment for new ovens. And here,' he ran his finger down the page, 'there is £25,000 for a van.'

'Does Ozzy know you have these?' I asked.

'No. He is using new software. I need to give everything to the accountant in January, so I logged in with his email.'

'Didn't you need his password?'

'Oh, the boy is an idiot. He has used the same password since school. His mother's maiden name and his year of birth. I am no William Gates, but I know my son.'

I scanned the pages of payments in and out. Mehmet was right, there were lots of transactions that I didn't recognise. I did a quick tally and, if some of the cash payments were to be believed, we had far more customers than capacity. Mehmet was scrupulously honest, but his practice of using a drawer instead of a till meant that he relied on meal slips for records of his cash sales.

'You're right,' I said. 'There's no way we've had this many cash sales. Have you checked whether GR Commercial Catering Equipment exists?'

'They have a website. There is an invoice.'

'Do you think Ozzy could have bought stuff and just not told you?'

'It says the ovens were bought two months ago, Katie.'

I sighed heavily, as I contemplated what I had to do next.

'This is not going to help matters, but I think you need to know. A while back, I bumped into Ozzy on a night out and he persuaded me to keep some money in my bank account for him. He said he'd sold a property in Turkey and he was going to buy you a new van. He didn't want you finding out about the money because he wanted to surprise you.'

Mehmet looked perplexed. 'How would I find out?'

'He said his bank statements are delivered here.'

'They are not!'

Mehmet puffed up, ready for an argument, so I hastened to continue, before we became bogged down in his outrage. 'I realise that now. He moved the money out again, yet the van never appeared. This looks like maybe he did buy a van. If so, where is it? There's something else. Remember the day you gave us the Christmas tree? He asked me to keep another £40,000 for him.'

'Why would he do this?'

'I don't know. There was no proper explanation. I realised afterwards that he'd guilted me into it. Then…well, you know the day when we came up with the plan to hide my identity? You came into the kitchen and we were a bit too close? He wasn't flirting with me. He was threatening me because I refused to let him use my bank account anymore.'

Mehmet looked like I'd just offered him a mug of vaginal discharge. 'Katie darling, I'm so sorry. I need to speak to my boy about this bloody cooking of the books. I have to find out what is going on. Will you stay with me while I call him?'

'Of course I will. I'm really sorry, Mehmet. I didn't want to tell you because I knew you'd be hurt.'

'I feel sick in my heart, but it is not your fault. Bloody stupid, stupid boy. What am I going to tell his mother?'

'Don't think about that now. Let's find out what's going on first,' I said, hoping against hope that there would be some reasonable explanation.

Mehmet dialled Ozzy's number and I could hear the muffled ringing. It rang. And rang. And rang. Eventually, a tinny voice said, 'You're through to Ozzy. Leave a message. Cheers.'

'Ozzy, it is Dad what is going on what is this oven and this van I have seen the books I know you are up to something call me [Turkish rant] this is your father speaking.'

Mehmet hung up and drew a deep breath. 'I do not like voicemail.'

There wasn't much more either of us could do. I asked Mehmet whether he intended to phone the police, but he said he wanted to talk to Ozzy first, so I gave him a quick hug, reminded him that I'd be late tomorrow because I was taking FB to the vet, and left him sitting, despondent, at the breakfast bar.

Christmas Eve dawned, grey and cheerless, and I lifted a raggedy FB into his pet carrier, ready for the trip to the vet. All the way there on the bus, I murmured comforting sounds into the plastic box on my knee. I knew in my heart that this might be FB's last big adventure, so I didn't care about making friends with strangers on the bus or patting puppies in the vet's waiting room. 'Oh, FB,' I whispered to him, 'I think you might be going to the big wheel in the sky.' The vet was kind and understanding, telling me he could do lots of tests, but they were unlikely to make a difference. FB was an older hamster and, whatever ailed him, it might be kinder to let him go than prolong the illness with little hope of a cure. This vet had time to listen to all the wonderful things about FB. He didn't mind me blubbering and hiccoughing through a rambling tale about the time FB fell asleep behind a sofa cushion and we nearly flattened him. He gave me time to stroke FB and kiss his little head, before taking him away to administer the injection. I couldn't watch. Despite being a wife and mother, despite working, despite all the difficult times I'd faced in my life, the decision to put FB to sleep felt like the first proper, grown up decision I'd ever made. Lordy, how was I going to break it to Rachel that I'd killed our hamster?

The vet promised to deliver FB back to me in an urn and, weighed down with guilt, I boarded the bus alone. I spent the journey planning FB's funeral. As the bus sped along, the plans became increasingly elaborate, so that by the time I reached Putney, I was googling 'can you hire hamsters to pull a mini carriage.' FB would love a little cortege to take him to his final resting place in Westminster Abbey. Did you need the Dean's permission to inter a hamster or could you just dig a little hole in the grass outside? I phoned Rachel to break the bad news and ask how she thought we should say goodbye to FB. She agreed that Westminster Abbey was a wonderful idea, but maybe the cortege and a twenty-one tiny gun salute were taking things a little too far. Also, she didn't think you could buy mini cannons and we might be arrested if we started firing cannons outside the Abbey. We agreed I'd leave FB on the mantlepiece until she came back.

The café was almost full by the time I arrived. I slipped in through the back door and found Mehmet in the kitchen, berating Carly about bloody sandwiches. No longer the shrinking violet, she was giving as good as she got. 'Don't take your bad temper out on me. There's nothing bloody wrong with the bloody sandwiches!'

'No swearing in my bloody kitchen,' cried Mehmet. He was about to march off in a rage when he spotted me pulling on an apron. 'She is getting the bloody sandwiches wrong,' he appealed.

'Thanks for covering for me, Carly,' I told the beleaguered girl. She flashed me a quick smile and scuttled off front of house to deal with difficult customers who, today at least, would be a breeze compared to doing battle with Mehmet. I pulled out a chair and gestured for him to sit. 'I know you're upset, Mehmet, but you can't take it out on Carly. She's just a kid doing her best.'

Mehmet sat down and put his face in his hands. 'Ozzy didn't call me back. I went to his flat this morning and nobody was there. No reply on the phone. No reply on the text. I tried the what's up and I don't know if I am working it properly. Here, look.'

He handed me his phone and I opened WhatsApp. He'd sent Ozzy a selfie of his left nostril. I quickly typed out a message asking Ozzy to get in touch, pressed send and returned the phone to Mehmet. 'Have you checked with his friends and his work? Maybe something's happened to him.'

'I phoned his friend Gary. They were out last night. He thinks Ozzy got my message because he left in a bad mood. His work said he called in sick this morning. There is nothing wrong with the bloody stupid boy. He is hiding from me.'

'Are you going to call the police?'

'Ah, Katie, to call the police on your own child. It is a hard decision.' Mehmet suddenly stopped talking and looked at me, tears in his eyes. 'I'm so sorry. I forgot to ask about FB.'

'He's gone. Another very hard decision. They'd done everything they could for him and he wasn't getting better, so I had to let him go.'

'That is sad news, my dear Katie.'

'It's for the best, I suppose. I'll miss the little beggar. It'll be weird when I go back to the flat tonight.' I gave myself a little shake. 'Come on, Mehmet. You and I can't sort our problems right now, so let's do our best to enjoy Christmas. I'll get cracking on these lunch orders. You put your happy face on and go see the customers. Then we'll clear up and get everything ready for tomorrow.'

The day went by quickly. Mehmet and I blocked our worries by focusing on work. In the spare moments between orders, I prepared our Christmas dinner. It was a slightly different affair, in that I had replaced pigs in blankets with slices of sucuk, the stuffing was hazelnut and apricot, there was gungo peas and rice for Bill and, alongside the Christmas pudding, I was serving ekmek kadayıfı with kaymak or custard. Something for everyone, I thought, as I peeled the sprouts.

I remembered last Christmas and reflected that never in a million years would I have imagined that this year I'd be spending it with a disparate bunch of people in a café in Putney. I wondered if Tony and April had received my Christmas card and, if they had, would they toss it in the bin? I didn't think Tony would throw it away, rather he'd brood on it, perhaps tuck it away in his desk drawer, and eventually pen a considered reply. I really had been in two minds about getting in touch. I wanted to go home and the idea of the press finding out about me, with the possibility of Tony being doorstepped by journalists, was unbearable. Perhaps I'd done so much damage that Tony and April wouldn't want me back anyway. Perhaps Roberta and I were doomed to roam the earth forever. A hundred years from now, robot minstrels would sing songs about the sad Tale of Frock. What a mess you've made, Katie.

Mehmet closed the café at 4pm and Scott arrived to help him arrange the furniture. They dashed to and fro in the little van, bringing armchairs, a television and a small sofa from wherever Mehmet kept his stash of all the things Meryem wouldn't let him have in the house. We pushed these to one side, in front of a stack of tables and café chairs, then joined two of the café tables together to create a table large enough to accommodate our Christmas feast. Judy arrived with a plastic Santa Claus tablecloth, napkins and a revolting arrangement of artificial flowers and tinsel, which she proudly told us was a centrepiece that she'd turned out every Christmas since 1983. Then she left, saying she was off to share a sherry with Bill. I imagined that slightly more than a sherry was planned, although I made my brain stop there. I definitely didn't want to imagine any more. It was worse than thinking about your parents doing it. Stop it, Katie. Stop it now.

Aviana had arrived with Scott, so I distracted myself by forcing her to peel potatoes. Aviana did not do menial tasks, as she kept reminding me. It is quite difficult to make your own child do things, but it is surprisingly easy to order other people's children around. They don't know you well enough to tell you to bugger off. I handed the potato peeler to Aviana and, taking a leaf out of Ozzy's book of guilt, sternly reminded her how lucky she was to be spending Christmas with her family. That seemed to do the trick and I soon had a nice, big pot of peeled potatoes ready to boil and roast the next day.

With everything good to go for Christmas day, it was time to go back to my empty flat. Mehmet offered me the usual lift as far as his garage, but I declined, saying we'd been closed for hours and it was so cold outside that I doubted anyone would be hanging around. Scott and Aviana walked part of the way with me, intending to peel off to get a taxi. Before we parted ways, I dug around in my handbag and pulled out two small parcels. 'Almost forgot to give you these,' I told them.

'Thank you.' Aviana, hair tucked in a green hat, nose and cheeks pink from the cold, looked like a pretty elf. 'I left yours under the tree in the café. Merry Christmas, Katie…erm…Sarah.'

I looked around. The street was almost empty. 'I think we're safe enough with Katie. Merry Christmas to you both.'

Aviana and I hugged, then Scott, who was not a hugger, gave me an affectionate fist bump, before we went our separate ways; me to clean a hamster cage, drink wine and watch old movies, Scott and Aviana to a swanky party in a hotel.

Christmas in London with new friends and being sort of famous. Who'd have thunk it?

CHAPTER 18

I arrived at the café early(ish) the next morning, nursing a prosecco hangover, having boozed my way through the sad task of clearing away FB's things the night before. I'd wept over his little ball and imagined that the spot where he lay in his cage, just that morning, was still warm. By the time I'd finished putting everything away, the bottle was two thirds gone. I drank the final third over a rerun of Home Alone, during which I somehow convinced myself that I'd abandoned April and ended up in a snotty mess of tears once more.

Fortunately, I'd made some carrot juice with ginger for Bill and left it in the café fridge, although by the time I'd reached the level of functioning human being, there wasn't much left. Ginger was supposed to be an aphrodisiac, wasn't it? Poor Bill and Judy. They'd never know what they'd missed. Woah! Shut up, Katie's treacherous brain. We did not want to go down that path of imagination again. Seriously, was I turning into some sort of pervert?

I put an apron on over my sparkly Christmas dress and shoved the turkey in the oven, almost forgetting to set the timer because I'd segued into googling "do they eat turkey in Turkey?" I smiled. That was such a Tony-like question. While I was at it, I had a quick peep on social media to check on Tony and April. Weirdly, nothing. Not even pictures of a scantily clad April living it large at a Christmas Eve party.

Not even a 'Merry Christmas to all my friends' post. I checked the JT Productions website. Error – not found. What on earth had befallen them? I checked the Facebook pages of close friends and family. They were all having a lovely Christmas and they definitely would not be grinning away in their Christmas jumpers if Tony and April had suffered a disaster. In fact, I was surprised to see that Tony's parents were spending the day with friends, rather than their darling son.

The back door opened and Mehmet came in, rubbing his hands and blowing warm breath on his fingers. 'Hello and happy Christmas, Katie. You look tired. Are you okay? Did you drink all the wine last night? You need fur of the dog.'

'Merry Christmas. I'm okay, thanks to some of Bill's carrot juice. The turkey's on and I was just about to make a latte. Do you want one?'

'Yes please. It is bloody freezing out there.'

I switched on the coffee machine and topped up the beans. While I steamed a jug of milk, Mehmet rummaged in the cupboard for proper cups, not the ridiculous glass things we gave the customers. He emerged holding two large mugs, which proudly declared themselves the property of 'The World's Best Farter' and 'Mum, Wife, Total F*cking Legend.' Mehmet thought for a moment, then handed me The World's Best Farter. 'Gifts from Ozzy,' he explained.

'Have you spoken to him yet?' I asked.

'No. He is still an immune avocado.'

'Incommunicado. Have you thought any more about contacting the police?'

'Tomorrow I will call them. Let us just enjoy today with our friends. And I have good news. Meryem called last night. She is coming home on 3rd January. This is exciting, yes?'

'That's the best news! I didn't tell you this because I didn't want you to worry about me leaving, but I wrote to Tony and April saying I'd like to go home once Meryem's back.'

Mehmet frowned. 'What have they said about this?'

'Nothing. They haven't replied. Looks like we both have immune avocados.' I grinned to let him know I was okay with not receiving a reply, although, on the inside, I was worried and a little hurt.

We were interrupted by the slamming of the back door. Judy and

Bill came into the kitchen, shivering despite the many layers they were evidently wearing. They looked like a couple of overstuffed cushions. For once, Judy was wearing a smart, padded jacket instead of her old gardening coat, although she still wore the ubiquitous headscarf under her woolly hat. Bill was always smartly dressed, but today he had a flower pinned to his overcoat. The two of them began to strip off layers of coats, hats, scarves and jumpers, all the while bickering about a game of Scrabble they'd been playing the night before.

'Judy,' said Bill in his gorgeous, gravelly lilt, 'you know that smoove isn't a word.'

'Course it is. Now, we're gonna smoove fings over and have a lovely day,' she replied, winking impishly at me. 'Merry Christmas, my darlings.'

Judy was wearing make-up in honour of the occasion. I didn't think I'd ever seen her looking anything other than slightly grubby. She walked dogs, did gardening and fetched shopping for, what she called, "the old people." Permanently dressed in an old coat, wellies and headscarf or hat, she had an air of the bag lady about her. However, not today. Today, she was kicking off the wellies and pulling a pair of slippers out of her handbag.

'Merry Christmas. You look great,' I told her.

'Oh, you ain't seen nothing yet,' she said, breezily. 'I'm just nipping to the loo. Back in a mo.'

While we waited for Judy, I put the potatoes on to boil and gave Bill the last of the carrot juice.

'I'm really sorry. There was loads but…bit of a hangover this morning.'

'Thank you for going to the trouble. Wow!'

For a moment, I thought Bill was completely blown away by my carrot juice, but I followed the direction of his gaze and there was Judy, resplendent in a pleated skirt, pretty blouse and cameo brooch, with a fabulous hairdo straight out of the 1940s. Joan Crawford waves. Definitely wow.

Bill hurried over to Judy and offered her his arm. 'May I escort the most beautiful woman in Putney to the ball?' he asked.

'Why, yes you can, kind sir,' she said. The two of them shuffled off to lay claim to armchairs and figure out how to access Netflix on

Mehmet's telly. Mehmet followed, to switch on the Christmas lights and offer them a glass of sherry.

Alone in the kitchen, I sipped my coffee and scrolled through that day's news. Lots of heart-warming stories about families reunited, a celebrity who'd spent vast sums creating a grotto for his daughter, record donations to homeless charities, could this be KT…hang on… rewind. There was a photograph of me with Scott and Aviana taken last night. We were well wrapped up against the cold and my head was turned to the side, so you'd have been hard pressed to say it was definitely me, but a KT sighting could not be a good thing. I googled 'KT chef' and, sure enough, there were articles speculating that KT was a woman. Bloody buggering barnacles. I took my phone through to Mehmet. 'Just as well I wrote to Tony. Look! I'm fifty percent outed!'

Mehmet put down the tinsel he was hanging around the television and Bill paused the YouTube clip of the Two Ronnies they were attempting to watch. Everyone crowded around the tiny phone screen.

'That could be anyone, love,' said Judy.

'Yes, but now they know I'm a woman. How long before they make the link between KT and Katie? I know you all call me Sarah in the café, but I wasn't always Sarah and it won't take much for one of the regular customers to remember and put two and two together.'

Bill looked at me like I'd totally lost it. 'Why worry about something you can't control? What's the worst that can happen? So, your family find out from the media. You already sent the hard message, child, when you ran. They either want you back or they don't.'

On hearing this, my first reaction was to shriek, 'They can't find out!' then I realised that Bill was right. I'd done what I could to hide from the press, cushion the blow and start making my way back to Tony and April. When I left, I'd been convinced it was for the right reasons yet, over time, I'd become convinced that I'd done irreparable damage to our relationships. However, the truth was probably somewhere in the middle. The ball was in the other court now and I had no control over the press or Tony and April's reactions, so there was little point in getting steamed up about things.

'You're right, Bill. I need to chill out. I've been so worried that I've wrecked things with Tony and April and I wanted the chance to explain to them. But if things happen, then they happen.'

Judy patted my arm and said, earnestly, 'You left them for a reason. Remember that and have confidence in it.'

I stared hard at her. This was the first time I'd seen her without a headscarf and she looked a little familiar.

'Judy?'

'Yes?'

'Have you ever written a book?'

Judy sniffed and turned her head away. 'I have no idea what you're talking about, love.'

'You do so! You're Irma Ford-Tinklebecker!'

She whipped her head back to face me and cackled. 'Alright, you got me.'

Mehmet was looking at us, confused, and I explained about the self-help book that had given me the resolve to stay on the train. 'How on earth…Why didn't you say something?' I asked Judy.

She shrugged and grinned mischievously. 'I wrote it years ago and only sent it off to publishers last year because I needed some money for a new boiler. Pension doesn't stretch to boilers. Anyway, they liked it and I sent them a photo of me from about thirty years ago for the cover. Made enough for the new boiler and gave the rest to charity.'

'But you're so…cantankerous.'

'I love a bit of cantanker, me. Amuses me no end.'

'Did you know about this?' I asked Bill.

'Yes. It's why I tell her off when she takes the cantanker too far.'

'Bloody hell.'

'No swearing in my café. Not even about annoying old ladies,' Mehmet chided. 'Here is the important thing. Are you still a racist, Judy?'

'Course not, love. I'm sorry, I just like winding you up. There you go, Katie. Getting outed ain't so bad.'

For a moment, Mehmet looked like he wanted to throttle her, but the impulse gave way to his natural bonhomie and he was soon beaming at Judy and telling her what a very good racist she was. I shook my head and sighed. Bonkers, the lot of them.

We decided to open our presents before lunch. Mehmet didn't normally exchange Christmas presents but, given the rather unusual situation in which we all found ourselves this year, he'd decided to join in with a few gifts from himself and Meryem. He had wrapped everything in brightly patterned silk scarves. For me, there was a selection of spices. Judy received a new umbrella and Bill, with his sweet tooth, a box of Turkish Delight. Half an hour later we each had a small pile of bubble bath, sweets and sundries.

Judy had given Bill a book of Christmas cracker jokes and he was merrily chortling away, reading the odd one out loud. As I took the turkey out, I heard him say, 'Listen to this one. What does Santa do in the garden? Hoe Hoe Hoe. Ha! Okay, what about -'

Spotting me, Mehmet cut him off. 'Here is the turkey. Shall we sit at the table?' To me, he whispered, 'Good timing. Thank you.'

The four of us sat patiently while Mehmet carved, then there was a friendly scramble for roast potatoes and a slightly less enthusiastic passing round of the sprouts. Crackers were pulled, resulting in much eye rolling as Bill insisted on reading out all the jokes. We compared and swapped the small plastic gifts and donned our paper crowns. Once more fit for wine, I popped a bottle of prosecco and filled our glasses. Mehmet didn't have any wine glasses, so we used the latte glasses.

'To dear friends,' Mehmet said, raising his glass.

'To dear friends,' we echoed.

'And to absent friends and loved ones,' I said.

'To absent friends and -'

The reply was cut off by a loud rap on the door. We looked at each other, all of us wondering who on earth could be calling at a closed café on Christmas Day.

'It must be Scott and Aviana,' said Mehmet, getting to his feet.

Taking his keys from his pocket, he pulled back the edge of the blind and peered through the window. We had no idea what he'd seen, but it caused him to hurry to the door and fumble in his haste to unlock it. He swung the door open and a large man dressed in black filled the frame.

'Mehmet Deniz?'

'Yes?'

'DS Ridley. This is my colleague, DC Mortimer. Can we come in?'

'Yes?'

DS Ridley stepped forward and Mehmet nervously shuffled back to let the two men enter. They were trailed by a couple of uniformed officers, who stood silently by the door. The room that, until a few moments ago, had been filled with laughter, was now silent as we watched the strangers, waiting uneasily for an explanation for the interruption.

DS Ridley spoke first. 'Mr Deniz, are you the father of Osman Deniz?'

'Yes, that's Ozzy. What's happening? Is my son alright?'

'And are you the owner of Café Deniz?' DS Ridley continued, ignoring Mehmet's questions.

'Yes. What is going on? Where is Ozzy'

'Mehmet Deniz, I'm arresting you on suspicion of money laundering. You do not have to say anything -'

The rest of the caution was lost as the room erupted.

Judy screeched, 'You leave him alone,' and launched herself at DS Ridley. DC Mortimer stepped between them and bore the brunt of a beating with a Christmas cracker. He grabbed her wrists, deftly snatched the cracker and firmly steered her back to the table. 'Sit down and stay there,' he ordered.

He had clearly mistaken Judy for a nice, little old lady, a notion which was soon dispelled when he turned his back and she began pelting him with roast potatoes. DC Mortimer spun around just in time to see a well-aimed potato flying directly towards his head. He ducked and the potato smashed into the forehead of DS Ridley. Mehmet took the opportunity to dart away from the policeman and scuttle around the table to stand behind myself and Bill. It was four on four and we had brussels sprouts.

A uniformed officer made a beeline for Judy, but Bill grabbed the turkey and stepped in front of her. 'Oh no you don't,' he cried, brandishing several pounds of cooked meat.

There was a brief pause, as we all wondered exactly what Bill intended to do with the turkey. I doubt even Bill himself knew. His body stiffened and he grasped the legs then, spinning like a shot putter, he hurled the bird at the oncoming policewoman. It hit her square in the face and, just for a second, she looked like a turkey in uniform. The bird slid slowly down, leaving a trail of grease and gravy, and the policewoman used her sleeve to wipe the goo from her eyes.

'Stop! Get back!' she shouted, through tears. Her uniformed colleague, seeing that she was in difficulty, had started towards Bill and Judy. He adopted a conciliatory tone, trying to persuade Bill to put down a plate that Bill had picked up and seemed ready to use as a frisbee. Lowering the plate, Bill moved to one side and Mehmet and I seized the opportunity to launch a hail of brussels sprouts at the cops.

'You will never take me, po-po!' shouted Mehmet.

'Po-po, Mehmet? Really?' I said, as I pulled a bowl of carrots towards me, ready for the next round.

'I think you bloody undercooked these, Katie darling,' he roared, as a sprout bounced off the nose of the policewoman.

'It's just as well I did.' Laughing, I turned to Mehmet, expecting a cheeky reply, only to see him clutching his arm and grimacing. He had gone very pale. I dropped my handful of green grenades and grabbed a chair.

'Sit here, Mehmet. STOP!' My anguished shriek caused everyone to pause. Judy, arm raised to throw another potato, whirled round. Bill, who had grabbed the gravy boat and was once more looking unsure as to his next move, froze. The police officers, hands protecting their faces, lowered their arms.

'I think Mehmet's having a heart attack. Quick, help me.'

Telling one of the officers to call an ambulance, DS Ridley strode quickly to Mehmet's side. 'Here, help me get him on the floor. Mr Deniz, we're just going to sit you on the floor so you don't hurt yourself. An ambulance is on its way. Do you have any medication?'

Mehmet shook his head, no. Supporting him on either side, we lowered him gently to sit on the floor, back against the wall.

'Is there any aspirin here?' asked DS Ridley.

'I don't know. I'll go look.'

DS Ridley signalled to one of the uniformed officers to accompany me and I set off to search the first aid box in the kitchen.

The cop positioned herself between me and the back door, ready to pounce should I decide to abandon my friend and make a run for it. I was wearing heels for the first time since I'd practised in my own kitchen all those months ago. If I did decide to take off, it would be more of a wobbly hobble than a run.

I don't know if Mehmet and Meryem were expecting disaster to strike, but the first aid box contained enough supplies to keep an army on its feet. There was every conceivable shape and size of sticking plaster and a range of painkillers, cough sweets, bandages and antiseptic. Sadly, no aspirin.

Returning to the dining area empty-handed, I surveyed the room. There was food everywhere. Three rather bedraggled police officers were being berated by Judy.

'Get away from him. Stop crowding him. This is your fault. What did you think you were doing, coming here on Christmas Day? It could have waited and now look at him. Look what you did. If he dies, I'll sue.'

'Nobody is going to die. Come on, sit down,' said Bill.

Judy ignored him and continued her rant. 'Money laundering, I ask you. This is the most honest man you'll ever meet. And look what you've done to him. He's at death's door and you're just standing there like a big pillock hoping you can arrest him. Well, you ain't arresting him. If there's anybody needs arresting, it'll be that little toerag Ozzy. Sorry, Mehmet. I've heard the way he talks to you. He don't treat nobody with respect. Bill, get your phone out. I want this all on video so I can put it on the Twitter.'

'Judy, neither of us know how to do videos on our phones and we're not even on Twitter. Now, will you please sit down. Mehmet needs calm and you're not helping.'

Judy crossed her arms, sighed a loud harumph and reluctantly sat down next to Bill. 'Can we at least watch the Queen's speech while we're waiting for the ambulance? Mehmet likes the Queen's speech. Don't you Mehmet?' She raised her voice, as though Mehmet's illness had rendered him partially deaf.

In the interests of peace and quiet, DS Ridley switched the television on. After a few adverts for Christmas specials and some llamas doing a bizarre synchronised dance around the BBC logo, the Queen came on to offer her reflections on the past year and wish the nation her best.

'This year, it has been more important than ever to cherish those we hold dear.'

I didn't listen to the rest. I was too busy watching Mehmet and keeping an ear cocked for the sound of sirens. Eventually, an ambulance drew up outside, blue lights flashing. Two paramedics arrived and asked us all to stand back while they did their assessment. With efficient kindness, they asked their questions, took Mehmet's blood pressure, gave him some medication and explained to him what was going to happen.

'I'll go with him,' I said, as the paramedics wheeled him into the ambulance.

'No.' DS Ridley put a hand out to prevent me from following. 'All three of you are under arrest for assault.' He nodded at his colleagues and they drew handcuffs from their belts. Over the sound of three police officers administering cautions, I could hear Judy protesting, 'I'm eighty-six, you know. I've got dementia an' all.'

The officers led us out of the building, towards the waiting police van. A small crowd had gathered outside and I spotted a few people filming us on their phones as we stepped into the van. Judy didn't help matters. She couldn't make the step up, so she stood outside the van yelling, 'Justice for the Putney Three!' until two officers grabbed an arm each and gave her a boost. Just before they closed the doors, she managed to shout a final call to action. 'Ain't you got homes to go to? It's Christmas Day for gawd's sake. Free the Putney Three!'

'That's enough now,' said Bill, reaching across the seat to hold her hand. 'We'll be okay. When we get to the police station, ask for a duty solicitor, then don't say anything until you've seen them.'

'You don't understand, Bill. I ain't been this excited since I set the pick 'n' mix on fire in Woolworths in 1983.'

'Dare I ask?'

'Lit a fag, dropped me lighter in the flying saucers and tried to put them out with a can of hairspray. Whoosh!' She grinned and winked at me. 'Got myself a fireman's lift, though.'

I obligingly laughed, but my heart wasn't really in it. I was too worried about Mehmet and confused about Ozzy. Was Ozzy on the run from the police? Is that why Mehmet couldn't find him? Something else was bothering me too.

My thoughts were interrupted by Bill. 'You're very quiet, Katie. Are you alright?'

'Yes, I was just thinking. You know, on the way into the van, I could have sworn I saw...never mind. How are you bearing up?'

'I'm fine. What's the worst they can do to a man my age? They're not going to jail me for throwing a turkey. Now, who wants to play I Spy?'

When we arrived at the police station, the officers opened the van doors to find three people bickering about something beginning with F.

'That does not begin with F and there's no way we could have guessed it.'

'Yes, it does. It's my middle name. Judy Effel.'

'Ethel. ETHEL. It begins with an E. There isn't even an F in it.'

The bickering continued as we entered the custody suite.

'And handcuffs does not begin with an A.'

'Cheating is not winning.'

'We can say what we like, but it's what we tell ourselves in here that counts.' Judy gestured to her heart. 'I'm a winner on the inside.'

'Don't you quote Irma at me, old lady. She…you…also said to be honest with yourself.'

I turned to the custody officer, stoic behind his high desk. 'Don't trust a word she says. She's a big cheat.'

'Name?' he asked Judy, completely disinterested in the finer points of I Spy.

'Judy Effel Loughton.'

'How do you spell it?'

'Eff Ell.' Judy cackled at her own joke.

The man sighed. 'Loughton.'

'L O U G H T O N.'

'Date of birth?'

'You should never ask a lady her age.'

This went on for some time. We established that Judy was, in fact, eighty-four and damned determined to see the duty solicitor. She asked four times and was eventually led to a cell, protesting all the way.

'You know she's going to be an absolute pain in the arse, don't you?' I asked the custody officer. 'Could you put Bill in with her? He's her responsible adult. Honestly, you'll have a much easier day if you put them in together.'

There was a buzzing noise. The custody officer pressed a button. The buzzing noise stopped. There was another buzz. The custody officer pressed a button and it stopped. The buzzing started again and I could hear Judy's muffled voice, 'Ain't nobody going to answer?'

The custody officer looked quizzically at Bill, as if trying to decide whether the old man posed a threat, then he sighed and slowly nodded. 'Alright. I'll make an exception.'

Bill and I were far more cooperative than Judy and I soon found myself in my own two star accommodation, complete with stainless steel corner toilet, surveillance camera and a faint smell of vomit. Oh great, I could have a wee on telly. I immediately resolved that I didn't care if my bottom was about to explode, there was no way I was doing a number two. But what if a number one unexpectedly turned into a number two? Because that sometimes happens to ladies. Although Tony had looked at me like I had two heads when I asked if men ever had unexpected number twos. Apparently, it was one or the other for men, and never the twain shall meet. Still, the facilities had improved in the decades since my last arrest. They were quite clean and there was a little bed roll. I settled down for a snooze to blow the last of the hangover cobwebs away.

Lord knows how many hours later, I awoke to the sound of my cell door opening. A policewoman told me that my solicitor was ready for me and asked if I'd like anything to eat or drink.

'A cup of tea would be nice.'

'I'll take you through to see your solicitor and bring you a cuppa,' she said, giving me a kind smile.

She took me to an interview room, where a grey-haired man in a very expensive suit sat in a plastic chair. He stood up to greet me, extending his hand. 'Charles Forbes, Forbes and Miller. I'm your solicitor.' He handed me an embossed business card. Very fancy.

I explained what had happened and said there was no point in denying it. I'd become caught up in the moment and thrown my fair share of sprouts. What I really needed was advice about Mehmet's arrest.

'They arrested him for money laundering. There's no way he was involved in that, but Ozzy would be. Mehmet was going to tell the police on him.'

I told Charles about Ozzy putting money in my bank account, about Mehmet hacking the accounting software and about the unusual transactions in the books.

'I reckon Ozzy has been using the café and me to launder money. I can give the police access to my bank account and give them the password Ozzy always uses. I'm not bothered what happens to me, but I can't have them arresting Mehmet for something so serious that I know for a fact he hasn't done. Also, someone needs to tell Meryem that Mehmet's ill. Can you find out if anyone has called her?'

'Okay, let's get the officers in and we'll see what they have to say.'

The interview went as well as it could have. I was suitably contrite and admitted to throwing sprouts. To be fair, it was one of the more monumentally stupid things I'd done. The police were just doing their jobs. At worst, we'd ruined their Christmas Day and at best, their colleagues would never let them live it down. When the tape was switched off, Charles explained that I had some information about the money laundering and I was willing to come forward as a witness. After a brief consultation, the interviewing officers told me that they would speak to DS Ridley. Would I like another cup of tea? Maybe a biscuit? A hobnob would be lovely, thanks.

Before they could leave, I asked if anyone had been in touch with Meryem. I was told that they'd spoken to an auntie, who was apparently very nosy, and she was rallying the family.

Two cups of tea later, DS Ridley arrived, dressed in what was clearly a borrowed clean shirt and tie. His belly hair poked through the gaps between the buttons and the collar was so tight I swear he had petechiae. I'd been half hoping they'd put me back in my cell because, with all the tea, I really needed to pee. However, as everyone was now being so nice to me, I didn't have the heart to put them to any more trouble. I just crossed my legs and gave DS Ridley my witness statement. He told me that Mehmet was doing well and that Ozzy had been arrested. Although he couldn't give me all the details, he warned me that Ozzy had been involved with an organised crime gang, importing large quantities of drugs into the UK. 'They're not known for intimidating witnesses, but you need to understand that you could be called to give evidence.'

'I do understand. I can't let Mehmet take any of the blame, though. I'll tell you everything I know.' And I did. The whole tale, from my arrival in London to my conversation with Mehmet that morning, although I may have skipped a few bits, like causing poomageddon in Rachel's bathroom. Despite DS Ridley seeming rather keen to get to the part about Ozzy's password, I made sure to include plenty of important details about FB. After this, I'd be going back to a cold, empty flat, so it was nice to talk about FB, even if DS Ridley thought a state funeral in Westminster Abbey was only a remote possibility.

DS Ridley said they would be releasing the Putney Three under investigation for the assault and took me back to the custody suite to retrieve my belongings. Opening the plastic bag that contained the few pieces of my life I'd managed to grab before they slapped the cuffs on me, it occurred to me that I had possibly hit rock bottom. A criminal record, a dead hamster and a dear friend laid low. I could really use a Tony and April hug right now. Even a spray of widdle from an overexcited Archie would be welcome. Also, there was a set of false teeth in this bag. Where on earth had they come from?

As I tottered out of the custody suite, I caught sight of my reflection in a glass door. Shiny dress, high heels, mascara like a panda. I couldn't help but be reminded of one morning, what seemed a lifetime ago, when I'd watched my daughter doing the same walk of shame. This time, though, there was no frazzled mother waiting to deliver a speech about growing up and taking responsibility. Instead, on walking through the door to reception, my heart leapt to see my partners in crime, Bill and Judy. They rushed to my side and enveloped me in hugs, Judy chanting, 'The Putney Three are Free.' I handed Judy her teeth and hugged them both back. For once, I was glad to be wearing high heels, as over their heads I could see someone else. Someone who made my heart leap just that little bit higher. 'Tony,' I gasped.

PART FOUR
KATIE, TONY, APRIL & ARCHIE

CHAPTER 19

Tony was feeling quite curmudgeonly. The bench was digging into the back of his thighs, he was bored and the elderly couple next to him were embroiled in a loud argument about a game of Snap they were playing. Well, the woman was loud. She was denouncing the man as having an unfair advantage because he had bigger hands than her. The man was telling her that this would settle things once and for all because there was no way she could cheat.

Tony was just about to stand up and stretch his legs, when the door to his right opened and a woman in a sparkly dress emerged. Katie. The old couple abandoned their game and rushed towards her, arms outstretched, and hugged her. Tony could feel his heart pounding hard in his chest, as a rush of adrenaline flooded through him. He'd thought long and hard about the moment he'd see Katie again, carefully planning what he would say. The one scenario he hadn't anticipated was shaky hands and wobbly legs. However, the shock of seeing his wife after so many months had set off a chain reaction and it took a few moments before he felt steady enough to get to his feet.

At first, he didn't think Katie had noticed him. She was smiling and laughing at the elderly woman, who appeared to be singing something about the Putney Three. Then Katie glanced over the heads of the overjoyed couple and he saw her do a slight double-take. Their eyes locked and she gasped, 'Tony.'

Katie detached herself from her enthusiastic welcoming party and approached her husband. He looked distinctly wobbly, which was unsurprising because her own heart felt like it was flip flopping all over the place. The sight of his face, with all its familiar lines, seemed to encapsulate all that she had missed over the months and she could feel the tears begin to well up.

'I'm so sorry,' she whispered.

Tony held out his arms and she took a tentative step forward, looking at him as if to check he really meant it. Through his own tears, he smiled at her and she took the final step, sinking into his chest, the two of them melding together in a familiar embrace borne of years of shared laughter, sadness and love.

'It's okay. I was an idiot. I'm sorry too,' he told her, stroking her hair.

They stood there, holding each other, stretching out the moment as they greedily drank in the smell and feel of each other, the closeness that they'd missed for so long. Until…

'SNAP! Hee hee. Them big hands didn't do you no good after all. Is it true what they say? Big hands, big -'

'Judy!' snapped Bill and Katie, in unison.

Katie introduced Tony to Bill and Judy. It felt very odd, this clash of her before and after lives. She had a thousand questions, but Tony forestalled her. 'We'll have plenty of time to talk things through later. First, we have a slight problem.'

Katie looked at him curiously. How could there be another problem before they'd talked about all the problems that had led them here? Didn't they already have their full quota of problems?

'There's a press battalion waiting for you outside. Something to do with you being a mystery chef?' said Tony.

'Oh, bugger. They've finally caught up with me then. How long was I in there?'

'Six hours.'

'The duty solicitor took his time.'

'That weren't no duty solicitor,' Judy interjected. She held out her phone and Katie read the text message.

'Merry Christmas, Putney Three. You're all over Facebook. Sending daddy's chum Charles to the rescue. Free the Putney Three. Aviana x' There was a photograph of Aviana and Scott dressed in Christmas jumpers, blowing kisses at the camera.

'Aw, bless them. They look so cute,' Katie cooed.

'Is that Aviana the model?' asked Tony. 'I can see we have a lot to catch up on. But first, this mystery chef business?'

'Right, yes. I was cooking at Mehmet's café while his wife was away and it just sort of took off. Aviana posted something and it went viral. I didn't want you finding out where I was through the media. Sorry, that's not as bad as it sounds. I'll explain better later. Anyway, I told her just to say I was a bloke called KT. Then the press started trying to find out who KT was. Someone photographed me with her yesterday, so it was only a matter of time before they cottoned on. I expect it all came out when we were arrested. It wasn't exactly discreet.'

'I know. I was there.'

'Aha! So, I *did* see you at the back of the crowd. I thought I was imagining things. Why were you there?'

'I've been looking for you for days.'

'I sent you my address.'

'You said you'd written it on the back of the Christmas card, but you forgot, you twit. I spent days tramping around every Turkish restaurant looking for you. I'd been to Café Deniz twice and they told me their chef was called Sarah.'

'Ah, long story. I'll fill you in later. Anyway, it looks like I'm no longer the Banksy of the culinary world, so we're going to have to run the gauntlet. I don't suppose anyone's called a cab?'

Bill pointed at Katie's face. 'I wouldn't normally comment on a lady's make-up, but I think you need some fixing. You take care of that and I'll take care of the rest.'

Twenty minutes later, they stepped through the front doors of the police station into a barrage of questions and flashes. Tony went ahead of Katie, clearing a path to a waiting limousine, and Bill and Judy brought up the rear, the driver quickly slamming the car door closed to cut off the stream of shouted questions.

'Where to?' asked the driver, settling himself back behind the wheel.

They froze or a moment, staring at each other. In the rush to leave, nobody had given any thought to where they were actually going. While Katie was fixing her make-up, Bill had asked Scott and Aviana for help with transport, hence the limo, and Tony had called April, who was currently clearing out the contents of The Dorchester minibar, to tell her he'd found Katie.

'I know,' she'd said through a mouthful of crisps. 'They're livestreaming it now. Can you hurry up and come out please? This is very boring.'

'Make sure you go to the corner shop in the morning and replace those crisps. They'll be charging a fortune,' Katie shouted into the speaker. She mentally kicked herself. Her first words to her daughter in months and she was wittering on about bloody crisps. 'I love you, darling.'

'Yeah, love you too, Mum. We need to have some serious words, though. After all the nagging you've done about *me* getting in trouble and here's Dad bailing *you* out. You really need to grow up and be responsible.'

Now, Katie slumped back in the plush limo seat, suddenly very tired. 'I know we're all frazzled, but would you mind if we go to the hospital to see how Mehmet's doing?'

Bill and Judy, who both looked like they needed an early night, asked if they could be dropped off at home on the way, but Tony was content to delay the family reunion while Katie checked on her friend. He knew they had a lot to talk about, a lot to catch up on, but it could wait.

The months following Katie's disappearance had wrought changes in him, chief among them a decision to be more open. Initially, he'd been closed off, and this had led to arguments with April. Like Katie, she wore her heart on her sleeve, and his determination to plough on without acknowledging the gaping hole left by his wife had frustrated April. She needed to talk about her mother. She needed to obsess over why Katie had left and explore how she felt about that. She needed to talk to the only other person who was experiencing the same loss. Tony, on the other hand, had spent most of the first month closeted in his study, working late into the night and formulating plans for how things would operate without Katie. He had left April to look after the house and Archie, without realising that, on a domestic level, he'd simply replaced his wife with his daughter. April had eventually marched into the study one evening and screamed at him that if he didn't come out and start talking, then she too would be leaving. Plus, she was not his fucking maid. She threw a book at him and yelled, 'Here, read this!' before storming out.

Tony had picked up the book. Some self-help nonsense by Irma Ford-Tinklebecker. He glanced at the cover. Hmm, probably some perfect American housewife, who'd done a course in counselling and thought she was better than the rest of them. Touchy feely bollocks. He considered tossing it in the bin, but stopped himself, reasoning that if the world is telling you something, then sometimes you need to listen. He wasn't doing very well on the husband and father front right now, so there was no harm in reading a book that might offer a few tips. He turned to a random page. "Are you telling yourself or are you listening to yourself? Sometimes we are so busy telling ourselves how things should be, that we forget to listen to ourselves and learn how things truly are. Understanding and accepting how you feel is an important step towards being able to connect with others. After all, being your best you isn't a solo journey. Like any good journey, you will need help along the way." Hooked, Tony had read on.

With Judy and Bill safely delivered to their respective homes, Katie and Tony suddenly found themselves alone.

'Is April okay? Is she mad at me?' Katie tentatively asked.

'She's fine. I think she was confused and angry at first, but about a month in she told me in no uncertain terms that she could see why you left. I'll be honest, I just locked myself away and did the bare minimum necessary. She ended up doing most of the housework and looked after Archie while I went away for work. In the end, she threatened to leave and I realised you were right. I'd been taking you for granted and we'd stopped being a partnership. Everything was revolving around my work and whatever was convenient for me. I hadn't been supportive over April. I was just taking the path of least resistance because parenting felt like too much effort and got in the way of work. It was easier to bung her the odd fiver, tell her to behave herself and leave the heavy lifting to you. I'm really sorry.'

'Lordy, I'm sorry too. I know how important your work is and without it, we wouldn't have the life we do. It must have been awful for you both when I left. I'm not sure I did a very good job of explaining it all in my letter.'

'Erm…about that…' said Tony, 'I only got the letter when we opened the Christmas cards. Sorry, you know how useless I am about opening post.'

Katie was silent for a moment, as she contemplated whether it was too soon to tell her husband he was an enormous twat. Yep. Things were probably too raw for name calling. 'So, if you didn't get the letter, what did you do?'

'Well, we realised a couple of days later that you were missing, so we called the police.'

'A couple of *days*?!'

'Oh, of course, you won't know about this. April had a huge fight in the pub and ended up in hospital.' Tony saw the look of alarm on his wife's face and hastened to reassure her. 'She was fine. A concussion and a few stitches. No lasting damage. We didn't get home until the Saturday morning and that's when we realised you hadn't come home the day before.'

'What was the fight about?'

'Something to do with a jealous ex-girlfriend and April going out with Davey.'

'For fuck's sake, Davey!'

'No, no, she wasn't really going out with Davey. It's a long story. I'll let her explain. Look, I think we're here.'

Tony was right. The car was turning into a road which led to a huge Victorian building. A vast expanse of red brick, with its modern cousin, an ugly 1960s panelled monolith, looming behind. Katie tapped on the dividing glass and asked the driver if he wouldn't mind waiting for them. He didn't mind. He was getting paid double time for this.

Pulling the limo to a halt in front of the pillared portico, the driver got out and came round the car to open the door. A group of smokers, puffing their way towards future hospital visits, stared at the couple exiting the vehicle, wondering if they were movie stars or VIPs. Katie had never felt so self-conscious in her life and felt some sympathy for people whose lives are played out in the public arena. She wanted to shout, 'Katie Frock, ordinary person,' before the realisation hit that she was no longer an ordinary person. Her life, too, was now being discussed in the newspapers and on social media. She'd checked her phone on the way to the hospital and, sure enough, there was a video of her arrest and headline after headline claiming to have identified the elusive KT. By morning, there would be interviews with old school friends, who would, no doubt, be eager to spill the beans about how she was the first one in their class to get fingered. Katie couldn't think of anything else she'd been first in at school.

As she and Tony headed to the reception desk, Tony muttered, 'We've been spending far too much time in hospitals and police stations this year.'

'That's your tax dollars at work. The Frock-Meadows have had their money's worth.'

'Meadows-Frock,' he grumbled, reflexively.

Their surnames had long been the subject of good-humoured debate. Katie hadn't wanted to bow to tradition and take Tony's surname, yet neither of them could agree on the double-barrelled version. The one thing they did agree on was that it didn't really matter. They could call themselves the Broccoli-Parsnips, as long as they were happy. Which, in the main, they had been.

They found Mehmet, propped up in bed and being fussed over by a gaggle of elderly women. His face broke into a huge smile when he saw Katie and he held out his arms for a hug. Relieved to see him looking well, she happily squeezed him until, fighting for breath, he wheezed, 'Okay, you can let bloody go now.'

Katie introduced Mehmet to Tony, and Mehmet introduced them both to the nosy aunties.

'What have the doctors said?' Katie asked.

'Bloody tests, test and more tests. Don't worry, Katie darling. They poked and prodded me. High blood pressure only. They are saying maybe it was a panic attack and they will do some more poking tomorrow, when everything is open again.'

'I'm so relieved. Is Meryem coming home?'

'Yes. First flight on Tuesday. I am so happy to see her, but I am so worried about Ozzy. And I am ashamed. I was a fool to let him look after the money.'

'You weren't a fool, Mehmet. He's your son, so how could you have known? At least you'll have Meryem to support you. Have the police been?'

'Oh yes, they left just before you arrived. Resisting arrest and assault. I have to go to see them when I am out of here. They told me that you gave them the whole story and I am glad. It is better that all the cats are out of the bags now.'

'I'm sorry that it doesn't help Ozzy, but I couldn't bear for them to think that you were involved. Listen, don't worry about the café. We'll clean it up, won't we Tony? Have you seen that KT has been outed?' Katie got out her phone and showed Mehmet the video of the arrest. Mehmet's shoulders began to shake and, at first, she thought she'd triggered another attack. She glanced at Tony, about to ask him to get a doctor, when Mehmet began to laugh.

'Oh, that is bloody priceless. Free the Putney Three,' he chortled, wiping tears from his eyes.

They left Mehmet, still merrily giggling, and made their way back to the limo.

'Your place or mine?' said Tony.

'Yours. Definitely yours. I can't wait to see April.'

The limo dropped them off at The Dorchester. Katie didn't think she'd ever been in such a posh hotel. She was quite looking forward to this, her only regret being that Roberta couldn't come along for the ride. However, looking at her gorgeous, amazing husband, she decided that, tonight, there may be no need for Roberta.

'Why were you wandering around Putney on Christmas Day?' she asked, while they waited for the lift. 'Everything's closed.'

'I don't know. I just couldn't sit still, doing nothing. We got your card and decided to come down here to look for you. I didn't want to ruin April's Christmas, so I booked the best hotel I could find and we wandered around, asking in every café and restaurant. We even tried the kebab shop on Martin Road, not that I could imagine you working in there. The owner made us buy a kebab before telling us he'd never heard of you. Just as well I checked the Scores On The Doors before I ate it! Anyway, I was so antsy this morning that April told me to go out for another wander around. I'm glad I did. Mind you, it was a shock seeing you being put in the back of a police van.'

'From police van and cell to limo and The Dorchester in one day. I reckon I'm doing quite well.' Katie grinned at him and stepped into the lift.

April was overjoyed to see her mother. She jumped off the bed, almost spilling a tray of tiny Christmas puddings that were balanced precariously on a bedside table, and glued herself to Katie in a tight hug. Yes, Mum was an utter pain in the arse for leaving her and yes, Mum needed a good telling off, but, for now, April's heart was bursting with joy. She whipped her phone out and took a selfie, all three of them squashing their heads together and grinning like maniacs. 'Look who's back!' she announced on Instagram.

Tony ordered bottles of champagne and they sat on April's bed, eating tiny Christmas puddings, an old Christmas movie playing in the background, while they caught up on all their news. April couldn't remember ever having had such a happy Christmas. Admittedly, she had drunk rather a lot of the mini-bar and Dad would kill her when he saw the bill, but this really was the best Christmas ever.

Much later, having tucked a comatose April into bed, Katie and Tony repaired to Tony's room.

Katie looked around at the plush décor, poking her head into the bathroom and eyeing the marble. 'This place must cost a fortune. How on earth can we afford it?'

'It's alright. I sold Archie.'

'You what!'

Tony couldn't keep a straight face. 'Just joking. I sold the company.'

'You what!'

'Sold the company. Jack married Mia and wanted to move to Italy. I needed to make changes at home. So, we agreed to sell up.'

'Mia?'

'Italian lady. Lovely woman. Huge…diamonds. Anyway, her family are some sort of nobility, so Jack's currently swanning around some palazzo, getting fat on pasta. Phones me once a week to remind me I'm still a twat.'

That night, Katie and Tony talked and talked and talked. They did other things too and Katie decided that she'd been perfectly correct, no Roberta required. There was a tense moment, when Tony suggested they try out the shower together. In the end, they agreed that a bath would be far safer, and the early hours of Boxing Day found them steeped in hot water and bubbles, wondering if they should call the caretaker to extract one of Tony's exceedingly long toes from the tap.

Tony had been circumspect as to what he'd been doing since he sold the company, telling Katie, 'All in good time.' She didn't press him, choosing instead to simply enjoy the moment. And enjoy they did until, spooning in a tangle of sheets and blankets, they fell fast asleep.

CHAPTER 20

The tube was almost empty on Boxing Day. All the sensible people were at home with their families, rather than trekking across London to clean up the aftermath of a food fight with the police.

Tony, Katie and April stopped at the flat to collect some supplies, then made their way to the café. A few reporters were hanging around the front, so they slipped in the back door. Katie switched on the coffee machine and they went into the main café area to survey the damage.

The table was almost stripped of food, but the chairs lay, tipped over, on a floor that was slick with vegetables and turkey grease. The turkey itself had landed on a statue of a reindeer and hung, suspended from the antlers, like a grotesque nosebag.

'Right,' said April, tying her hair into a neat ponytail, 'let's start by cleaning the area by the door. Then we can move the furniture into the clean part and start on the rest.'

'Alright, Miss Bossy Boots. Who put you in charge?' said Katie.

'I've discovered that I quite like being in charge. I'm far better at telling other people what to do than I am taking orders.'

'She really is,' said Tony. 'Lord help me if I forget to do the dishes when it's my turn. It's your fault, you know. You created this monster.'

'Come on parents. Chop chop. Dad, you start sweeping. Mum, get the mop.'

They'd barely started cleaning when Katie heard a knock at the back door. She rushed to unlock it and saw, to her relief, that it was Scott and Aviana.

'Come in. I thought you were journalists. We saw a few hanging around the front earlier.'

'We come bearing gifts,' said Aviana, pulling some bin bags from her expensive handbag. 'We hoped someone would be here. Thought we could help with cleaning up.'

'It's so good to see you both. Come through and I'll introduce you to Tony and April. They turned up out of the blue yesterday and… well…I think I'm going home.'

Aviana gave Katie's arm a little squeeze and said how happy she was. Scott proffered a hand, which Katie ignored, opting instead for a hug. He stood stiff and unyielding, but when she released him, he said, 'That was surprisingly okay.'

April, of course, recognised Aviana immediately. There was a brief OMG moment, where she became completely tongue-tied, although she soon regained her equilibrium when Aviana explained that she'd never done cleaning before and could April please tell her what to do. Bossy April immediately asserted herself, handing Aviana a bin bag and a cloth and pointing her towards the table. Scott was packed off to the kitchen to do the dishes.

Bill and Judy arrived, ostensibly to help, but in reality, to sit around pointing out the bits that the cleaning crew had missed. Bill eventually pitched in with drying the dishes. However, Judy clearly felt that the one thing they needed today was an annoying person. She switched on the television and found an episode of Judge Judy.

'Now, there's a lady who knows what's what,' she announced to the room. 'There ain't enough Judys in the world. Well, there's Richard and Judy. But they ain't on the telly no more. She's a lovely woman. Why ain't she on the telly no more?'

It was like a stream of Judy consciousness, set against the noise of a blaring television. Within minutes, everyone was shouting at Judy to put her hearing aid in and turn the telly down.

'Sorry, I can't hear you. The telly's too loud.'

The argument was resolved by Tony, who wrestled the remote control out of her grasp and switched the thing off.

'Go into the kitchen and make the coffees,' he told her.

'But I don't know how to work the machine. I'm eighty-nine, you know.'

'No, you're not. Get Scott to do it and take over the dish washing from him. I assume you know how to work a tap and a dish cloth?'

Judy smiled beatifically at him. 'Did you two not…,' She mimed a nudge and a wink, '…last night? Is that why you're so grumpy? I may be eighty-five, but at least I'm getting some.'

'Judy!' Bill was standing by the kitchen door, looking mortified.

'Coming, lover boy,' she cooed, throwing a stage wink in Tony's direction. Unrepentant to the last, she shuffled off to annoy Bill and Scott.

Tony turned to Katie. 'Is she always like that?'

'Pretty much.'

'It's odd, though. There's something familiar about her. I can't quite put my finger on it.' Tony gave himself a little shake and picked up his sweeping brush. 'Never mind. I'm sure it will come to me.'

By late afternoon, the café was looking spick and span. They had all downed tools and were sitting at the table, drinking coffee and watching Home Alone.

Katie gazed around the room, wondering if this would be the last time she saw the café. They couldn't reopen without Mehmet and, even if they could, there was nowhere to put the armchairs and television. The police had seized Meryem's iPad, where Katie had stored all her recipes and cooking tips. She imagined the contents would come as something of a disappointment to DS Ridley. He'd be excited to find evidence of drug trafficking and all he'd get was a bloody great set of instructions for making crème anglaise without lumps.

'Tony and April are going home tomorrow,' she told her friends. 'I'm staying on for a few days. I have to collect FB's ashes and I want to see Mehmet and Meryem before I go. And I should phone Rachel to let her know what's happening.' A whole London life to unpick.

'You'll see us before you go, won't you?' asked Scott, anxiously.

'Course I will. And it's not like I'm disappearing off the face of the earth.'

'Yeah, because you'd never do that, would you?' April gave her mum her best sarcastic smirk.

'Well, I for one will miss you,' interjected Bill, before an argument could erupt. 'We both will. We all will.'

He put an arm around Judy, who nodded in agreement. 'Cheer up, you lot. It's oh voyeur, not goodbye,' she said.

'Au revoir,' corrected Bill.

'Tomato, tomayto. Come on, love, I'll let you walk me home. If McDonalds is open, we can share a bag of chips.'

'Fries.'

'This is England. I'll have none of that foreign muck.'

There was a flurry of coats, hats, scarves and gloves, as everyone got ready to leave. The others were going out the back door when Judy put a hand on Tony's arm to stall him.

'I know the two of you have gone through a tough time and there's a lot of making up to do. Yet I can see how much love there is between you. Hold on to that and you'll be okay. You're a good man, I know it. You need to know it too. Forgive her, forgive yourself and you'll both be fine.'

Tony was surprised to hear such wise words from such an annoying old woman. 'Thanks Judy. You know, I was saying this earlier, I feel like I know you from somewhere.'

'That's because I'm the woman of your dreams. Hear that, Bill? I'm the woman of Tony's dreams.' Judy cackled and rushed to catch up with Bill.

Pulling the door to, Tony reflected that leaving this place and these friends would be hard for Katie. Almost as hard as it had been for her to leave him and April. Wherever she went, she sowed the seeds of warmth and love. All those months ago, she'd felt like she'd lost herself. Tony had never fully subscribed to the notions of 'finding yourself' and 'being on a journey', but he'd make an exception here. He could see how Katie shone when they were all together in the café. With these people and in this place, she was the girl he had fallen in love with. Tony hoped the changes he'd made at home would help her hold onto that girl when she came back.

April walked down the back lane, arm in arm with her mother. 'You're definitely coming home, aren't you Mum?'

'Yes. Definitely,' said Katie.

'Good. Because Dad was miserable when you were gone, nobody would come to the police station with me and Archie has adopted a teddy. And when I say adopted, I mean he really, really loves that teddy. Teddy has to be washed every few days, otherwise he gets…crispy.'

'Goodness, how undignified. I shall have words with him. Right, let's get back to the flat and pack my bags. Your father said he's booked The Dorchester for me until next week and I've never been known to turn down the chance to steal good toiletries.' Katie tightened her arm and pulled April a little closer. 'I do love you both. That never went away. I wonder what I'll do when I get back, though.'

Bloody hell, thought April, she better like what Dad's got planned.

New Year's Eve fireworks lit the London sky and the air was filled with the smell of gunpowder, as crowds gathered along the Thames to see in 2022. Further upriver, a small group of people gathered around a tiny, wooden longboat, arguing about whether they should set it on fire. One of them was holding a phone, from which an Australian voice complained loudly that she was missing lunch for this, so could they please get on with it?

Katie reverently opened a box and tipped FB's ashes into the longboat.

'I'm sorry, little friend. You were such a good hamster and we will miss you forever. We couldn't bury you somewhere fancy because we don't want to get arrested again. So, may you go in peace the Viking way, only we're not setting fire to anything because we don't know how to get you in the water if the boat's in flames and, anyway, Mehmet forgot the matches. Any last words for FB, Rachel?'

Rachel's tanned face filled the phone screen. 'Little mate, we're gonna miss you. When I get back, it won't feel right without you. You had a happy life full of toys and dog biscuits. Go with honour, into the water.'

Judy, Bill, Mehmet, Meryem and Scott aimed their torches at the river and Aviana turned the phone so that Rachel could watch while Katie gently lowered the longboat into the river. Together, they looked on as the small vessel bobbed out of range of the torchlight.

'Bye, FB,' shouted Rachel. Then, 'Lovely to see you all, but there's a barbie with my name on it, so if you don't mind…Happy New Year.'

When Rachel had gone, the friends made their way back to Putney Bridge, where a driver was waiting to take Scott, Aviana and Katie back to their respective abodes. Katie was going home tomorrow and this was possibly the last time they would all be together.

'Oh, love,' said Judy, 'I ain't going to lie. I won't be coming up North to visit you. Too cold, what with my chilblains. And them trains! Lord knows what's been on the seats. I hope you'll stay in touch and come down to us.'

'Same goes for both of us,' said Bill. 'Except it's not chilblains, it's old age. Please call and let us know how you're getting on.'

'Are you saying I'm old? I'm only seventy-nine, I'll have you know!'

Bill and Judy wandered off, arm in arm, bickering happily.

Katie smiled fondly after them. 'Next time I'm down, it'll probably be for their wedding. Please say you'll persuade them to get married.'

'I think we've had enough stress for one lifetime. Can you imagine Judy planning a wedding? What is it they say? Bridezilla.' Meryem laughed at her own joke. 'Thank you for looking after everything while I was away. I'm so sorry about Ozzy.'

'Please don't be sorry, Meryem. You and Mehmet gave me more than you can ever know.'

'I tell you what I'll give you. A bloody big thump in the ear if you don't get in the car. It is like metal monkeys out here.'

'Oh, Mehmet, I'll miss you most of all.' Katie hugged Mehmet tightly. 'Thank you for everything.'

Mehmet quickly ran a finger under one glistening eye. 'Now look what you've done. I am leaking. Go now, Katie darling. Call us tomorrow so we know you are home safe.'

Katie got into the back seat of the car, beside Scott and Aviana, closing the door behind her with a resounding thunk. As the car pulled away, she twisted around in her seat to wave goodbye, but Mehmet and Meryem were already hurrying away, arm in arm, through the cold night.

By the time the car reached The Dorchester, Katie had said her goodbyes to Scott and Aviana. Scott had reluctantly granted her a final hug and Aviana had taken their final selfie together.

Walking into the hotel lobby, Katie encountered a group of cheerful drunks, who were performing an impromptu Auld Lang Syne. Grabbing her hands, they swept her into their circle and she soon found herself enthusiastically bellowing the official English version of the old Scottish favourite, 'We'll tak a cup of la, la, la, la, la, la, la Auld Lang Syne.' A gloriously uplifting end to her adventures and sign from the gods that it was time to look forward to the next chapter. Going home.

CHAPTER 21

The journey back North was very different from the one South, when Katie had been filled with self-doubt and anxiety. The woman who arrived in London was hesitant and unsure of herself. The woman leaving London had gone viral, thrown sprouts at a policeman and grassed up a drug trafficker to save a friend. In a city full of strangers, she had made a surrogate family and created a life for herself. This time, Katie threaded her way through the crowds and negotiated the Kings Cross ticket barrier with ease.

She pulled her suitcase along a platform that must surely be the longest platform in the universe. Coach M. Coach M. Seat 12. M12. She'd treated herself to first class. After nearly a week in The Dorchester, nothing else would do. Nevertheless, she'd made sure to book a table seat, in the hope that a nice train BFF would come along.

Ah, here it was, coach M. Katie stashed her suitcase, settled into her comfortable chair and took out her phone to text Tony. 'On train. See you in a few hours. Love you xx' The reply came immediately. 'Okay.' She reflected that Tony may be more in touch with his emotions these days, but his texting clearly hadn't improved.

She had just begun to shift the contents of her handbag so she could get to her book, which was firmly wedged between her purse and Roberta, whom Katie had decided could not be trusted to behave herself if left in a suitcase, when a very well-groomed woman in her mid-fifties took the seat opposite. Katie flashed her a quick smile and continued to tug, trying to dislodge the book. The woman leaned across the table and, in a low voice, said, 'Are you alright? Can I help?'

'I'm okay. Just…one…more…pull…should do it…ah!'

Roberta clearly could not be trusted in a handbag either, for she leapt out and hit the woman, still leaning across the table, square in the face. Roberta bounced off the woman's forehead, bounced off the table and was about to make a bid for freedom, when Katie snatched her up and stuffed her back into the handbag, where she lay merrily buzzing away.

'Sorry about that,' said Katie, frantically trying to find the off switch. 'Just as well I washed her this morning.' She glanced at the woman, who sat frozen, a look of astonishment on her face. Oh bugger, thought Katie, am I about to get chucked off the train? She wasn't sure how she'd break that one to Tony and April. Sorry, not coming home after all, assaulted fellow passenger with a sex toy.

'I know who you are!' the woman exclaimed. 'You're that KT person.' She extended a manicured hand. 'Daniella Dankworth. I believe you told my PA to eff off.'

Katie extended a sticky hand, thanks to a rogue packet of sweets which had burst somewhere in the depths of her bag. 'Oh. Sorry about that too. I'm not doing very well with you, am I? Can we start again? Katie Frock.' She withdrew her sticky hand from Daniella's, rummaged around in her bag some more and extracted a packet of wipes, proffering a small damp square like it was a flag of surrender.

Daniella took it, wiped her hands then wiped her forehead. 'No problem. You learn to be pretty robust in the food world. Now, tell me all about what inspired you to cook Turkish food.'

The next three hours sped by as the two women shared recipes, kitchen horror stories and celebrity gossip. As Aviana was the only celebrity Katie knew, her part in the celebrity gossip was relatively minor. Daniella, however, was a mine of useless trivia and, by the time they arrived at their destination, Katie had the low down on who had permanent garlic breath, who swore by crushed bananas as a pile treatment and consequently left wet patches on chairs wherever they went, and who groped Daniella's bottom at a film premiere then had to leave early due to a broken toe caused by a well-placed stiletto heel. 'It was the eighties, darling. We had to defend ourselves against the perverts.'

Daniella didn't seem perturbed by the experience and it put Katie in mind of Maggie and her stoicism in the face of the casting couch. Never mind that these women weren't angry or didn't think of themselves as victims. Never mind that they were able to laugh it off. Katie was angry on their behalf. Sensing this, Daniella told her, 'It seems strange now, but at the time this sort of thing was normal. Socially acceptable, even, especially in show business. Things are so much better these days and there's no point in me getting angry about something that happened thirty-five years ago.'

Katie told Daniella about Maggie, silently praying that Maggie would forgive her for blabbing. Daniella frowned. 'Yes, that sort of thing used to happen a lot. It sounds like your friend dealt with it in her own way, with some humour. Still, nowadays you'd hope that man would be jailed.'

'I doubt Maggie would want to rake it all up again. I think she was pleased enough that she'd almost bitten his Bobby off.'

As the train pulled into the station, the two women exchanged numbers. Daniella helped Katie off the train with her suitcase and they made their way to the ticket barriers.

'I always hate these barriers. I can never get my ticket to work,' Daniella confided.

'There's a trick to that. Follow me.' Katie led Daniella towards a bored looking guard, slouching by the wide barrier. 'Excuse me,' she said. 'Can you tell us which tickets we're supposed to put in the machine? I can't seem to find the right one.'

The guard straightened up and pressed a button. 'Happy New Year, Katie. Happy New Year, Daniella,' he said.

Katie thought he was going to salute, but he seemed to stop himself and stepped aside to let them through. At that moment it hit Katie. He'd known her name. She was famous! How very weird.

She looked around the concourse and spotted two familiar faces by the arrivals board. Having bade Daniella a fond goodbye, with promises of getting together to plan an appearance on Daniella's show, Katie rushed as fast as her suitcase wheels would allow towards Tony and April. There were hugs and kisses all round, then Tony led the way to the car.

'Was that Daniella Dankworth?' April asked. Katie nodded, the cold air outside the station and the effort of wheeling the suitcase at Tony's pace having stolen her breath.

'You're, like, a celebrity or something now. It's dead strange you knowing famous people. Is Dad going to have to iron your stuff while you swan off around the world? Because that would be funny. It hasn't even been a week since you were all over the news, you know, and I've got thousands of followers on Insta.'

As Katie listened to April babble on about whether they'd get invited to celebrity parties and what would she even wear to a celebrity party, she couldn't help smiling to herself, recalling that only six months ago, her daughter had called her a drudge. At the time, Katie had privately agreed with her, yet she knew that neither of them saw her like that now. She wondered what the next six months had in store and realised that, far from thinking of life going back to normal, she was viewing her homecoming as the beginning of the next big adventure.

Tony hoisted the suitcase into the car boot. He was so relieved to finally have Katie back, but also a little worried about the next part. Normally when he was worried, he would do something to occupy his mind until the feelings went away or he came up with a practical plan. However, he had learned the hard way that it was better to get it out there. As Katie got into the front passenger seat, he called April over. 'I'm worried she won't like this. Do you think we should leave it until tomorrow? Give her time to settle in at home first?'

'Dad, you made the first impulsive decision of your life. She's going to love it.'

'Okay, but if she hates it, I'm telling her it was your idea.' Tony grinned at April to show he was joking and got into the car.

'Seatbelts on? Everyone ready?' he asked. April and Katie agreed that they were good to go. 'Before we get home,' Tony said, 'we're going to make a quick detour. April and I have something we want to show you.'

'Ooh, surprises. I like surprises. Hang on, you haven't sold the house have you? Because I would have to get back on the train to London.'

'Nothing dreadful. Your kitchen is still there, I promise.'

'Righty-ho, then. Lay on Macduff.'

Forty-five minutes later, Tony pulled into the Plough car park. He glanced at April in the rear-view mirror. Their eyes met and they both suppressed a nervous smile. Katie was wittering on about how lovely it would be to see Maggie and Bob and how beautiful the pub looked in the winter sunshine, with all the decorations, and were they going to have lunch because she was absolutely starving.

'We'll see about lunch. First, let's get ourselves inside,' said Tony.

They made their way across the car park, trying not to slip on the frosty tarmac. The pub door was festooned with a Christmas wreath and, as she pushed it open, Katie was assailed by the pub smells of beer and food. She inhaled deeply, glorying in the familiarity of it all. There was Davey, propping up the bar as usual, but looking surprisingly smart and sober. There was Maggie, giving someone a telling off. There was Bob, cleaning glasses behind the bar and smiling fondly at his firebrand wife. Who was making the pies, she wondered.

Maggie was the first to spot them. She came rushing over to welcome Katie back. 'Although, you could have warned me about that daughter of yours. She's a wee demon in the kitchen. Runs the place with an iron fist. Even Bob does as he's told. And Bob hasn't done as he's told since 1993!'

From behind the bar, an unrepentant Bob laughed and waved hello. As the group made their way to the bar, he rang the closing time bell. Every customer stopped what they were doing and looked around, confused. Surely the pub wasn't closing? They'd only just started on their pies.

'Hear ye, hear ye,' shouted Bob, like an olde worlde town crier. 'Today we welcome back our Katie and we have an important announcement to make.'

Tony and April stepped forward. Bob handed them a sheet of paper and together they said:

. . .

'Five months ago you disappeared,
    And left us in a state,
    We couldn't work the washing machine,
    Or mop, or clean a plate.
    Somehow, we learned to function,
    And it made us realise,
    How well you had looked after us,
    And baked delicious pies.
    We're glad that you've come home,
    Now we'd like to share our news,
    Bob and Mags are retiring,
    They're going on a cruise.
    The pub in which you're standing,
    Has new names on the doors,
    Those names are Frock and Meadows,
    Yes, the pub is ours and yours.

April stepped forward and handed Katie a blue box, decorated with an oversized silver bow. 'We bought the pub, Mum. You can cook whatever you want. We can do it together.'

The look on her face was filled with such vulnerable hope that Katie could feel herself welling up. She looked at Tony and could see him anxiously biting his lip. She opened the box and peered inside. It was the key to the front door of the pub.

Smiling through her tears, she managed to hiccough, 'Thank you. Oh, thank you.'

Relieved, Tony came over and put an arm around her. 'I believe the next round's on us,' he shouted.

As happy patrons scuttled to the bar to claim their free drink, Maggie came over with a bottle of champagne.

'Sit yourselves down and pour a glass,' she told them. 'There's someone missing from this celebration and I'm just away to get him.'

A few minutes later, she led that someone into the pub. He was small, hairy and clutching a rather crispy-looking teddy in his mouth. Katie leapt out of her seat. 'Archie!'

Archie was overjoyed to see his favourite human. He wanted to punish her for going away and had given much thought as to how many weeks he should spend ignoring her when she came back. However, his doggy heart was now filled with such happiness that he decided to put his plans on hold in favour of licking her entire face and doing an excited pee on the carpet.

As Katie scrabbled around on the floor, trying to mop up the wet patch, it occurred to her that if fame ever went to her head, she need only remind herself of this moment. Job done, she disposed of the damp cloth and tissue, and returned to the table, where Maggie, Bob, Tony and April were waiting for her.

Tony raised a glass. 'To Maggie and Bob. May your retirement dreams come true.'

'Maggie and Bob,' they chorused, lifting their glasses.

Maggie drank deeply, wiped her lips and raised her own glass. 'To April, Tony and Katie. Oh, and Archie. May you all live happily ever after.'

EPILOGUE

Six months later.

Tony dashed into the study, coat tails flying and his tie askew. 'Hurry up. The car's outside. I told April you're running late and we'd meet her there.'

Katie waved him away and turned back to the screen. 'Sorry, I have to go, Mehmet. We've had the new logos through for the KT's franchise. I'll email them to you. I'll be in London on Thursday to record Daniella's new show and I'll come over to the café afterwards. Give my love to Meryem.' She blew a kiss to her friend and business partner, and closed the screen.

'Come on,' shouted Tony, who was hovering impatiently by the front door.

Katie slipped her feet into a pair of outrageously expensive shoes, luxuriating in the knowledge that she'd earned every penny she'd paid for these. No matter that Tony had wailed 'HOW MUCH?', the agreement stood. All money went into one pot, all decisions were made as a family, all parties were consulted, everything out in the open and up for discussion – except when it came to shoes. Now that Katie had posh places to go, she needed posh shoes. Well, perhaps not *needed*, but getting dolled up for posh places certainly made for some great shopping trips with Suzy. Katie brushed an Archie hair off the front of her dress, donned her hat and pronounced herself ready.

Half an hour later, April stood by the altar. She could see Mum sitting in a pew, hat slightly askew and lipstick on only her top lip. Honestly, you'd have thought she could have made more of an effort. She was probably so thrilled with the new shoes, she forgot to finish her make-up. Even now, she was looking down at the flipping things. She'd barely glanced at April and it was April's big day! What was the point in trussing yourself up in endless metres of fine satin if your mother was more interested in her own shoes?

April looked at Davey. He'd turned out to be rather handsome. It had taken quite a bit of effort to get him off the booze and into shape, but he definitely looked rather tasty in a frock coat. Dad looked handsome too, in a dad way. He'd given Davey so much support in getting the furniture restoration business going. When Becca wrote that article, none of them had anticipated that glossy magazines would come calling. Poor Davey had barely been able to cope with the sudden interest and the influx of orders. It all came at a good time for Dad, though. Helping Davey had helped him too.

Suddenly, organ music filled the air and everyone stood. Startled from her inner musings, April stepped back and looked down the aisle. Da da de dum, da da de dum. There was Becca, radiant in white satin, her father by her side. April glanced at Davey and could see him holding back tears. Even Dad, the best man, was looking a touch misty-eyed. She clasped her small bridesmaid's bouquet tightly to stop herself from flapping her hands, as tears sprang to her own eyes. Get a grip, April. In twenty years' time, Davey and Becca would be looking at their wedding album and saying, 'Here's another one of April with mascara down her face.'

That evening, the grounds of the Northumberland Grand were filled with the sounds of music and laughter, as hundreds of guests danced the night away in the Grand marquee. Inside the hotel itself, a young man was waiting, impatiently, outside the ladies' toilets. He banged on the door. 'Come on, April, I'm dying out here.'

April opened the door and beckoned him in. 'Come in. It's okay, there's nobody here.'

They stood by the sinks and eyed each other anxiously, the tension in the air palpable. April broke the silence. 'Curtis, whatever happens, I just want you to know that I love you and I'm the luckiest girl in the world to have met you. When you interviewed me at the police station, I wasn't nervous about the fight. I was nervous because I fancied the pants off you and I was trying to figure out how to ask you out.'

Curtis reached over and brushed her cheek. 'I'm glad you didn't, because I would have had to say no. Against the rules and all that. But if you're the luckiest girl, then I must be the luckiest bloke. I'm so glad I went to the Christmas karaoke at the Plough and got the chance to ask *you* out.'

They both looked down at the plastic stick on the counter. It was time. April turned the stick over. Two lines. 'Fuck-a-doodle-do, Mum's going to kill me.'

AFTERWORD

I hope you enjoyed this book. If so, I would be grateful if you could take a moment to pop a review or a few stars on Amazon.

You can hear more about my books and get access to exclusive material by subscribing to my newsletter via my website, https://theweehairyboys.co.uk . You also can drop me a line using the contact information on the website or treat yourself to a signed copy of one of my books.

Did you know that there's a Losers Club on Facebook for fans of the Losers Club series? Yes, you really can join Losers Club, although our fellow Losers are far more interested in cake and chocolate biscuits than diet sheets. I think it is best described as a warm, friendly and creatively bonkers place. Please do join us.

Other than this you can find me at:

Facebook Growing Old Disgracefully (blog)

Yvonne Vincent - Author

Instagram @yvonnevincentauthor

Threads @yvonnevincentauthor

X (Twitter) @yvonnevauthor

Tik Tok @yvonnevincentauthor

Amazon Yvonne Vincent Author Page

Until the next adventure.

Yvonne

ALSO BY YVONNE VINCENT

Losers Club

The Laird's Ladle

The Angels' Share

Sleighed

The Juniper Key

Beacon Brodie

The Losers Club Collection: Books 1 - 3

The Losers Club Collection: Books 4 - 6

The Big Blue Jobbie

The Big Blue Jobbie #2

Frock In Hell

You can find all of these via my website at https://theweehairyboys.co.uk or on Amazon.

Printed in Great Britain
by Amazon